THE GHOST OF BLACKWOOD HALL

WHEN Mrs. Putney seeks Nancy Drew's help in recovering her stolen jewelry, the search for the thieves takes the teen-age detective and her friends Bess and George to the colorful French Quarter in New Orleans. But the quest is hampered by the strange behavior of Mrs. Putney and two young women who are being victimized by so-called spirits. How can Nancy fight these unseen perpetrators of a cruel hoax? And how can she help the gullible victims when the spirits warn them not to have anything to do with Nancy?

The young sleuth's investigations lead her to a deserted old mansion haunted by a phantom organist. How Nancy uses her own ghostlike tactics to outwit the ghost of Blackwood Hall and aids the police in capturing a group of sinister racketeers will keep the reader tense with suspense.

The ghostly figure was wading deeper into the water

The Ghost
of
Blackwood Hall

BY CAROLYN KEENE

PUBLISHERS   *Grosset & Dunlap*   NEW YORK

PRINTED IN THE UNITED STATES OF AMERICA

Contents

CHAPTER I

A Mysterious Message

"If I ever try to solve a mystery with a ghost in it, I'll use a smart cat to help me!" Nancy Drew remarked laughingly. "Cats aren't afraid of ghosts. Did you know that, Togo?"

Laying aside the book of exciting ghost stories which she had been reading, the slim, titian-haired girl reached down to pat Togo, her fox terrier. But, as if startled or annoyed by her words, he scrambled up and began to bark.

"Quiet, Togo!" ordered Hannah Gruen, the family housekeeper, from the living-room arch-way. "What's wrong with you?"

But Togo, hearing the sound of a car door slam-ming, braced his legs, cocked his head, and barked more excitedly than ever. An automobile had stopped in front of the house, and a middle-aged man was hurrying up the walk.

"It's Mr. Freeman, the jeweler," said Nancy in surprise.

A moment later the doorbell rang sharply, and Nancy hastened to open the door.

"I can't stay long," Mr. Freeman said, speaking rapidly. "I shouldn't have left the jewelry store to come here, only it's important!"

"But Dad isn't at home, Mr. Freeman."

"I came to see you, Nancy. I want you to help an old customer and friend."

The jeweler indicated the parked car. "Mrs. Putney is out there waiting. I tried to get her to talk to the police, but she refused. She won't even tell me all the details of the theft—says there's a good reason why she must keep the matter to herself."

By now, Nancy's curiosity was aroused. "Please bring Mrs. Putney in," she said. "If there is some way I can help her, I certainly will. But if she is unwilling to talk—"

"She'll tell you everything," the jeweler advised in a low voice. "You see, you're a *girl*."

"What has that got to do with it?"

"You'll find out," the jeweler said mysteriously. "Mrs. Putney is a widow. She lives alone and is considered rather odd by her neighbors. I've known her for years, however, and she's a fine woman. She needs our help."

Before Nancy could ask why she needed help, he ran back to the car. After a brief conversation, the woman emerged and the jeweler led her up the walk to the house.

"This is Mrs. Henry Putney, Nancy," Mr. Freeman introduced her, adding, "Nancy Drew is the best amateur detective in River Heights."

From her father, Carson Drew, an outstanding criminal lawyer, Nancy had inherited both courage and keen intelligence. The first case Nancy had worked on with her father was *The Secret of the Old Clock*.

Recently she had solved the mystery of *The Clue in the Old Album*. Although only eighteen years old, Nancy's ability was so well known that anyone in River Heights, who was in trouble, was likely to seek her assistance.

Stepping aside so that the caller might enter the living room, Nancy studied Mrs. Putney curiously. She was a woman well past middle age, and the black of her smartly cut dress accentuated the thinness of her body. Her expression was sad, and in the faded eyes there was a faraway look which made Nancy vaguely uneasy.

Mrs. Gruen greeted the newcomers, chatted a few moments, then tactfully withdrew. Nancy waited eagerly for the callers to reveal the purpose of their visit.

"I shouldn't have come," Mrs. Putney said, nervously twisting a handkerchief. "No one can help me, I'm sure."

"Nancy Drew can," the jeweler declared. Then from a deep pocket of his coat, he withdrew a leather case which bore traces of dried mud.

He opened the case and displayed a sizable collection of rings, necklaces, and pins. He held up a string of pearls to examine.

"Clever imitations, every one!" announced the jeweler. "When Mrs. Putney brought them to me to be cleaned, I advised her to go at once to the police."

"I can't do that," Mrs. Putney replied. "There must be no publicity."

"Suppose you tell me everything," Nancy suggested.

"You promise never to reveal what I am about to tell you?" her visitor asked anxiously.

"Of course, if that is your wish."

Mrs. Putney looked at the jeweler. "I cannot speak in your presence," she said haltingly. "I was warned never to tell any man or woman of this matter."

"That's why I brought you to a *girl detective*," the jeweler said quickly, directing a significant glance at Nancy. "You'll be breaking no confidence in telling Nancy everything. And now I must be getting back to the store."

Bidding them good-by, he left the two together. Satisfied, Mrs. Putney began her story.

"I'm all alone now. My husband died a few months ago," she revealed. "Since then I have had strange premonitions. Shortly after my husband passed away, I had an overpowering feeling the house was to be robbed."

"Clever imitations, every one!" the jeweler announced

"And it was?" inquired Nancy.

"No, but I did a very foolish thing. I gathered all the family jewels, put the collection in this leather case, and buried it."

"Somewhere on your grounds?"

"No, in a secluded clearing in the woods about ten miles from here."

Nancy was amazed that a woman of Mrs. Putney's apparent intelligence should commit such a foolish act. However, she remained silent.

"I decided I'd been unwise, so this morning I went there and dug up the leather case," Mrs. Putney continued. "Then I took the collection to Mr. Freeman to have the pieces cleaned. The moment he saw them he said they were fake."

"Someone stole the real jewelry?"

"Yes, and substituted these copies. I prized my husband's ring above all. It breaks my heart to lose that."

"This is a case for the police," Nancy began, only to have Mrs. Putney cut her short.

"Oh, no! The police must learn nothing about what happened!"

Nancy regarded the woman intently. "Why are you so opposed to talking to anyone except me?" she asked.

"Well, I'm afraid if I call in the police there will be a lot of publicity."

"Is that your real reason, Mrs. Putney?" Nancy was certain that the widow was deliberately withholding the truth. "If I am to help you, I must know everything."

After a pause Mrs. Putney, speaking in a whisper, said, "One night, several weeks ago, my dear husband's spirit came to me. I awoke, or thought I did, and heard a far-off voice. I'm sure it was Henry's. He instructed me to bury the jewels in a place which he described in minute detail and warned me never to reveal to any man or woman that he had told me to do it. Otherwise he would never permit me to hear from him again."

"But he didn't say anything about not telling a girl?" Nancy asked.

"No. That is why I risked coming to you. I need your help desperately. Oh, I hope my coming won't spoil everything!"

Nancy, who did not believe in ghosts or spirits, nevertheless respected Mrs. Putney's belief and was diplomatic in her reply.

"I'm sure that coming to me will not spoil anything," she said. "You must have been robbed by someone who saw you hiding your jewelry, and who knew its value."

"But I told no one my plan."

"I'd like to see the place where you buried the leather case. Why don't we drive out there now in my car?"

"If you like," the widow agreed halfheartedly.

Nancy explained to Mrs. Gruen that she would be gone for an hour or so. Nancy's mother was not living. For many years, the Drew household had been efficiently run by Hannah Gruen, who had been with the family so long that she was regarded as one of them. She loved Nancy as a daughter, and worried a great deal about her whenever the young detective undertook to solve a mystery.

Taking Togo along, Nancy and Mrs. Putney drove through the countryside to the edge of a dense woods which bordered the highway. At Mrs. Putney's direction, Nancy turned down a narrow side road, crossed an old-fashioned covered bridge, and finally parked beneath an arch of thickly interlaced tree limbs.

As the two alighted, a gentle breeze rippled Nancy's hair and stirred the leaves overhead. The rustling in the branches seemed to make Togo uneasy. He pricked up his ears and began to growl.

"Quiet, Togo!" Nancy ordered. "You'd better stay in the car," she added, raising the windows part way. "You might race off into the woods."

"Follow me," Mrs. Putney directed, setting off through a path that curved among the tall trees.

The widow reached a small clearing a few hundred yards from the roadside and halted. Without speaking, she pointed to the center of a grassy place where a section of earth had been dug up.

Nancy glanced around carefully. On all sides, the clearing was shielded by a dense growth of bushes. Quickly she set about inspecting the spot where the leather case had been buried.

The ground was soft, for it had rained hard during the night. If there had been footprints other than those of Mrs. Putney, they had been washed away.

As Nancy straightened up, she heard a car pass along the road. It slowed as if the driver intended to stop, then speeded on.

Nancy continued systematically to search the area for evidence. She was about to abandon the task when her gaze fell upon a scrap of paper which had snagged at the base of a thorny bush. Picking it up, Nancy noticed that it was a page torn from a catalog. On one side was the advertisement:

"BEAUTIFUL LIGHTS, $10.00." On the other, "NO ASSISTANTS."

Doubtful as to the value of the find, Nancy nevertheless slipped the paper into her purse. As she did so, her eyes came to rest upon a long, shiny piece of metal a few feet away.

Before she could pick it up, an agonized scream cut through the silent woods!

CHAPTER II

The First Clue

NANCY whirled around and was relieved to see that Mrs. Putney was safe. The bloodcurdling scream must have come from the road.

"What was that?" The widow was trembling.

"Someone's in trouble!" Nancy exclaimed. "It was a woman's voice!"

Nancy began running in the direction of the road. Mrs. Putney followed as fast as she could.

Out of breath, Nancy reached the place where she had left her convertible. Togo was jumping from seat to seat, barking excitedly.

"Maybe you know something, old boy," Nancy said, and let him out on a leash.

She allowed him to lead her a short distance down the road. He began sniffing the ground, where Nancy noticed some fresh tire prints. Before they reached the first bend in the highway, she heard the muffled roar of a car engine.

"A car must have been parked just out of sight!" she murmured. "Now it's pulling away!"

Though she and Togo ran, the automobile had disappeared by the time they rounded the bend. The dog at this point seemed to lose interest.

"The woman who screamed must have been in the car," Nancy decided. "But who was she? And why did she scream?"

It was too late to attempt pursuit. Thoughtfully Nancy walked back to her own car, where Mrs. Putney anxiously awaited her.

"Did you learn anything, Nancy?"

"Nothing of importance. No one seems to be around here now."

"It was such a horrible scream." Mrs. Putney shivered. "Please, let's leave. I feel so uneasy here—as if unfriendly spirits were watching!"

Nancy suddenly remembered the object in the grass which had drawn her attention just before she had heard the scream. "I'd like to return to the clearing for a minute or two," she said. "Mrs. Putney, why don't you wait here in the car?"

"I believe I will," the widow agreed, quickly getting into the automobile. "But please hurry!"

"I will," Nancy promised.

She started off through the woods with Togo. Though she did not for an instant share Mrs. Putney's belief that "spirits were watching," the woods depressed her.

"I've allowed Mrs. Putney's ghost talk to get on my nerves!" Nancy chided herself.

As she approached the spot where Mrs. Putney had buried the jewelry, Togo began to act strangely. Twice he paused to sniff the air and whine. Once he looked up into Nancy's face as if trying to tell her something, and growled.

"Togo, what is it?" Nancy asked. "One would think—"

She gazed alertly about the clearing. It was deserted, yet every rustle of the leaves seemed to warn her to be careful.

Rather annoyed at her misgivings, Nancy went to the spot where she had been about to pick up the metallic object. Though she looked everywhere, the young detective was unable to find it.

Now more than ever alert, she carefully looked at the ground. In several places the grass had been trampled by herself, Mrs. Putney, or by someone else.

Togo began to sniff and tug at his leash. The dog led her to a depression in the ground which was hidden by bushes. Plainly visible in the soft earth were the prints of a man's shoes.

Stooping down, she examined the footprints thoroughly, measuring them with her hand. Obviously they were fresh. The narrowness of the shoe, and its length, led Nancy to believe that the man who had walked there was tall and thin.

"So that's why I can't find the piece of metal!"

she decided. "He came and picked it up while I was investigating the woman's scream! And probably," Nancy thought ruefully, "she was with him, and her scream was to frighten me away."

Though the trail was indistinct, Nancy could follow the footprints to the shelf of land which overlooked the clearing. The stranger had concealed himself there, watching!

"If he didn't go off in the car, he may not be far from here now," Nancy decided uneasily. "He may be the jewel thief!"

Nancy's attractive face tightened as she realized that danger might be lurking in the forest. She was convinced that the theft of Mrs. Putney's buried treasure was no ordinary affair.

"Only a very clever thief would have taken the trouble to substitute fake pieces of jewelry," she thought. "No doubt it was done to keep Mrs. Putney from discovering her loss and reporting the theft to the police."

Wasting no further time in reflection, Nancy followed the footprints. When the marks were no longer visible, Togo sniffed the ground intelligently, and led her to the road, where he stopped.

"So the man did go off in the car," she sighed.

With Togo trotting along beside her, Nancy returned to her convertible.

"I'm so glad you're back," Mrs. Putney said, greatly relieved. "I was beginning to worry."

En route to River Heights, Nancy said nothing

of her findings, except that she thought the footprints might have been made by the thief. Her
companion now seemed only mildly interested,
and responded absent-mindedly to questions.

When they came to the city, Mrs. Putney requested that she be dropped off at Mr. Freeman's
jewelry store. Reminding her that the case of fake
jewelry had been left at the Drew home, Nancy
asked what should be done with it.

"I'll get it later," Mrs. Putney decided.

Nancy was pleased to have the case left in her
possession, and promptly asked permission to
show the jewelry to her father.

"By all means do so," Mrs. Putney said. "Only
please be careful not to reveal what I told you
about my husband or his instructions."

Nancy promised. After leaving the widow, she
drove directly home. When her father arrived
from his office, she had the collection spread out
on the living-room table in front of her.

"Well, well! What's going on here?" the lawyer
exclaimed, pausing to stare. "Have you been rob-
bing jewelry stores lately, Nancy?"

Carson Drew was a tall, distinguished-looking
man of middle age, with keen, twinkling blue eyes
like those of his daughter. He and his only child
were companionable and shared a delightful sense
of humor. Nancy sprang up to hug him.

"Dad, I had the most exciting afternoon!"

"Ha! Another mystery!" the lawyer said with a mock groan.

"I think it's going to be a very interesting one. Just look at this fake jewelry!"

Mr. Drew examined the pieces one by one, while Nancy related some of the story.

"One or two facts I can't tell," she said reluctantly. "Mrs. Putney swore me to secrecy."

"I don't like that, Nancy."

"Neither do I, Dad, but in a day or so, she'll change her mind. Meanwhile, I can't pass up a good mystery!"

"I suppose not," her father replied. "The point is, if you're determined to try to help Mrs. Putney, you must be very cautious."

Mr. Drew picked up a jewel-studded pin, studied it a moment, and added, "Whoever made this is a clever craftsman. He must have plotted every move far in advance, for it takes time to make imitations like this."

"Dad, do you suppose a River Heights jeweler made these pieces?"

"Possible. However, I'm sure our jewelers are honest merchants, and if they made the imitations, they did so in good faith."

Nancy replaced the jewelry in the leather case.

"Tomorrow I'll show these pieces to a few of the River Heights stores, and perhaps someone can identify the work."

Soon after breakfast the next morning, Nancy set forth on a tour of jewelry stores. Bigelow Company was the last establishment at which she called, and there luck was with her. Mr. Bigelow, one of the owners, stated positively that the imitations had not been made by his firm, but he gave Nancy a suggestion.

"Look for a man named Howard Brex," the jeweler said. "He was a salesman and former designer for a New Orleans house. Used to sell jewelry to me. Not a bad-looking fellow—tall, dark, slender, and a smooth talker. He was a slippery character, though. Finally went to prison for fraud. Maybe he's been released."

Nancy became excited upon hearing this description of Brex. The footprints in the woods had been those of a tall, slender man!

After thanking Mr. Bigelow for the information, Nancy hurried to her father's office. Perching herself on his desk, she asked him if he had any information about Howard Brex in his files. Ringing for his secretary, the lawyer sent for a certain loose-leaf file and fingered through the B's.

"Brex was released a few months ago from a Louisiana penitentiary with time off for good behavior," Mr. Drew revealed. "You think he may be your thief?"

"Oh, I do," she replied, thrilled at the possibility that she had uncovered a real clue.

The arrival of a client cut short further conversation. Nancy telephoned Mr. Bigelow from the outer office and got the name of Brex's former employer in New Orleans. Then she started for home, a plan of action in mind.

Upon arriving at the Drew house, she was pleasantly surprised to find two friends, Bess Marvin and another girl, George Fayne, on the front porch.

George, her dark hair cut in an attractive short style, was deeply tanned. By contrast, her plump cousin Bess was blonde and fair-complexioned.

"I may have some news for you," Nancy hinted as they entered the house. She left Bess and George in the living room and went to telephone Mrs. Putney. After assuring the widow that her two assistants were girls, Nancy obtained reluctant permission to explain the circumstances of the case to Bess and George.

Rejoining the girls, Nancy said, "How would you two like to go to New Orleans with me?"

CHAPTER III

Tracking a Thief

"NEW ORLEANS!" Bess and George exclaimed.

Nancy smiled at her friends. "I'm working on a new case," she said. "Right now, I'm looking for a tall, dark man."

Bess giggled. "What would Ned say to that?"

Nancy blushed as she replied that the man she was after was probably a thief. Furthermore, the place to start looking for him was New Orleans. She told them the story, saying Brex's former employer should be able to recognize the craftsmanship in any imitation jewelry Brex might have made.

"Dad promised me a trip," Nancy said. "I know he can't go with me now. Tonight I'll ask him if you girls can take his place; that is, if you'd like to go."

"Would we!" exclaimed George.

"While we're investigating this Brex person,

George and I can do some sightseeing," remarked Bess. "New Orleans is such a romantic city!"

A twinkle came into Nancy's eyes. "I'm taking you girls along for protection," she said.

"Oh, we won't desert you." George grinned. "But all work and no play isn't any fun."

That evening Nancy discussed the plan with her father. He readily gave his consent.

Not only might a conference with Howard Brex's former employer bring results, he agreed, but there was a possibility that the suspect might even pawn the stolen articles in his home town.

"It's the most likely place for him to have a fence," declared the lawyer.

As Nancy hurried to the telephone to call her friends, he warned her to be careful in following up the clue in the distant city. To Nancy's delight, George and Bess also received permission to make the trip.

Hannah Gruen helped Nancy pack, while Mr. Drew made plane and hotel reservations. Before leaving, Nancy telephoned to Mrs. Putney to ask permission to take the imitation jewelry to New Orleans.

"I appreciate your efforts," the widow said, "but I'm sure nothing will come of the trip."

"Why do you say that, Mrs. Putney?"

"Last night I had another message from my departed husband. He said the thief who stole my jewelry lost it in a large body of water, and it'll never be recovered!"

Nancy was skeptical of the widow's messages but wisely did not argue with Mrs. Putney. She simply said she would be leaving in the morning with her two friends, and promised to report to the widow immediately upon her return.

The next day the three girls boarded the plane for New Orleans. The day was perfect for flying. An attractive hostess served them a tasty lunch and spent most of her spare time chatting with them.

Once, when the plane stopped briefly to pick up passengers, the girls alighted for a little while to stretch their legs. Upon taking their seats again, they noticed that a dark-haired woman in her late thirties had taken the empty seat next to Bess. She regarded the three intently as they sat down, and smiled in a friendly manner.

"Is this your first plane trip?" she asked Bess.

"No!" Bess replied. Then, not wishing to be rude, she added, "We're going to New Orleans."

"You'll love the city!" the woman declared. "Where are you staying?"

Bess told her. Nancy, seated in front of them, was sorry their hotel had been named. She had wanted to keep their visit to New Orleans as secret as possible. When they reached their hotel George scolded her cousin.

"You'll never learn to be a detective, Bess," she

said severely. "You can't tell who that woman on the plane might be."

Nancy, acting as peacemaker, said, "Let's forget it, girls, and do some sightseeing. It's too late to call on Mr. Johnson, Howard Brex's former boss, today. We'll go there in the morning."

Nancy's friends soon found that she did not intend to spend the time in mere sightseeing. Whenever she came to a jewelry shop, or a pawnshop that was open, she insisted that they go in and look at the jewelry on display.

The trip proved to be pleasurable, if not profitable. Their inquiries led them into many sections of New Orleans. The French Quarter, where the buildings were charming in their elegance of a bygone day, interested them most. Beautiful ironwork, delicately tinted plaster walls, old courtyards, once the center of fashionable Creole family life, fascinated the girls.

On a balcony, a bright-colored parrot chattered at them in friendly fashion. A smiling woman, bearing a basket of flowers, stopped to sell a flower to each girl. On all sides, the visitors saw interesting characters, and heard the soft-spoken dialect which was a blend of French, Cajun, and Gumbo.

Bess sighed contentedly. "If I could only spend a month in this lovely old city!" she said.

"It would be nice," Nancy agreed. "But come on. Here's another shop."

It was the fifteenth they had visited, and even Nancy was becoming weary. She had not seen any trace of the stolen jewelry.

"Let's quit," urged Bess. "I'm starved. Suppose we go to one of those famous restaurants and have oysters baked with garlic, and Creole shrimp, and—"

"And take on five pounds," scoffed George, looking with disfavor at Bess's generous weight.

But the girls ate sensibly and went to bed early. In the morning they accompanied Nancy to the jewelry firm for which Howard Brex had worked. Mr. Johnson, the head of the company, was most cooperative. He studied the imitation jewelry which Nancy showed him, and compared it to some pieces of his own which Brex had made.

"I'd certainly say that all of these were made by the same man," Mr. Johnson declared.

Then he told the girls what he knew of his former salesman. "He was a fine craftsman and made excellent designs," Mr. Johnson said. "Too bad he got into trouble."

"I understand he's been released from prison," Nancy said. "Have you any idea where he is?"

"Not the slightest, but I'll be glad to let you know if I hear anything."

Nancy left both her hotel address and that of her River Heights home. She was in a thoughtful mood as she accompanied her friends on their round of sightseeing and to lunch in a quaint restaurant.

"New Orleans is wonderful!" Bess exclaimed. Counting on her fingers, she added, "We've seen the banana wharf, the market, the garden district, and that old cemetery where all the dead are buried in tombs above the ground."

"That's because this place is below sea level," said George. "Say, do you suppose that guide thought we believed the story about the tomb which is supposed to glow at night with an unearthly light?"

"He said spirits come out and weave back and forth like wisps of fog," said Bess.

"That's just what they are—fog," George declared practically.

"Oh, I don't for a minute believe in ghosts," Bess replied quickly.

"I wish we had time to go to Grand Isle, the haunt of Lafitte and his men," said Nancy.

"Who is he?" Bess asked.

"He was a famous pirate," Nancy replied. "According to tradition, when burying treasure, he always murdered one of his band and left his ghost to guard the hidden loot!"

As the girls left the restaurant and started up the street, Nancy happened to turn around. Emerging from the door of the restaurant was a woman.

"Girls," Nancy said in a whisper, "don't look now, but the woman who was on the plane just came out of our restaurant. I think she was spying on us!"

"Why would she do that?" Bess asked.

"If she follows us, then I'll be convinced she's trying to find out what we're up to in New Orleans," Nancy replied.

To prove her point, the young sleuth turned down one street and up another. The woman did the same.

"I'm going to try something," Nancy said quietly. "Two can play this game."

It was easy for the girls to dodge into three different shops as they rounded another corner. Their pursuer, confused, stood on the sidewalk for several seconds, then turned and walked back in the direction from which she had come. Cautiously Nancy emerged, then Bess and George.

The girls trailed the woman for several blocks. Though there were many pedestrians on the street, they were able to keep their quarry in sight. Apparently she was in a hurry, for she walked quickly, not once slackening her pace. As they rounded a corner, she suddenly disappeared into an alley. Nancy darted forward, just in time to see the woman enter a building.

When she and her friends reached it, Bess was not in favor of continuing the search. Nancy insisted the place was innocent-looking enough, and walked through the open arch. In the distance the girls could hear low singing.

They proceeded down a dimly lighted hall, and in a moment the girls stood beside the door beyond which the singing was coming. A placard on it read: *Church of Eternal Harmony*.

Bess, intrigued, lost her fears and urged that they go inside. Nancy hesitated. At that moment the door opened. A man with long white hair and a beard invited them to enter.

"Our admission is reasonable," he said, smiling. "Only two dollars. If the spirit speaks, your questions will be answered."

Still Nancy hesitated. She realized now that a séance was going on inside. Having no desire to spend two dollars so foolishly, she was about to retreat, when Bess walked boldly into the room beyond. George followed, and Nancy was forced to go along.

After paying admission they seated themselves on a bench near the door. The singing had ceased, and as the girls' eyes grew accustomed to the dim lights, they could see that a number of people sat on benches scattered about the place.

On one wall hung a life-size portrait of a woman swathed in white veils up to her eyes. Long dark hair fell below her shoulders. Every face in the room was upturned, gazing at the portrait.

Presently the white-bearded man announced

that all would have to help summon her spirit.

"Let us sit around this table," he intoned.

Bess stood up to go forward, but Nancy pulled her back to the bench. Several others in the room arose and seated themselves on chairs around an oblong table. The old man took his place at the head of it, his back against the wall, a few feet beyond the portrait.

"Let no one utter a sound," he requested.

Silence fell upon the room. Nancy strained her eyes toward the table, watching intently. The white-bearded man sat perfectly still, looking straight ahead of him. Presently a smile flickered over his face.

"I feel the spirits approaching," he said in a scarcely audible voice.

The words were hardly out of his mouth when three raps were heard. The old man, looking pleased, interpreted the sounds as meaning, "I am here," and invited the participants to ask the spirit for answers to their problems. He explained that one rap would mean Yes, two No, and five would mean that danger lay ahead and the questioner should take every precaution to avoid it.

For several seconds no one spoke. The spirit gave three more sharp raps. Then, shyly, a woman at the table asked:

"Will my child be ill long?"

There came two sharp raps, and the questioner

gave a sigh of relief. Another silence followed. Nancy felt Bess lean forward. Out of the corner of her eye, Nancy had noted that her friend was completely entranced by what was going on. Realizing that Bess was about to ask a question, and fearful she might say something about Mrs. Putney's mystery, Nancy leaned over and whispered into her friend's ear:

"Please don't say anything!"

"Silence!" ordered the old man at the table. "Do you wish to drive away our friendly spirit? Ill luck follows him who disturbs the work of the spirit."

As he spoke, the dim lights faded out. The room was in complete darkness.

Suddenly, on the wall above the portrait, a faint glow appeared. It grew larger, until the whole portrait seemed to be taking form. Bess and George, seated on either side of Nancy, huddled close to her.

Bess nervously clutched her friend's arm until Nancy winced from the pressure. The next moment the three girls gasped.

The portrait had come to life!

The white-bearded man arose from his chair.

"Good people," he said, "Amurah has come to us to speak. But she will answer only the most important questions. Approach no closer, or her lifelike spirit will vanish on the wind."

"Oh, Amurah, tell me, please," implored a young woman from a far corner of the room, "if Thomas comes back to me, shall I marry him?"

Amurah lowered her eyes, then nodded.

"Oh, thank you, thank you," the young woman exclaimed, delight in her voice.

Again Nancy could feel that Bess was about to ask a question. Quietly she laid a finger across the girl's lips. The light around the portrait began to fade.

"Alas, the spirits are leaving us!" the white-bearded medium interpreted.

A few seconds later the lights came on in the room. The old man, arising, made a low bow to the portrait, then announced he regretted that the spirits had not been able to remain long enough to answer the questions of all those present.

"Should you wish further knowledge," he said, "you may seek it from Norman Towner, a photographer, who has a direct connection with the spirit world. From time to time messages appear upon Mr. Towner's photographic plates."

The man ushered his clients from the room, but not before each of them had paused to look at Amurah. George had the temerity to touch the canvas. There was no question but that it was only a portrait. Upon reaching the street, the three girls paused.

"Wasn't it wonderful!" Bess exclaimed, adding

that they should go at once to the studio of Norman Towner.

"Nonsense," George said. "You've already spent two dollars and got nothing for it."

"That's because Nancy wouldn't let me ask a question," Bess argued. "Maybe I'll get an answer when I have my picture taken."

To George's amazement, Nancy encouraged the visit. Not having seen the woman they had followed to the séance, Nancy felt she might have gone to the studio.

By inquiring for directions from pedestrians, the girls arrived at length at a courtyard entered by means of a long passageway. At one side of it a flight of iron stairs led to a carved door which bore the photographer's sign.

"Up we go!" George laughed, starting ahead.

The studio, though old and a bit shabby, was well furnished. The proprietor, a short man with intent dark eyes and an artist's beret cocked over one ear, appeared so unusually eager that the girls wondered if he had many customers.

Nancy inquired the cost of having individual photographs made. The price was reasonable, so the three friends decided upon separate poses.

After the pictures had been taken, the photographer disappeared into the darkroom. Soon he returned with two dripping plates. The pictures on them of George and Bess were excellent. To

Bess's disappointment, however, not a trace of writing appeared on the glass.

"Where is my friend's picture?" inquired George, referring to Nancy.

The photographer returned to the darkroom for it. When Nancy glanced at the wet plate, she inhaled sharply. Just beneath her photograph were the words:

Beware your client's request.

"Spirit writing!" Bess gasped.

"Yes, a message from someone in the other world is warning you not to go on with your work," the photographer said slowly, with emphasis on the word "warning." "Young lady, do not take the warning lightly."

"No, I won't," said Nancy.

She had just glimpsed in the photographer's darkroom the woman they had seen on the plane! The next instant the door closed, and the lights in the studio went out. The room, with its one window heavily curtained, was in complete darkness.

A chill breeze suddenly wafted into the studio. Nancy felt a clammy hand brush across her face and fumble for her throat!

CHAPTER IV

A Strange Adventure

BESS screamed in terror. George, with more presence of mind, groped along the wall until she found a light switch she had noticed earlier. In another moment the room was bright again.

Both girls gasped in horror at what they saw. On the floor, almost at their feet, lay the photographer, unconscious! Bess started toward the man, but checked herself as George demanded:

"Where's Nancy?"

Their friend had vanished from the studio!

In their alarm, the cousins temporarily forgot the photographer. Frantically they ran into the darkroom, then into an adjoining kitchenette.

"Nancy!" George shouted. "Where are you?"

There was no answer.

"Nancy's gone and that photographer isn't regaining consciousness," Bess wailed. "What shall we do?"

"We must call the police," George decided.

Rushing out of the studio and down the iron steps, the girls ran through the deserted courtyard to the street. Fortunately, a policeman was less than half a block away. Hurrying up to him, George and Bess gasped out their story.

Immediately the patrolman accompanied the girls to the studio. As they entered, the photographer stirred slightly and sat up.

"What happened?" he mumbled.

"That's what we want to know," demanded the policeman. "What goes on here?"

"I was showing these girls a plate I'd just developed, when the lights went out. Something struck me on the head. That's all I remember."

"What became of the girl with us?" Bess asked.

The photographer, pulling himself on to a couch, gazed at her coldly and shrugged.

"How should I know?" he retorted.

"And where is the plate with the writing on it?" George suddenly demanded.

"The spirits must have been angry and taken it," the photographer said. "I've known them to do worse things than that."

The policeman appeared to be skeptical. He searched the building thoroughly, but no trace of Nancy or of the missing plate could be found.

Worried over Nancy's safety, and scarcely knowing what to do, Bess and George demanded the arrest of the photographer. The policeman, however, pointed out that they had no evidence against the photographer.

"Now don't you worry, young ladies. Your friend can't be far away. We'll have some detectives on the job right away. But I'll have to ask you to step around to the precinct station and give us a description of Nancy Drew."

Shortly afterward, Bess and George, considerably shaken, returned to their hotel. There, nervously pacing the floor, they debated whether to send a wire to River Heights.

"If Nancy doesn't show up in another half hour, we'd better notify Mr. Drew," Bess quavered. "To tell the truth, I'm so scared—"

"Listen!" George commanded.

Footsteps had sounded in the corridor, and now the door of the suite was opening. The two girls waited tensely. Nancy tottered in. Her hair was disheveled and her clothing wrinkled and soiled. Wearily she threw herself on the bed.

She greeted them with a wan smile. "Hello."

Bess and George ran to her solicitously. "Are you all right? What happened?"

Nancy told them how the hand had clutched at her throat when the lights went out in the studio.

"I tried to scream and couldn't. I was lifted bodily and carried out of the room."

"Where?" George asked.

"I couldn't see. A cold, wet cloth was clapped over my face. I was taken to the basement of a vacant house not far away and left there, bound hand and foot."

"How did you get away?" George questioned.

"I kept working until I was able to wriggle out of the cords. Then I climbed through a window and came straight here."

"Did you get the number of the house?" asked George. "I think we should get a policeman and investigate."

Nancy nodded. "We'll go to the police station as soon as I have a bath and change my clothes."

While Nancy was dressing, the girls discussed their recent experiences. George and Nancy were equally sure the photographer had resorted to trickery in putting the message on the plate.

"He could do it easily," George argued. "Maybe he used a plate which already had been exposed to the printed words."

"I believe there's more to it than that, George," Nancy told her. "I think the woman who spoke to us on the plane figures in it. I saw her at the studio," Nancy disclosed. "I'm convinced the photographer was part of a scheme and only pretended to be knocked unconscious. We must get that plate with the message on it."

"It's gone," said George.

This news added to Nancy's suspicions about the whole adventure. As soon as she was dressed, the girls returned to the police station, and an officer was assigned to accompany them. A careful search was made of the vacant building where Nancy had been imprisoned, but not a clue could be found. Even the cords which had bound her had disappeared.

To their surprise the policeman remarked soberly, "This isn't the first time queer things have happened in this section of the city."

No additional information was gained by calling on the photographer, who maintained his innocence in the affair. Bess and George obtained their pictures, but the man insisted that the plate with the spirit writing had disappeared.

When the girls were in their hotel suite once more, George remarked, "Queer about the warning message—'Beware your client's request.' Do you think it meant Mrs. Putney's case?"

"I'm sure it does. But," Nancy said with a determined smile, "now I'll work even harder to solve the mystery!"

"Nancy," said Bess, "is there anything else we can do down here? I feel we should go home and report to Mrs. Putney."

"Maybe she's had another message!" said George.

"Do you suppose she goes to séances?" Bess asked, "and then later dreams she's hearing her husband talk to her?"

"It's possible," Nancy replied. "But it would be hard to get her to admit it."

Bess and George were glad to leave New Orleans. Nancy's experience had frightened them, and they felt that some sinister motive was back of her temporary abduction. Nancy herself was reluctant to leave.

"I think several people were involved in an effort to get me out of the way so that I couldn't find out too much," she said.

Despite the danger, she thought a further search should be made for the mysterious woman. Yet she agreed there was some justice in the girls' argument that Mrs. Putney should be consulted.

Learning that a plane which stopped at River Heights left within an hour, the girls quickly packed and reached the airport just in time. The trip home was uneventful, but during the flight, Bess revealed that she had a little mystery.

"That's what I wanted to ask Amurah," said Bess. "You remember Mrs. White, who comes to our house once a week to clean? She has a daughter, Lola, who is eighteen. Her mother's terribly worried about her."

Nancy recalled the woman, a very gentle, patient person who had suffered a great deal of misfortune. At present her husband was in a sanatorium, and she was struggling to pay the debts his illness had piled up.

"Where does the mystery come in?" Nancy asked.

It seemed that lately, Lola, ordinarily good-natured and jolly, had become unnaturally subdued. She acted as if she were living in a dream world. Mrs. White said there had been no broken romance, nor had her daughter lost her job.

"In fact," said Bess, "Lola earns good wages at a factory and used to give her mother most of the money. Now she gives her practically nothing but won't say why. Something has happened to her," Bess insisted. "Oh, Nancy, won't you go to see Lola? Maybe she'll tell you what's wrong."

"All right, I will," Nancy promised.

Nancy kept her promise the day after she returned from New Orleans. After calling Mrs. Putney and making an appointment for the following day, she started for Lola White's home, wondering what she would say.

Evidently Bess had told Mrs. White she might expect the visit from Nancy. No sooner had Nancy rapped, than the door was opened by Lola's mother. It was evident that she had been crying.

"Oh, Nancy, I'm so relieved you've come!" she said, her voice trembling. "Lola didn't go to work today. Ever since breakfast she's acted like someone in a trance. Please see if you can do something for her!"

CHAPTER V

The Figure in White

"LOLA dear, Nancy Drew is here to see you," called Mrs. White.

The woman had led the way to the back yard, where her daughter sat motionless, staring into space.

"It is quite useless," sighed Mrs. White. "She will talk to no one."

"Oh, Lola needn't talk," Nancy said in a friendly voice. "I came to take her for a little ride in the country. It's a beautiful day."

"Yes, it is!" Mrs. White agreed. "Lola, wouldn't you like to go for a ride, dear?"

Lola, though looking none too pleased, made no protest. Once in the car, she sat in silence, gazing ahead as if hypnotized.

Nancy pretended to pay no attention as the car sped along the picturesque river road. The prolonged stillness seemed to wear upon Lola, who kept pushing back her long blond hair. Several times she glanced at Nancy. Finally, unable to bear the strain, she asked:

"Why did you bring me out here?"

"To help you if I can." Nancy smiled. "You're worried about something to do with money, aren't you? Is it about your job?"

"Well, sort of," Lola confessed. "It's just that my wages at the factory aren't mine any—" She broke off and gazed forlornly at Nancy.

"Why not tell me everything?" Nancy urged. "Perhaps I can help you."

"No one can. I've pledged to give away almost every cent I earn."

"Whatever induced you to do that, Lola? To whom are you giving the money?"

"I can't tell you," the girl replied, her head low and her voice scarcely above a whisper.

"Do you feel that's fair to your mother? She must need part of your earnings."

"That's what worries me," Lola said miserably. "I've pledged myself and I can't get out of it. I don't dare tell Mother the truth either. Oh, I'm in a mess! I wish I were dead!"

"Now that's silly talk! We'll find a way out of this. If I were you I'd ignore the pledge."

"I don't dare," Lola said fearfully.

Nancy told her that any legitimate organization would not take money to the point of depriving

Mrs. White of needed support. If Lola were paying money to unscrupulous persons, she should have no qualms about breaking the pledge.

"You really think so? If only I dared!"

"I'm sure that your mother would tell you the same thing."

"I guess you're right," Lola admitted. "Maybe I've been foolish."

For another half hour, Nancy talked to the girl in a friendly way, seeking to learn to whom she had pledged her salary. Lola, however, would not reveal the information.

When Nancy finally drove her home, Lola thanked her and promised to follow her advice. The next day Nancy was pleased to hear from Bess that Lola White seemed to be herself again.

"Splendid!" Nancy commented. "I only hope whoever was taking her money will leave her alone now."

As soon as Bess had gone, Nancy hurried to the widow's home. Mrs. Putney herself opened the front door of the big house.

"Oh, I'm so glad you came," she cried excitedly. "While you were gone I remembered something I had forgotten to tell you. In the directions given me by my dear husband as to where I should conceal my jewelry, he mentioned specifically that I was to look for a sign of three twigs placed on the ground and that I should bury the jewel case two steps from the sign in the direction of the big walnut tree. When I reached the clearing I found the three twigs lying crossed on the ground, just as the spirit had directed me."

"Oh, Mrs. Putney, I wish you had told me about this when we were at the spot before!" exclaimed Nancy.

She glanced at her wrist watch. "It's only four o'clock. I'll pick up my friends and drive out now to see if the crossed twigs are still there."

When the girls reached the clearing in the woods, there lay the three crossed twigs. The position seemed too perfect for Nature to have placed them there. Yet Nancy doubted that they were the same ones which Mrs. Putney had seen. Rain and wind would have displaced the others.

"The thief may use this method to communicate with his confederates," Nancy mused. "But why would—"

Her voice trailed off. Through the trees Nancy had seen a flash of white.

"Someone's over there," Bess whispered uneasily.

"Let's try to get closer without being seen!" George urged.

Taking care not to step on dry twigs, the girls entered the woods. Through the bushes, they could see the back of a young woman with long blond hair.

"That almost looks like Lola White!" Nancy exclaimed.

The girl appeared to be reaching high into the crotch of a black walnut tree.

"She's hiding something there!" Nancy whispered excitedly.

The girl suddenly moved off in the opposite direction. Soon she disappeared.

Nancy went quickly to the big walnut. Standing on tiptoe, she reached into a hollow in the trunk of the tree. Triumphantly she pulled out a sealed envelope. The others crowded around her.

The envelope bore no name or address, but on its face was a crude drawing of three crossed twigs!

"Wow!" said George. "The mystery deepens!"

"What's inside?" Bess asked in awe.

"If I had one guess, I'd say money," Nancy replied. "I feel justified in opening it, too, for I'm sure it was meant for the person who stole Mrs. Putney's jewelry."

The other girls agreed. Carefully Nancy slipped her thumb under the flap, gradually peeling it free. Inside was a sheet of paper and ten five-dollar bills.

There was no message but the name "Sadie." So the girl had not been Lola!

"I wonder who the girl was," said George.

"What I want to know is why she left the money here," said Nancy. "We must overtake her and find out!" On second thought she added, "Maybe the thief will come to the tree to get the envelope. I'll stay here. You two go."

"She's hiding something!" Nancy whispered

The cousins darted off, leaving Nancy alone beside the black walnut tree. Carefully Nancy put the envelope back in the hollow, and sat down a little distance away to watch.

As Nancy sat with her back to a tree trunk, she thought she heard the soft pad of steps. She straightened up, listening intently, but heard nothing.

"Probably some animal," Nancy decided.

Nevertheless, she glanced about carefully. Her skin prickled, as if in warning that some stranger might be nearby.

"Nerves!" she told herself.

At that moment Bess and George, unsuccessful in their pursuit of the blond girl, were returning. Coming within view of the big walnut tree, George was astonished to see a strange sight. Though no wind was blowing, a leafless branch of a tree behind the walnut seemed to bend slowly downward.

"Bess, look—" she began, then ended lamely, "Never mind! It's gone now."

"What's gone?" Bess demanded.

"A branch. I guess my eyes tricked me," George admitted.

Hearing the voices of her friends, Nancy quickly arose and came to meet them. Seeing that they were alone, she said in disappointment:

"You weren't able to overtake her?"

"We had miserable luck," Bess admitted. "We didn't even get close enough to see her face."

"We trailed her to the main highway, where she must have hopped a bus," George added.

"I think we should take the money with us," Nancy said. "I'll ask Dad what to do about it."

On tiptoe, Nancy reached into the hollow of the tree. A puzzled expression came over her face.

"The envelope's gone!" she exclaimed.

"It can't be!" insisted Bess.

Nancy groped again and shook her head. "The envelope is gone! But no one was here!"

"I've got an idea," said George. "Maybe someone climbed another tree, crossed over into the big walnut, and then snatched the letter from above!"

"The trees are so close together I suppose it could be done," Nancy admitted doubtfully.

"Wait a minute," George cried out excitedly. Then she told about the slowly bending, leafless branch.

Nancy peered intently up into the old walnut and the maple next to it. "No one there," she observed. "George, you're sure it was a branch and not a fish pole with a hook on the end that was used?" she asked.

"It could have been a pole."

"I understand several things now!" Nancy exclaimed, thinking aloud. "That metal object I saw near here the other day must have been part of a collapsible pole! I'll bet it belonged to the same person who was here today!"

"And the same one who robbed Mrs. Putney!" added Bess.

"George, did the stick bend down out of the tree, or did it come from the direction of the bushes?" Nancy asked.

"I couldn't see well enough to be sure," George replied. "But from where I stood, it appeared to bend down out of a tree behind the walnut."

The three went back to the convertible, agreeing that it might be a good idea to keep a lookout for visitors to the walnut tree. Obviously it was being used as a collection station by some-one extracting money from gullible people.

Later, as she drove homeward, Nancy began to wonder whether this might not tie in with Lola White's peculiar actions.

As she turned into her own driveway she no-ticed a dark-green sports car parked in front. The driver came to meet her.

"Hi, Nancy!" Ned grinned. "Guess I got here a little early."

"I'm late. Been working on a case. Please for-give me."

A week earlier she had accepted Ned Nicker-son's invitation to a sundown picnic planned by Emerson College students spending their summer in River Heights.

"I'll be ready in fifteen minutes," she promised.

While Ned waited on the porch, she rushed into the house, showered, and dressed. On her way downstairs, she paused in the kitchen to say good-by to Mrs. Gruen.

"It seems to me you're never home any more," the housekeeper replied. But she added with a smile, "Have a good time and put mystery out of that pretty head for tonight!"

"How could I?" Nancy laughed gaily.

Nancy had not asked Ned where the picnic was to be held. Therefore, she was surprised when she discovered that the spot selected was on the upper Muskoka River, less than a mile from the mysterious walnut tree.

"Want to do me a favor?" she asked Ned.

"Sure thing."

Nancy told him about the money in the walnut tree, its puzzling disappearance, and her suspicion that something sinister was going on.

"And you want to stop and have a look for more envelopes," said Ned. "Okay."

They found nothing in the tree, but the crossed twigs had been removed. Someone had been there! Ned promised to stop at the spot now and then to see if he could learn anything.

They drove on to the picnic spot, where their friends had already gathered. The aroma of broiling hamburgers made them ravenous.

Both Nancy and Ned were favorites among

their friends, and soon everyone was laughing and joking. After all the food had been consumed, some of the young people began to sing. Others went off in canoes.

"Let's go out on the river, Nancy," Ned suggested.

Nancy sat in the bow of the canoe, her paddle lying idle across the gunwales, while Ned paddled smoothly upstream. Moonlight streamed over the treetops and shimmered across the surface of the water. Presently Ned guided the canoe into a cove and let it glide silently toward shore.

"What a night!" he said. "I wish—"

Suddenly Nancy, who was facing the shore, sat bolt upright and uttered a low cry.

"Look over there, Ned!" she exclaimed in a hushed voice. "Am I seeing things?"

The youth, who had been watching the moonlight on the water, turned his head and was startled to see a ghostly white figure wading out into the river from the beach.

"Whew!" Ned caught his breath, nearly dropping his paddle.

As the canoe swung with the current, Nancy got a clear view of the figure in white.

The person wading deeper and deeper into the water was Lola White!

CHAPTER VI

A New Lead

"Quick, Ned!" Nancy cried, seizing her paddle. "She'll be in over her head in a minute. We must save her!"

Her companion needed no urging. He sent the canoe forward with powerful strokes.

"Lola, stay where you are! Don't move!" Nancy called to her.

The girl did not appear to hear. On she waded, holding her hands in front of her.

As Nancy had feared, the shallow water ended abruptly. The next instant Lola had stepped in over her head. The ducking seemed to bring her out of her trance, and now she began to struggle frantically. If she knew how to swim, she gave no evidence of it.

Fortunately, the canoe was soon alongside her. Quickly Ned eased himself into the water, while Nancy steadied the craft. He seized the struggling and terrified girl, then began to swim toward shore. In a moment they were in shallow water.

Nancy was waiting with the canoe, and the sputtering Lola was lifted into the bottom of the craft. The girl was only half conscious. Nancy bent low over her and caught the words, "the beckoning hand."

"Gosh!" Ned observed uneasily. "She's in a bad way!"

"We must get her home right away," Nancy decided. "And you, too, with those wet clothes."

Paddling as fast as they could, she and Ned started toward the picnic grounds where he had left his car. Midway there, Lola seemed to recover her senses. She sat up and gazed at Nancy as if recognizing her for the first time.

"Lola, why were you wading out into the water?" Nancy asked.

"I can't tell you," Lola answered weakly.

"You said something about a beckoning hand."

"I did?" Lola's eyes opened wide and an expression of horror came over her face.

"You thought someone was calling to you?"

Lola spoke with an effort. "I'm grateful to you for pulling me out of the river. But I can't answer your questions!"

Nancy said no more. Taking off her sweater, she put it around the shivering girl.

Later, when they reached the picnic grounds, she hurried Lola in secret to Ned's car, as the college group made joking remarks to Ned about his bedraggled appearance.

At the White home Nancy and Ned lingered only long enough to be certain that Lola had suffered no ill effects from her immersion.

"Please don't tell anyone what happened," Mrs. White pleaded. "Lola went out this evening without telling me where she was going. I can't imagine why she would go to the river."

"Perhaps to meet someone," Nancy suggested.

"So far as I know, she had no date. Oh, I do so need your help to clear up this mystery, Nancy!"

"I'll do everything I can," Nancy promised.

Upon returning home, the young detective sat for a long while in the Drew library, reflecting upon the events of the evening.

Nancy mused also about the many unrelated incidents that had taken place the past week. Into several of these the mysterious Howard Brex seemed to fit very naturally. Yet of his whereabouts since his release from prison, nothing was known.

Penning a brief note to Mr. Johnson, Brex's former boss in New Orleans, she described the crossed-twig sign, and asked if by chance it had any connection with the suspect and his jewelry designs.

For several days after the letter had been sent, Nancy and her friends kept a fairly close watch on the black walnut tree at the edge of the clearing.

But so far as they could determine, no one visited the tree, either to leave money or to take it away.

"We're wasting time watching this place," Ned commented after the third day. "Whoever it is you're looking for knows you've discovered the walnut-tree cache, and has probably moved to a safer locality."

Nancy was inclined to agree with him. She felt very discouraged, for it seemed that she was making no progress whatever in solving the stolen jewelry mystery. Because she could report no success to Mrs. Putney, she avoided calling upon her.

But a letter from Mr. Johnson, the jewelry manufacturer, brought startling results. He wrote:

> *The crossed-twig design you described was never used in any work Brex did for us. We have also looked through other jewelers' catalogs, but do not find anything like this design pictured.*
>
> *However, some time ago, a simple-minded janitor in this office building received from Chicago a letter bearing an insigne of crossed twigs. The man was urged to invest money in stock of the Three Branch Ranch on the promise of doubling his funds. The scheme sounded dishonest, and I persuaded him to ignore it. I would have reported the stock*

*sellers to the authorities, but unfortunately
the janitor destroyed the letter before I had a
chance to examine it.*

Nancy took Mr. Johnson's letter to her father,
who read it carefully, then offered a suggestion.

"Why not notify the postal authorities? It's
against the law, as you know, to use the mail to
promote dishonest schemes."

"Will you do it for me, Dad? Your letterhead is
so impressive!"

"All right, I'll dictate a letter to my secretary
this afternoon," the lawyer promised.

Nancy decided to write a letter of her own to
the Government Information Service to inquire if
they had any record of a Three Branch Ranch.
Three days later she received a reply. She was told
that no such ranch was listed.

"This practically makes it certain the stock
scheme is a swindle!" she declared. "The headquarters of the outfit may be in Chicago, but I'll
bet salesmen are working in other places." Yet it
was difficult for her to connect Brex, a clever designer of jewelry, with a crooked stock promotion.

Even though she had no conclusive information
to convey, Nancy decided to call upon Mrs. Putney to ask a few questions. Just as she was about to
leave the house, however, a taxi stopped in front,
and the widow herself alighted.

Mrs. Putney looked even more worried than on the previous occasion.

"Poor thing," Nancy said to herself. "I'd like to be able to help her!"

Nancy met Mrs. Putney at the front door, and cordially escorted her into the living room.

"I've come to see you, because you never come to my house," the visitor scolded Nancy mildly.

"I haven't been to see you lately, because I had nothing to report, Mrs. Putney. I intended to call today."

"Then I'll forgive you, my dear. If you were coming, you must have a clue."

"Several of them, I hope. Before I tell you what I suspect, I must ask you a rather personal question, Mrs. Putney. Do you own any stock in the Three Branch Ranch?"

Nancy's question seemed to take the widow completely by surprise.

"What—what do you know about the Three Branch Ranch?" she asked in a voice which quavered with emotion. Her faded eyes reflected stark fear.

CHAPTER VII

Matching Wits

ALARMED, Nancy called to Hannah Gruen, who came in hurriedly from the garden. Then she took Mrs. Putney's arm and led her to a chair.

"I didn't mean to upset you," said Nancy. "Please sit down, and Hannah will bring you a cup of tea."

While Mrs. Gruen was in the kitchen preparing the tea, Mrs. Putney rested quietly.

"How did you discover—about the ranch?" she finally asked in a voice scarcely above a whisper.

Nancy remained silent as the widow slumped back in her chair. When the housekeeper brought her a cup of tea, she sipped it obediently. Presently she declared she felt much better.

"Please forgive me for having distressed you so," begged Nancy.

"On the contrary, I should have told you sooner. Three days ago I had another message from my dear husband. He advised me to invest my money in a good, sound stock. Three Branch Ranch was recommended. That's why I was so startled when you asked me about it, Nancy."

"The message came to you at home?" Nancy inquired.

"No, through a medium. I heard of the woman and attended a séance at her home. It was very satisfying."

"Who is she, and where does she live?"

The question took Mrs. Putney by surprise. "Why, I don't know," she said.

"You don't know!" exclaimed Nancy. "Then how could you attend a séance in her home?"

"I learned of the woman through a friendly note which came in the mail. The message said if I cared to attend the séance, I should meet a car which would call for me that night."

"The car came?"

"Yes. It was driven by a woman who wore a dark veil. During a rather long ride into the country, she never once spoke to me."

"Yet you weren't uneasy or suspicious?"

"It all seemed in keeping with what I had understood to be the general practice in such things. The ride was a long one, and I fell asleep. When I awakened, the car stood in front of a dark house."

"You were taken inside?"

"Yes. The veiled woman escorted me to a room illuminated by only a dim, greenish light. When my eyes became accustomed to it, I saw a white, filmily clad figure lying on a couch. Through this medium, the spirit of my husband spoke to me."

At the recollection, Mrs. Putney began to tremble again.

"Your husband advised you to invest money in the Three Branch Ranch!" Nancy said. "What else did he tell you?"

"That I should listen to no advice from any earthly person, and keep what he told me to myself. Oh, dear!"

"What's the matter?" Nancy asked kindly.

"I've told too much already! I shouldn't have revealed a word of this to anyone!"

The widow arose and in an agitated voice asked Nancy to call a taxi.

"I'll drive you home myself," Nancy offered.

During the ride, the young detective avoided further reference to the subject which so distressed her companion. But as she left the widow at her doorstep, she said casually:

"I suppose you did invest money in Three Branch Ranch?"

"Only a little. I gave what cash I had with me to the medium, who promised to use it to purchase the stock for me."

"I don't like to worry you, Mrs. Putney, but I'm afraid you may lose the money you invested."

"Oh, I couldn't. My husband's judgment on business matters was excellent!"

"I don't question that, Mrs. Putney. But I have evidence which convinces me you were tricked by a group of clever swindlers."

Nancy then told of the letter she had received from the Government Information Service, saying no Three Branch Ranch was listed, and that the postal authorities had been notified.

"Promise me you'll not invest another penny until the outfit can be thoroughly investigated."

"I trust your judgment," the widow said. "I promise."

"And another thing. May I have the note you received telling of the séance?"

"I haven't it. I was requested to return it to the medium as evidence of my good faith."

"Oh, that's a bad break for us," Nancy said in disappointment. "Those fakers think of everything! The letter might have provided a clue!"

"What can we do?"

"Don't admit that you suspect trickery," Nancy advised. "Sooner or later, another séance will be suggested and you will be requested to invest more of your money. Phone me the minute you receive another communication."

"Oh, I will!" Mrs. Putney promised.

After leaving the widow, Nancy began to speculate on how many others in River Heights might have been duped into buying the phony stock. The first one to come into her mind was Lola White. The second was the mysterious Sadie.

"Lola probably signed up for a lot of stock, and is paying the bill little by little, out of her wages," Nancy surmised. "I must see her at once."

Lola was not at her place of employment. Upon being told that the girl had not appeared for work that day because of illness, Nancy drove to the White cottage. Lola was lying in a hammock on the front porch, gazing morosely at the ceiling. She sat up and tried to look cheerful.

"How are you today?" Nancy inquired. "No bad effects from the river?"

"I'm all right, I guess," Lola answered. "Thanks for what you did."

"We were just fortunate to be there when you needed us," replied Nancy. "By the way, do you feel like telling me why you were there?"

"No, I don't," Lola said sullenly.

Nancy did not press the matter. Instead, she asked her if she had ever heard of the Three Branch Ranch. Lola's eyebrows shot up, but she shook her head.

Then Nancy told Lola that her real purpose in coming to call was to ask if she were acquainted with a girl named Sadie.

"Oh, you must mean the one who works at the Save-A-Lot Market," Lola said. "I don't know her last name."

"Thanks a lot, Lola. I'll go to see her." As Nancy went down the porch steps she added, "Keep your chin up, Lola!"

Happy that she had obtained a lead, Nancy climbed into her convertible, waved to Lola, and sped away down the street.

When Nancy inquired at the market whether a girl named Sadie worked there, a tall blonde operating a cash register was pointed out. So busy that she was in no mood to talk, the girl frowned as Nancy paused and spoke to her.

"You're Sadie?" Nancy asked, uncomfortably aware that she was delaying a line of customers.

"Sadie Bond," the girl replied briskly.

"I'm trying to trace a Sadie interested in buying stock in a western ranch," Nancy said, keeping her voice low.

"You've got the wrong girl, miss," Sadie replied. "I don't have money to buy ranches."

Nancy smiled. "Then I guess I'm looking for some other person."

Having drawn a blank, Nancy decided that her next move should be to write an advertisement for the River Heights *Gazette*.

It read:

> *SADIE: If you are blonde and know of a certain walnut tree, a beautiful gift awaits you in return for information. Reply Box 358.*

The second day after the advertisement appeared, Nancy, with Bess and George, went to the *Gazette* office to ask if there had been any replies.

To their astonishment, nearly a dozen letters were handed them.

"Jumping jellyfish!" muttered George. "How many walnut-tree Sadies are there in this town?"

Carrying the replies to a nearby park, the girls divided the letters and sat down to read them. Several were from pranksters, or persons who obviously had no information about the walnut tree but were eager to obtain a free gift.

"Running that ad was a waste of money," Bess sighed, tossing aside her last letter.

Nancy, however, was deeply engrossed in a letter written on the stationery of the Lovelee Cosmetic Company. "Girls, listen to this!" she exclaimed.

" 'I have blond hair. Do you refer to a black walnut tree along the Muskoka River? What is the gift you are offering? Sadie Green.' "

"We must find out more about this girl right away!" Nancy declared.

She telephoned the cosmetic firm and learned that Sadie was the telephone operator. When Nancy spoke about the letter, the girl pleaded with her not to come to the office.

"I'll meet you in the park," Sadie promised. "I'll be there in a few minutes."

The three friends were afraid the girl might not keep her promise. But eventually they saw a young woman with long blond hair approaching.

"I can't stay more than a minute," she said nervously. "The boss would have a fit if he knew I skipped out!"

"Will you answer a few questions?"

"What do you want to know?"

"First, tell me, did you ever hear of the Three Branch Ranch?"

"Never," the girl replied with a blank look.

"Did you leave an envelope with money in the hollow of a tree near the river?" Nancy asked.

The girl moved a step away. "Who are you?" she mumbled. "Detectives? Why do you ask me such a thing?" Before Nancy could reply, she burst out, "I've changed my mind. Keep your present!"

With a frightened look in her eyes, Sadie whirled and ran off through the park.

"That girl is afraid to tell what she knows!" Nancy exclaimed. "But we may learn something by talking to her parents."

Inquiry at the Lovelee personnel department brought forth the information that Sadie lived with an elderly grandfather, Charles Green, on North James Street. The girls went directly there.

Old Mr. Green sat on the front porch in a rocker, reading a newspaper. He laid the paper aside as the girls came up the walk.

"You friends o' my granddaughter Sadie?" he asked in a friendly way. "She ain't here now."

"We're acquaintances of Sadie," Nancy replied, seating herself on the porch railing.

"If you're aimin' to get her to go some place with you, I calculate it won't do no good to ask." The old man sighed. "Sadie's actin' kinda peculiar lately."

"In what way?" Nancy asked with interest.

"Oh, she's snappish-like when I ask her questions," the old man revealed. "She ain't bringin' her money home like she used to, either."

Mr. Green, who seemed eager for companionship, chatted on about Sadie. She was a good girl, he said, but lately he could not figure her out.

From the conversation, Nancy was convinced that the case of Sadie Green was very similar to that of Lola White. After the girls had left the house, Nancy proposed that they drive out to the black walnut.

"I have a plan," she said.

Nancy did not say what it was, but after examining the hollow in the walnut tree, which was empty, she looked all about her. Then she tore a sheet from a notebook in her purse. Using very bad spelling, she printed:

My girl friend told me by leaving a letter hear I can get in touch with a pursen who can give infermation. Please oblige. Yours, Ruby Brown, Genral Delivry, River Heights.

"You hope to trap the man who took the fifty dollars!" George exclaimed admiringly. "But how do you know you'll get an answer? It seems pretty definite that the racketeers aren't using this tree as a post office any longer."

"We'll have to take a chance," said Nancy. "And if there is an answer, someone will have to call for it who answers to the name of 'Ruby Brown.'"

"George and I will," Bess offered eagerly.

Nancy smilingly shook her head. "You're well known as my friends. No, I'll have a stranger call for the letter, so that anyone assigned to watch the post office won't become suspicious."

Nancy arranged with a laundress, who sometimes worked at the Drew home, to inquire for the letter each day.

"Did you get it?" Nancy asked eagerly when Belinda returned the third day.

The good-natured laundress, lips parted in a wide grin, said, "I got it, Miss Nancy!"

Taking the letter, Nancy ran upstairs to her room to open it in private. She gasped when she read the message enclosed, which was:

> *If you're on the level, Ruby, go to Humphrey's Black Walnut for instructions. If you are a disbeliever, may the wrath of all the Humphreys descend upon you!*

CHAPTER VIII

The Ghost at the Organ

REREADING the message several times, Nancy speculated about the Humphreys and their connection with the black walnut tree.

Deciding it best to keep the contents of the message to herself, Nancy went to the River Heights Public Library, hoping to find a book which would throw some light on the Humphreys mentioned in the note. The name sounded vaguely familiar, and it had occurred to her that it might belong to one of the very old families of the county.

Finally Nancy found exactly the book she wanted. Fascinated, she read that a famous old walnut grove along the river once had been known as Humphrey's Woods.

Even more exciting was the information that a duel, fatal to one member of the family, had been fought beneath a certain walnut tree. The tree, known since then as Humphrey's Walnut, was marked with a plaque.

The article went on to say that Blackwood Hall, the family home, was still standing. Built of walnut from the woods surrounding it, the mansion had, in its day, been one of the showplaces along the river. Now the grounds were weed-grown, the old home vacant, and the family gone.

"It seems a pity to neglect a fine old place that way," Nancy thought. "Why would—"

The next sentence aroused her curiosity.

"It is rumored that Jonathan's ghost still inhabits the place!"

Nancy decided she must investigate Blackwood Hall, although she smiled at the thought of any ghost walking there.

But first she would find Humphrey's Walnut. When she returned home, Nancy telephoned Ned, asking if he were free to accompany her, and told him briefly about the letter.

"I'll pick you up in my car in five minutes!" he promised eagerly.

At Nancy's direction, Ned drove as close as he could to the ancient walnut grove by the river. Then they parked the car and started off on foot. They examined each tree for a plaque. It was not until they were deep in the grove that Nancy spied the dull bronze marker with its tragic account of how Jonathan Humphrey had died in a duel while defending his honor beneath the shade

of that tree. For fully a minute neither Nancy nor
Ned spoke; then Nancy's voice shook off the spell
of the place.

"I wonder if anyone will come," said Nancy.

"The note suggested that you were to receive
instructions of some kind," Ned remarked.

"Perhaps this tree, also, is used to hold messages. Do you see any hollow in the trunk,
Ned?"

The youth, noticing a deep pocket in the crotch
of the walnut, ran his hand into it.

"Say, something's crammed in here!" he said
excitedly. "Yes, it's a paper!"

"And addressed to Ruby Brown!" Nancy cried,
looking at it.

The message was short.

> Name the girl friend who suggested you
> leave that letter.

"Wow!" exclaimed Ned. "Looks as if you've
put your foot in it now, Nancy."

Nancy read the message again, then asked Ned
to put it back. "Come on!" she urged.

Nancy led the way back to the car and they
drove to the walnut tree where she had left her
first note signed "Ruby Brown." Again Nancy
printed a badly spelled message, asking for instructions on how to find the Humphrey tree.

"That ought to fool him." She chuckled as Ned
placed the note in the hollow of the tree. "He'll

think poor Ruby is dumb, which is exactly what I want him to think."

"Say, why don't you ask the police to guard the place?"

"Because I'm afraid I'll scare off the man altogether. I want to trap the mastermind behind this thing, not some errand boy."

For the next two days, no mail was received by General Delivery for Ruby Brown. On the third morning, in response to Nancy's telephone call, she learned a letter was at the post office. The laundress went to get it.

"What does our unknown friend write this time?" asked Bess, who had arrived at the Drew home just ahead of the maid. "Does he tell Ruby how to reach the Humphrey Walnut?"

"He says 'Ask Lola White.' "

"Lola!" exclaimed Bess. "That poor girl! Then she *is* involved in that swindler's scheme."

"I've suspected it all along," Nancy admitted. "The fellow is clever. He's suspicious that Ruby Brown is a hoax, but so far I don't think he connects her with me in any way. And it's my job to keep him from finding out."

"What will you do next?" asked Bess. "Talk to Lola?"

"Not right away," Nancy decided. "Unwittingly she might carry the information back to the writer of this note."

"Then what's the next move?"

"Dad says when you're confused—and I admit I am—you should sit back and try to arrange the facts into some kind of order," Nancy replied. "Dad also thinks a change of scenery is a good idea when you're in a mental jam."

"Where shall we go?" asked Bess.

"How would you like to go with me to Blackwood Hall?" asked Nancy. "The book at the library told various stories about this old mansion, which stands within a few miles of River Heights. It's haunted, has a secret tunnel, and is said to house the ghost of one Jonathan Humphrey who lost his life in a duel. Would you like to explore it with me?"

At first Bess insisted that wild horses could not drag her to the deserted mansion. But later, when she learned that Nancy had persuaded George to accompany her, she weakened in her decision.

"I'll go along," she said. "But I'm sure we're headed for trouble."

The trio set off at once, although a summer storm seemed to be brewing. As the girls tramped through the woods along the river, Nancy suddenly stopped short. Below her was the cove where she and Ned had rescued Lola White. The girls were not far from Blackwood Hall now. Could there be any connection between the sinister old place and the strange, hypnotic state in which they had found Lola that night?

Without voicing her thoughts to the others,

Nancy plunged on. At last they came within view of the ancient building. The three-story mansion, where several generations of Humphreys had lived, looked as black as its name, forbidding even by daylight. High weeds and grass choked off any paths that might once have led to the house.

The girls circled the mansion. The wind rattled the shutters and at intervals whistled dismally around the corners of the great structure. An open gate to what had once been a flower garden slammed back and forth, as if moved by an unseen hand.

Nancy walked to the massive front door, expecting to find it securely fastened. To her amazement, as she turned the knob, the door slowly opened on groaning hinges.

"Well, what do you know!" George muttered.

Bess tried to dissuade her friends from going inside, but they paid no attention.

Turning on flashlights, the three girls entered the big hall into which the door opened. The floor was richly carpeted, but Time had played its part in making the carpet worn and gray with mildew.

Velvet draperies, faded and rotted, hung from the windows of an adjoining room. Through the archway, the girls caught a glimpse of a few massive pieces of walnut furniture.

"This looks interesting," Nancy observed. "There's nothing to be afraid of here."

At that moment the front door banged shut behind them. Bess stifled a scream of terror.

"Goose! It was only the wind!" George scolded her. "If you keep this up, you'll give us all a case of the jitters."

"I'm sorry," said Bess, "but it's so spooky."

Just then a sound of sudden, heavy rain told the girls a storm had indeed begun.

Passing through what they took to be a small parlor, the girls found themselves in another long hall, running at right angles to the entrance hall. From it opened a huge room, so dark that their flashlights illuminated only a small section of it.

"Listen!" Nancy whispered suddenly.

As they paused in the doorway, the three distinctly heard the sound of organ music. Bess seized George's arm in a viselike grip.

"W-what's that?" she quavered. "It must be ghost music!"

"It couldn't be—" George began, but the words died in her throat.

At the end of the room a weird, greenish light began to glow. It revealed a small organ.

At the keyboard of the instrument sat a luminous figure.

Bess uttered a terrified shriek which echoed through the ancient house. Instantly the dim light vanished, and the music died away. The long room was in darkness.

Nancy raised her flashlight and ran toward the place where the phantom organist had appeared. Only the old, dust-covered organ remained against the wall.

"It looks as if it hadn't been touched for years," Nancy remarked.

"Oh, Nancy! Let's leave this dreadful place!" Bess wailed from across the room. "The house is haunted! Somebody's ghost does live here!"

Refusing to listen to her friends' pleas to wait, Bess rapidly retreated. A solid slamming of the front door told them she was safely out of the house.

George, keeping her voice low, commented, "To tell the truth, I'm a little nervous, too."

"So am I," admitted Nancy. "This place is haunted all right—not by a specter but by a very live and perhaps dangerous person."

"How did that 'ghost,' or whatever it was, get out of the room so fast? And without passing us?"

"That's what we must find out," Nancy replied, focusing her light on the walls again. "There may be a secret exit that the—"

She ended in midsentence as a girl's piercing scream reached their ears. The cry came from outside the mansion.

"That was Bess!" Nancy exclaimed.

Fearful, the two girls abandoned the search and

raced outdoors. The rain was coming down in torrents, making it difficult to see far ahead.

At first they could not locate Bess anywhere. Then Nancy caught a glimpse of her, huddled among the trees a few yards away. She was trembling violently.

"A man!" Bess chattered as her companions ran up to her. "I saw him!"

"Did you get a good look at him?" Nancy asked.

Bess had been too frightened to do this. But she was sure she must have surprised the person who had come from the direction of the house, for he had turned abruptly and entered the woods.

"Any chance of overtaking him?" Nancy questioned.

"Oh, no!" Bess had no desire either to lead or join an expedition through the woods. "He's gone. He knows his way and we don't. Let's go home, girls. We're wet through, and we'll catch colds."

"I'm going back to the mansion," Nancy announced.

"I'll come along," said George. "We'll hunt again for the hidden exit that the ghost at the organ must have taken!"

Bess reluctantly accompanied her friends. As they reached the massive front door, Nancy noticed that it was closed.

"I'm sure I left it open. The wind must have blown it shut," she remarked.

George tried to open the door. Though she twisted the knob in both directions and pushed hard, the door refused to budge.

"Bolted from inside," George concluded. "The ghost isn't anxious for company."

"I can't get it out of my mind that Blackwood Hall is part of this whole mixed-up mystery," Nancy remarked thoughtfully. "I wish I could get inside again!"

Nancy smiled to herself. Ned was coming to dinner. She would ask him to bring her back to Blackwood Hall that evening. Ghosts were always supposed to perform better at night!

"All right, let's go," she said cheerfully.

Before returning home, Nancy did a few errands, so it was after six o'clock when she reached her own house. Hannah Gruen opened the door excitedly.

"Mrs. Putney has been trying all afternoon to reach you by telephone. She wants to talk to you about something very important."

"I believe Mrs. Putney is going to attend another séance!" Nancy exclaimed.

Nancy hurried to the telephone and called the Putney number, but there was no answer.

"Oh, dear, I hope she won't be taken in again by the faker," Nancy said to herself.

Without the slightest clue as to where to find

Mrs. Putney, Nancy turned her thoughts toward the evening's plan. Ned, upon arriving, fell in eagerly with her idea of going to Blackwood Hall.

"I hope the ghost appears for me too," he said, laughing, when Nancy had told him the story. "Say, how about going there by boat?"

"Wonderful."

After dinner Ned rented a trim little speedboat, and in a short time they reached an abandoned dock some distance from Blackwood Hall. A full moon shone down on the couple as they picked their way through the woods.

"Listen!" Nancy suddenly whispered.

From far away came the sound of chanting.

"It might be a séance!" Nancy said excitedly. "If we hurry, we may get there in time!"

Running ahead of Ned, Nancy paid scant heed to the ground underfoot, and stepped ankle-deep into a quagmire. When she tried to retreat, the mud tugged at her feet. Ned caught her by the arm.

"Stay back, Ned!" she cried out.

The warning came too late. Already Ned had followed her into the quagmire. He, too, tried to extricate himself without success.

"It's quicksand!" Ned cried hoarsely.

Inch by inch, he and Nancy felt themselves sinking lower and lower into the mire!

CHAPTER IX

Another Séance

REALIZING how serious their situation was, Ned urged Nancy to pull herself out of the quagmire by using him as a prop and jumping to firm ground.

"No, don't ask me to do that," Nancy replied. "I might save myself, but you would be pushed so far down, I couldn't possibly get help in time to pull you out."

"If you don't do it, we'll both lose our lives," Ned argued. "Hurry, Nancy! We're sinking fast!"

Nancy refused to listen to his pleas. Instead, she began to shout for help, hoping that some of the chanters would hear her. Ned, too, called loudly until his voice was hoarse.

No one came, and they kept sinking deeper into the quicksand. Soon Nancy was up to her chest.

"I'm afraid there's no help for us," Nancy said despairingly.

The youth scarcely heard her, for just then his feet struck something hard and firm.

"Nancy!" he cried. "I've hit bottom!"

Before she knew what was happening, he grasped her beneath the armpits and tugged hard. The muck gave a loud, sucking sound as it slowly and reluctantly released its hold. A few minutes later Nancy was safe and sound and on dry, firm ground, though she was plastered from heels to head with mud.

"You all right, Ned?"

"I'm okay," he answered.

Nancy scrambled to her feet. Now she must get Ned out! Desperately she looked around for something she could use to rescue him.

"Hold everything, Ned. I'll be back in a jiffy," Nancy called. She had remembered the long painter with which they had moored the motorboat to the dock.

Nancy raced through the darkness to the riverbank. She flicked on the lights of the small speedboat, untied the stout Manila rope which tied it to the pier, and a few minutes later was back at the edge of the quagmire where Ned was patiently waiting. She threw one end of the rope to the boy who calmly tied a noose under his arms. He directed her to toss the other end over the limb of a tree and then pull steadily.

Nancy struggled desperately to pull Ned from the quicksand. As the rope tightened, Ned began slowly but surely to emerge from the mire. Soon he was able to help with his arms and legs, and at last he succeeded in scrambling to safety beside Nancy.

For several minutes neither was able to speak, so exhausted were they from their violent efforts. As the two looked at each other, suddenly both Nancy and Ned began to laugh hysterically.

"If you could only see what you look like!" they exclaimed in the same breath.

Covered with mud and shaken by their unfortunate experience, their one desire was to get into clean clothes. The mystery, they decided, as they started back toward the dock, must wait for another time.

Later, at home once more and in dry clothes, Nancy began to wonder if Mrs. Putney had returned and whether she had been attending another séance. On a chance, she telephoned, but there was no answer. As Nancy reflected on her own adventure, she recalled the sound of chanting she and Ned had heard. Could it have come from Blackwood Hall? she wondered.

Immediately after breakfast the next morning, Nancy called at Mrs. Putney's home. The widow, looking very pale and tired, was wearing a dressing gown.

"I was up very late last night," she explained.

Nancy struggled to pull Ned from the quicksand

Then she added peevishly, "Why didn't you call me yesterday? It seems to me you're always away when I need you," Mrs. Putney grumbled. "Oh, dear! No one seems interested in my affairs—that is, no earthly being."

Nancy, though annoyed by the woman's attitude, was careful to hide her impatience. She realized that Mrs. Putney was a highly nervous individual, upset by the death of her husband, and recent events, and would have to be humored.

The widow remained stubbornly silent about telling where she had been the previous evening. Nancy, following a hunch, remarked:

"By the way, what were you chanting last night just before the séance?"

Mrs. Putney leaned forward in her chair, staring at Nancy as one stupefied. For a moment she looked as if she were going to faint. Then she recovered herself and whispered:

"Nancy Drew, how did you know where I was last evening?"

"Then it's true you were at a séance again last night?"

"Yes, Nancy. I tried to call you yesterday afternoon to let you know that I had been invited to another invocation of the spirits. But I couldn't reach you. *She* took me there again last night."

"She?"

"The woman in the veil," Mrs. Putney explained. "Yesterday afternoon I was instructed by telephone to go to Masonville and have dinner at the Claridge. Afterward, the car would be waiting for me. We drove somewhere into the country," the widow went on. "It seems strange, but I fell asleep again and didn't awaken until it was time to leave the car."

Nancy thought it very strange, indeed. Had the woman been drugged?

"As I opened my eyes, a long, opaque veil was draped over my head. I was led a short distance, where I was told there were several other persons who, like myself, were veiled."

"Did you learn their names?" Nancy interposed eagerly.

"Oh, no. My companion warned that to avoid annoying the spirits, we were not to speak to one another or ask questions."

"Then you all sang?" Nancy prompted as the widow stopped speaking.

"Yes, a woman led us in a prayerful chant," Mrs. Putney continued, her voice growing wistful at the recollection. "After a while we were taken indoors and the spirits came. They spoke to us through the control."

"How can you be certain it wasn't a trick?"

"Because my husband called me Addie. My first name is Adeline, you know, but he always liked Addie better. No one besides my husband ever called me by that name."

"Tricksters easily might have learned of it,"

Nancy pointed out. "The information could have been obtained from neighbors or relatives."

Apparently not listening, Mrs. Putney began to pace the floor nervously. "The spirits advised each of us to contribute money to carry on their earthly mission," she revealed.

"And what is that mission?"

The widow gave Nancy a quick look and replied, "We're supposed to turn money over to the earthly beings who make spiritual communication possible for us. Full instructions will be sent later. I gave them only fifty dollars last night. I felt I had to do that because everyone was giving something."

"A profitable night's work for those people!" Nancy remarked caustically. "You mustn't give another penny."

Mrs. Putney gave Nancy a cold stare. "Everything so far has seemed quite honest to me," she said.

Nancy was dismayed to realize that the widow was fast falling under the spell of the phonies who were trying to fleece her.

"Don't forget your jewelry was stolen," Nancy reminded her.

"I'm sure these people had nothing to do with that, Nancy."

"Mrs. Putney, at any time during the séance did you hear cries for help?"

"Why, no," the woman replied, startled. "Everything was very quiet." Then she added, "When the séance was over, I was taken outside again and helped into the car."

"Still veiled?"

"Oh, yes." A faraway look again came into her eyes. "You know, the trip home was like a dream. To tell the truth, I don't seem to remember anything about it. The next thing I really knew was that it was morning and I was lying on the divan in this very room."

Nancy was greatly disturbed at hearing this. It sounded too much like the strange actions of Lola and Sadie. She asked Mrs. Putney if she had been given anything to eat or drink before leaving the séance. The answer was No. She had noticed no unusual odors, either. Nancy was puzzled; somehow, the mediums must have brought on a kind of hypnotic sleep.

"Please don't ask me to give up the chance to get messages from my dear, departed husband," Mrs. Putney said, forestalling what Nancy was about to request.

Instead, on a sudden inspiration, Nancy told her to continue attending the séances, but asked to be kept informed of what happened. Pleased, Mrs. Putney promised, not realizing that Nancy hoped in this way to get evidence against the group. Then, at the proper moment, she would expose their trickery.

"I'll have to get busy before these people become suspicious and skip," Nancy said to herself as she drove home.

When Nancy told her father about the strange occurrences at Blackwood Hall, he agreed that the place should be thoroughly investigated to find out if fake séances were being carried on there.

"Nancy, I'm afraid to have you go near that place again," the lawyer said. "It sounds dangerous to me. Besides, we have no right to search anyone's property without a warrant. Perhaps your crowd of spirit-invoking fakers have rented the Humphrey mansion."

"But, Dad, everything depends upon it. Won't you go with me, and maybe Ned too?"

On the verge of refusing, Mr. Drew caught the eager, pleading look in his daughter's eyes. Also, he realized that they might very well make important discoveries at Blackwood Hall and the thought intrigued him.

"Tell you what!" he offered impulsively. "If Ned can go with us, we'll start out right after lunch! And I'll take care of the warrant. Captain McGinnis will fix me up."

Nancy ran to the telephone. "With both you and Ned to help me," she said excitedly, "that ghost is as good as trapped now!"

CHAPTER X

The Secret Door

SHORTLY after lunch Nancy arrived at Blackwood Hall with her father and Ned. What Nancy had counted on as a clue to fit into the puzzle, as she had worked it out in her mind, proved to be a disappointment.

"I was so sure there were going to be automobile tracks here," she said. "Mrs. Putney told me she was driven right to the door of the place where the séance was held."

"But here's something interesting," her father called from a spot among the trees.

As Nancy and Ned ran over, he pointed to several deep, narrow tracks and some footprints. The tracks looked as if they had been made by a wheelbarrow, which had been used to make several trips.

"I believe someone was busy moving things out of the house!" Mr. Drew exclaimed. "Anything valuable inside?"

"Furniture," Nancy replied. "Most of it would be too heavy to move by wheelbarrow, though."

"It's more likely the scamps carried away evidence which might incriminate them if found by the police," the lawyer said grimly. "Mediums' trappings, perhaps."

"Wonder if we can get inside," Ned said.

When he attempted to open the door, he found it locked. Thinking it might only be stuck, he and Mr. Drew heaved against the door with all their strength, and suddenly it gave way. The lock was broken.

"Not a very cheerful place," said Ned as the three stepped into the hallway. "This dim light would make anybody think he saw ghosts."

Nancy peered into the adjoining rooms. So far as a hasty glance revealed, none of the furniture had been disturbed. It was possible, of course, that the wheelbarrow tracks had no connection with the fake mediums at all, and perhaps Mrs. Putney's séances in turn had no connection with the ghost of Blackwood Hall!

"Let's separate and see what we can find out, anyway," Nancy proposed.

"All right," Mr. Drew agreed. "But call me, Nancy, if you come upon anything suspicious."

Eager to examine the organ again, Nancy walked along the hall and entered the huge room which was almost in complete darkness. Ned and her father began to search the other rooms.

With scarcely a thought that she was alone, Nancy went directly to the old organ, which stood at an angle across one corner. Laying down her lighted flashlight, she seated herself on the creaking bench and tried to play. No sound came forth.

"Why, that's funny!" Nancy thought, startled. She tried again, pumping the pedals and pressing the keys down firmly. "I certainly didn't dream I heard music coming from this organ! There must be a trick to it somewhere!"

Now deeply interested, Nancy began to examine the instrument inch by inch with her flashlight. There was a small space along the side wall, large enough for a person to squeeze behind. Peering in curiously, she was amazed to see a duplicate set of ivory keys at the rear of the organ!

"Why, the front of the organ is only a sham!"

Eager to investigate, Nancy pushed through the opening. There she found a low door in the wall of the room. "So this is how the ghost vanished so quickly!" she told herself.

Nancy tried the door, which was unlocked. Flashing her light, she saw that a flight of stairs led downward. Cautiously she began to descend. Only after proceeding a short distance along a damp, musty corridor did she regret that she had not summoned her father and Ned.

"They may wonder what's become of me," she thought. "I mustn't be gone long."

Intending to make a speedy inspection, Nancy quickened her steps along the corridor.

"This must be the secret tunnel the book mentioned!" she said to herself.

Soon Nancy came to a heavy walnut door, blocking the passageway. Her light revealed an iron bolt. As she slid it back and pushed the door open, she drew in her breath in sharp surprise. A strange green light on the floor of the room beyond illuminated the back of a ghostly figure standing just ahead of her!

Simultaneously, the flashlight was struck from her hand. It crashed on the floor and went out. The green light also faded away.

Fearful of a trap in the inky darkness, Nancy backed quickly into the corridor, slamming the heavy door and bolting it. Her heart pounding, she felt her way along the tunnel wall. Finally she stumbled up the stairway and through the exit behind the organ.

"Whew, that was a narrow escape!" she thought breathlessly. "I must find Dad and Ned."

Nancy hurried from room to room, upstairs and down, but did not see either of them. She was tempted to call out their names but then thought better of it. Very much concerned, Nancy decided that they must have left the house to investigate the grounds.

As she circled the mansion, the young detective tried to figure out under which room the secret tunnel had been built, and where it led. She noted that there was no outside exit from the cellar as most old houses had. Remembering the length of the musty underground corridor, she could very well believe that the exit was some distance from Blackwood Hall—perhaps in the woods.

When ten minutes or more had elapsed and neither Mr. Drew nor Ned had appeared, a harrowing thought began to disturb Nancy. Maybe the two of them were prisoners in the tunnel room! They might have found the outside entrance to the tunnel and been captured!

Frightened by this possibility, Nancy wondered what to do. Her first instinct was to go to the police. Then she realized that she could not drive the car to get help, because her father had the keys in his pocket. She finally decided that she would have to go back to the underground room at the end of the corridor alone and find out if her father and Ned were being held captive.

Forgetting any thought of safety for herself, she entered the house again. She ran to the organ room and squeezed through the opening to the secret door. There she closed her eyes for several seconds until they became accustomed to the darkness, then carefully she picked her way down the steps and along the passageway.

Reaching the heavy walnut door, she stooped down to look under the bottom for a light beyond. There was nothing but blackness.

Trying not to make any noise, Nancy slid the iron bolt and cautiously opened the door a crack. The place was dark. When nothing happened, Nancy decided to take a chance, and called out:

"Dad! Ned!"

There was no answer. Yet she thought possibly the two men might be lying gagged or unconscious not far away, and she could not see them. Without a light she had no way of finding out.

Nancy listened intently for several seconds, but heard only the sound of her own breathing.

"I'll have to get a light and come back here," she decided finally.

As Nancy was about to leave, she suddenly heard a scraping, creaking sound somewhere overhead.

"Maybe it's Dad or Ned!" Nancy thought excitedly.

Hopefully she hurried to the first floor. Seeing no one there, she climbed the front stairs to the second floor. As she reached the top step, Nancy froze to the spot.

At the far end of the hall, a wraithlike figure was just emerging from the far wall of the hallway!

CHAPTER XI

The Tunnel Room

NANCY uttered no sound. As she watched in the dim light, the ghost flitted noiselessly up a flight of stairs at the end of the hall which evidently led to the top floor.

Without thinking, Nancy started after it on tiptoe. Despite the heavy carpet, a floorboard groaned beneath her weight. Did she fancy that the filmy figure ahead hesitated a moment, then went on?

As she mounted the steps to the third floor Nancy heard another creaking sound. At the top she was just in time to see the white-draped figure again vanish into the wall!

The wall was solidly paneled with black walnut. Though Nancy searched carefully, running her fingers over every inch of the smooth wood panels, she could find no secret door or spring that might release a sliding partition. Returning to the second floor, she examined the panels there also, but without success.

Of one thing Nancy was convinced. The old house harbored more than one sinister character, how many she did not know. There was the figure at the organ, the one who had knocked her flashlight from her hand, the man who had scared Bess almost out of her wits, and now, the apparition she had followed up the stairs. Surely these could not all be one and the same "ghost."

"The one that went up the stairs was a live man or woman, I'm sure of that! But what was he up to?"

Knowing that a further investigation at this time would be worthless, Nancy started once more to look for her father and Ned.

After a futile search of the house and grounds, she decided:

"There's just a chance that they went back to the car and are waiting for me." She hurried down the road.

As she reached the place where the car had been parked, she halted in astonishment.

The automobile was gone!

Before she could examine the rutty road for tire prints, she heard the sound of hurrying footsteps. Whirling, she saw her father and Ned coming out of the woods.

"Nancy, thank heaven you're safe!" Ned exclaimed, hurrying to her side.

"But where's the car?" Nancy demanded.

"The car's been stolen!" Mr. Drew said grimly. "Ned and I heard voices outside and ran to investigate."

"Did you find out who it was?"

"No. But we caught a glimpse of a man streaking through the woods," Ned replied. "He was too far away for us to get a good look at him, and he gave us the slip."

"By the way, here's something I picked up near those wheelbarrow tracks that lead back through the woods," Mr. Drew remarked.

The lawyer handed Nancy a tubular piece of metal which appeared to have been taken from a collapsible rod such as magicians and fake mediums might use.

"Why, this piece is similar to the one I saw in the clearing the other day!" Nancy exclaimed.

"And look what I found on the kitchen stairway!" Ned exclaimed.

From his pocket he drew forth a miniature short-wave radio sending set.

"Does it work?" Mr. Drew asked eagerly.

"I'll see. Messages couldn't be sent very far with it, though."

"Could you tune it to send a message to the River Heights police station or a prowl car?"

Ned made some adjustments on the set, and began sending a request to the police asking that men be dispatched at once to Blackwood Hall. He gave the license number of the missing car and asked that it be rebroadcast over the police radio.

While they waited hopefully for action in response to Ned's call, Nancy related her adventures. She described the underground passageway, the strange appearance and disappearance of the "ghost," and the peculiar scraping sounds she had heard.

"If the police don't show up soon, we'll investigate the ghost room with my flashlight," Mr. Drew declared.

"Look!" Nancy cried out. "There's a car coming up the road."

The three quickly stepped behind some bushes and waited to see if they could identify the occupants of the approaching automobile before revealing their presence. To their relief, it was a State Police car.

"My message must have been relayed to them!" Ned exclaimed. "Swell!"

Two officers alighted, and the trio moved out of hiding to introduce themselves. Upon hearing the full details of what had happened, the troopers offered to make a thorough inspection of Blackwood Hall.

Nancy, Mr. Drew, and Ned accompanied them back to the mansion.

The police looked in every room but found no trace of its recent tenants. When they tackled the secret tunnel, Nancy stayed close behind, eager for a glimpse beyond the walnut door. It proved to be a tiny, empty room with no sign of a mysterious green light, a ghost or a human being. Furthermore, the room had no other exit.

"Is this little room under the house? Or is it located somewhere under the grounds?" Nancy asked one of the officers.

After making various measurements the men announced that it was located under the house, almost beneath the stairwell. It was not connected with the cellar, and no one could hazard a guess as to its original purpose.

"You may have thought you saw a ghost, but don't tell me anyone can get through a locked door," one officer chided the girl.

"I actually did see a figure in white," Nancy insisted quietly. "Something or someone knocked the flashlight from my hand. See, it's over there by the door."

In all fairness, Nancy could not blame the troopers for being a trifle skeptical. She almost began to doubt that she had ever had a frightening adventure in this spot.

Observing Nancy's crestfallen air, Mr. Drew said to the troopers, "Obviously this old house has been used by an unscrupulous gang. When they discovered we were here to check up on them, they moved out their belongings—my car as well."

"Stealing a car is a serious business," one officer commented. "We'll catch the thief, and when we do, we'll find out what has been going on in the old Humphrey house. Meanwhile, we'll have one of our men keep a close watch on this neck of the woods."

"No use sticking around here now," the other trooper added. "Whoever pulled the job has skipped."

"I'm going to keep working on this case until all the pieces in the puzzle can be made to fit together—even the ghosts!" Nancy told her father.

"Here's a bit of evidence," said the lawyer, taking the piece of telescopic rod from his pocket.

One trooper recognized it at once as magicians' or fake mediums' equipment, and asked for it to hand in with his report. Ned turned over the pocket radio sending set which had proved so valuable in bringing the police.

Though the license number of Mr. Drew's car had been broadcast over the police radio, there was no trace of it that night. The following afternoon Mr. Drew was notified that the car had been found abandoned in an adjacent state.

Accompanied by Nancy in her convertible, the lawyer traveled to Lake Jasper just across the state line. His automobile, found on a deserted road, had been towed to a local garage. Nothing had been damaged.

"Some people have no regard for other folks' property," the attendant remarked. "Probably a bunch o' kids helped themselves to your car to go joy riding."

But Nancy and her father were convinced that the car had not been "borrowed" by any joy riders. It had been used by a gangster to transport some unknown objects from Blackwood Hall!

What were the objects, and where had they been taken? Here was one more question to which Nancy must find the answer.

Nancy and her father had just returned home when Bess Marvin came bursting in. "Lola White has been talking wildly about you in her sleep!" Bess said ominously.

"What's so serious about that?" Nancy inquired.

"Lola's mother says she raves about a spirit warning her to have nothing more to do with Nancy Drew! If Lola does, the spirit will bring serious trouble to both of you!"

CHAPTER XII

Nancy's Plan

"Lola believes that a spirit has warned her to have nothing more to do with me, or we'll both be harmed!" Nancy exclaimed.

"That's what she said," Bess answered. "I knew it would worry you."

Her face serious, Nancy started for the telephone. Bess ran after her.

"Are you going to call Mrs. White or Lola," she asked.

"No, I'll go to see them. But first I'm going to call Mrs. Putney." As Nancy looked for the telephone number in the directory, she added, "Members of a sinister ring of racketeers, posing as mediums are convinced that I'm on their trail. To protect themselves, they're having the so-called spirits warn their clients against me!"

"Do you think Mrs. Putney has been warned against you too?" Bess asked.

"We'll soon know." Nancy dialed the widow's number.

"Oh, Mrs. Putney, this is Nancy," the girl began. "I—"

A sharp click told her that Mrs. Putney had hung up. Nancy dialed again. Though the bell rang repeatedly at the other end of the line, there was no response.

"It's no use," she said at last, turning to Bess. "She refuses to talk to me. She must have been warned and is taking the warning seriously."

"What'll you do?"

"Let's go to her home," Nancy proposed. "This matter must be cleared up right away."

As the two girls arrived at the widow's home, they saw her picking flowers in the garden. But when she caught sight of the car, she turned and walked hastily indoors.

The girls went up the porch steps. They knocked and rang the doorbell. Finally they were forced to acknowledge that the woman had no intention of seeing them. Nancy was rather disturbed as she and Bess returned to the car.

"I'm afraid those swindlers have outsmarted us," she commented. "But not for long, I hope!"

She drove at once to the White home. Lola herself opened the door, but upon seeing Nancy, she backed away fearfully.

"You can't come in!" she said in a hoarse voice. "I never want to see you again."

100 THE GHOST OF BLACKWOOD HALL

"Lola, someone has poisoned you against me."

"The spirits have told me the truth about you, that's all. You're—you're an enemy of all of us."

Mrs. White, hearing the wild accusation, came to the door.

"Lola, what are you saying?" she said sternly. "Why haven't you invited our friends in?"

"Your friends—not mine!" the girl cried hysterically. "If you insist upon having them here, I'll leave!"

"Lola! How can you be so rude?"

Nancy was sorry to see Mrs. White berate her daughter for an attitude she felt was not entirely the girl's fault.

"I'll leave at once," Nancy said. "It's better that way."

"Indeed you must not," Mrs. White insisted.

"I think perhaps Lola has reached the point where she can work out her own affairs," Nancy said, but with a meaningful glance at Mrs. White, which the latter understood at once.

Nancy and Bess drove away, but pulled up just around the corner.

"I intend to keep watch on Lola," Nancy explained. "She may decide to act upon the suggestion that she straighten out her affairs herself."

"What do you think she'll do?" Bess asked.

"I'm not sure. But if she leaves the house, I'll trail her."

It became unpleasantly warm in the car, and Bess soon grew tired of waiting. Recalling that she had some errands to do, she presently decided to leave her friend.

Time dragged slowly for Nancy, who began to grow weary of the long vigil. Just as she was about to give up, she saw Lola come out of the house and hurry down the street.

Nancy waited until the girl was nearly out of sight before following slowly in the automobile. At the post office Nancy parked her car and followed Lola into the building where she watched her mail a letter.

"I'll bet she's written to those racketeers!" Nancy speculated.

Cruising along at a safe distance behind Lola, Nancy saw her board a bus, and followed it to the end of the line. There Lola waited a few minutes, then hopped an inbound bus, and returned home without having met anyone.

"Either she had an appointment with someone who didn't show up, or else she simply took the ride to think out her problems," Nancy decided.

Of one thing she was fairly certain. The old tree in the woods was no longer being used as a post office. Instead, the racketeers were instructing their clients to use the regular mails.

On a sudden impulse Nancy drove her car back to the post office to make a few inquiries. The clerk might remember a striking blonde like Lola. As she was approaching the General Delivery window, she saw a familiar figure speaking to the clerk. It was the woman that she and the girls had seen on the plane and who had followed them in New Orleans!

Darting behind a convenient pillar, Nancy heard the woman asking whether there were any letters for Mrs. Frank Immer.

The clerk left the window and soon returned shaking his head. The woman thanked him, then left the building. When Nancy was sure the coast was clear she followed. Starting her car, Nancy kept a safe distance behind the woman. A few minutes later she saw her quarry disappear into the Claymore Hotel.

Nancy drove around the hotel once or twice, looking for a place to park. It was some time later that she approached the hotel clerk's desk. Examination of the register revealed no guest by the name of Mrs. Frank Immer, nor had anyone signed in from Louisiana.

"But I saw Mrs. Immer enter here," insisted Nancy. "She wore a large black hat and a blue dress."

The clerk turned to the cashier and asked if he had seen anyone answering the description.

"Maybe you mean Mrs. Frank Egan," the cashier volunteered. "She just checked out."

"How long ago?"

"About ten minutes."

The cashier could not tell Nancy where the woman had gone, for she had left no forwarding address. From a bellhop she learned that Mrs. Egan had directed a taxi to take her to the airport.

"She said something about going to Chicago," the boy recalled.

"Thanks." Nancy smiled.

Determined that Mrs. Egan should not leave the city without at least answering a few questions, Nancy sped to the airport. To her bitter disappointment, as Nancy pulled up, a big airliner took off gracefully from the runway.

"Mrs. Egan probably is aboard!" she groaned.

Nancy checked and confirmed that a woman answering the description had bought a ticket for Chicago, in the name of Mrs. Floyd Pepper.

"My one chance now of having her questioned or trailed is to wire the Chicago police!" Nancy decided. "I'll ask Dad to make the request."

She telephoned to explain matters, and Mr. Drew agreed to send a telegram at once.

Nancy, having done all she could in the matter, returned to the Claymore Hotel with a new plan in mind. She asked for some stationery with the

Claymore letterhead. When she arrived home her father was there.

"Dad, I want to find out if Mrs. Egan has any part in the séances, the stock deals, or the money that used to be put in the walnut tree," said Nancy. "Will you tell me honestly what you think of this plan? I'm going to type notes to Mrs. Putney, Lola White, and Sadie Green."

"Using Mrs. Egan's name?"

"That's the idea. If it doesn't work, then I'll try the name of Immer later. I won't try imitating Mrs. Egan's signature in the hotel register. I'll just type the name."

"But what can you say without giving yourself away?" asked Mr. Drew.

"I'll write that my plans have been changed suddenly," Nancy said. "I'll request them to send all communications to Mrs. Hilda Egan at the Claymore Hotel."

"When she isn't there? And why Hilda? Isn't the name Mrs. Frank Egan?"

"That's how I'll know the answers belong to *me*. I doubt if her clients know her first name, anyway."

Mr. Drew chuckled. "Anyone could tell that you have legal blood in your veins," he said. "But aren't you forgetting one little detail?"

"What's that?" Nancy asked in surprise.

"If Mrs. Putney, Sadie, Lola, or any of the others have ever had any correspondence with Mrs.

Egan, they'll be suspicious of the letters. They may question a typed name instead of one written in her own hand."

"How would it be," said Nancy, "if in the corner of the envelope, I draw the insigne of the Three Branch Ranch!"

"Well, here's hoping," said Mr. Drew a trifle dubiously.

Later that day Nancy wrote the letters, then rushed over to the Claymore and persuaded the hotel clerk, who knew her to be an amateur detective, to agree to turn over to her any replies which might come addressed to Mrs. Hilda Egan.

"Since you say these letters will be in answer to letters you yourself have written, I'll do it," he agreed.

All the next day Nancy waited impatiently for word from the Chicago police in reply to her father's telegram. None came, nor did she receive a call from the clerk at the Claymore Hotel.

"Maybe my idea wasn't so good after all," she thought.

But on the second day, the telephone rang. Nancy's pulse hammered as she recognized the voice of the Claymore Hotel clerk.

"Nancy Drew?"

"Yes. Have you any mail for me?"

"A letter you may want to pick up is here," he said hurriedly.

CHAPTER XIII

Complications

THE letter awaiting Nancy at the Claymore Hotel proved to be from Sadie Green, the girl who worked at the Lovelee Cosmetic Company.

In the communication, which the girl never dreamed would be read by anyone except Mrs. Egan, she revealed she had received a bonus and would gladly donate it to the poor orphans cared for at the Three Branch Home.

". . . In accordance with messages from their deceased parents," the letter ended.

"So that's what they are up to!" Nancy thought grimly. "There's no greater appeal than that of poor, starving orphans! The very idea of trying to rob hard-working girls with such hocus-pocus!"

As soon as Nancy returned home, she promptly typed a reply on the hotel stationery warning Sadie that since certain unscrupulous persons were endeavoring to turn a legitimate charity into a racket, she was to pay no attention to any written or telephoned messages, unless they came from Mrs. Egan herself at the Claymore Hotel.

Nancy's next move was made only after she had again consulted her father. At first he was a little reluctant to consent to the daring plan she proposed, but when she outlined its possibilities, he agreed to help her.

"Write down the address of this shop in Winchester," he said, scribbling it on a paper. "Unless I'm mistaken, you can buy everything you need there."

As a result of Nancy's talk with her father and also with Ned Nickerson, another letter went forward to Sadie Green. The note merely said that the girl would be required to attend an important séance the following night. She was instructed to wait for a car at Cross and Lexington streets.

At the appointed hour, Nancy, heavily veiled, rode beside her father in the front seat of a car borrowed from a friend. In order not to be recognized, Mr. Drew had a felt hat pulled low over his eyes.

"Dad, you look like a second-story man!" Nancy teased him as they parked at the intersection. "Do you think Sadie will show up?"

"I see a blond girl coming now," he replied.

Nancy turned her head slightly and recognized Sadie. Making a slow gesture with her gloved hand, she motioned the girl into the back seat. Mr. Drew promptly pulled away from the curb.

The automobile took a direct route to the vicinity of Blackwood Hall. Nancy covertly watched Sadie from beneath her veil. The girl was very nervous and kept twisting her handkerchief as they approached. But when they got out and started walking, she gave no sign that the area was familiar.

Ned Nickerson had followed in another borrowed automobile which he concealed in a clump of bushes. Then he removed a small suitcase from the trunk, and started off through the woods.

Meanwhile, Nancy and Sadie, with Mr. Drew a little distance behind, approached Blackwood Hall.

"I hope everything goes through as planned," Nancy thought with a twinge of uneasiness. "If Ned is late getting here—"

Just then she saw a faint, greenish light glowing weirdly through the trees directly ahead. At the same moment came a strange, husky chant.

Nancy stepped to one side so that Sadie might precede her on the path. The girl gazed at the green point of light as one hypnotized.

"The spirit speaks!" Nancy intoned.

Simultaneously a luminous hand seemed to appear out of nowhere. It floated, unattached, and reached out as if to touch Sadie.

"My child," intoned an old man's cracked voice, "I am your beloved grandfather on your dear mother's side."

"Not Elias Perkins!" Sadie murmured in awe.

"The spirit of none other, my child. Sadie, I have been watching you and I am worried—most sorely worried. You must give no more money to the Three Branch Ranch or to any cause which my spirit cannot recommend."

"But, Grandfather—"

"Furthermore," continued the cracked voice, taking no note of the interruption, "follow no orders or directions from anyone, unless that person writes or speaks his name backward. Mind this well, Sadie, my child, for it is important."

The voice gradually drifted away as the green light began to grow dim. Soon there was only darkness and deep silence in the woods.

"Oh, Grandfather! Come back! Speak to me again!" Sadie pleaded.

"The séance is concluded," Nancy murmured.

She took Sadie by the arm and led her back to the waiting car. All the way home Sadie remained silent. Only once did she speak and that was to ask "the veiled lady" the meaning of the strange instructions issued by her grandfather.

Nancy spoke slowly and in a low monotone, "You are to reveal no information to anyone and take no orders from anyone unless he spells or speaks his or her name backward."

"I don't understand," Sadie said.

"There are unscrupulous people who seek to

take advantage of you. Your grandfather's spirit is trying to protect you. He has given you a means of identifying the good and the evil. You have been in communication with a Mrs. Egan, have you not?"

The blond girl nodded. And Nancy continued, "Should Mrs. Egan approach you again, saying 'I am Mrs. Egan,' then beware! But should she say 'I am Mrs. Nage,' then you will know that she is to be trusted, even as you trust the spirit of Elias Perkins."

"Oh! I see now what Grandfather meant," Sadie said, and became silent again.

At Cross and Lexington streets, the girl left the car. Nancy and her father drove on home, to find Ned awaiting them.

"How did I do?" the youth demanded in the cracked voice of Elias Perkins as they entered the house together.

Nancy chuckled. "A perfect performance!"

"You don't know the half of it," Ned joked. "I almost messed up the whole show."

As the three enjoyed milk and sandwiches in the Drew kitchen, the young man revealed that he had nearly lost the hand from the end of the rod.

"Next time you want me to perform, buy a better grade of equipment!" He laughed, biting into another ham sandwich.

Ned was referring to the props used during the séance, which Nancy had purchased earlier that day at a store in Winchester. These included a telescopic reaching rod, and the luminous wax hand, as well as a bottle of phosphorus and olive oil, guaranteed to produce a ghostly effect when the cork was removed, which would disappear again at the required moment when it was stoppered.

"When I took the bottle from the suitcase, I nearly dropped it," Ned confessed. "And what's a séance in the dark worth without a spooky light?" he added, laughing.

On the following day, Nancy called at Sadie's home. Sadie was at work, but elderly Mr. Green, eager for companionship, told Nancy everything she wished to know.

"That granddaughter o' mine ain't so foolish as I was afeared," he said promptly. "This morning she says to me 'Grandpa, I've made up my mind to save my money and not give it away to every Tom, Dick, and Harry who asks me for it.' What do you think o' that?"

"Splendid!" Nancy approved. "I hoped Sadie would have a change of heart."

To test Sadie further, Nancy asked Ned the next day to telephone the girl at the Lovelee Cosmetic Company.

"I want to prove a couple of things," she said.

"First of all, I want to find out whether Sadie is really following my instructions, and second, if she knows the name of Howard Brex."

Ned began to laugh. "How would you pronounce Brex backward?"

Nancy smiled too. "Guess you'll have to use his first name. 'Drawoh' is easy."

While Nancy listened on an extension at the Drew home, Ned made the call. He addressed the girl as Eidas instead of Sadie and added, "This is Drawoh speaking."

"My name ain't Eidas, and I don't know what you're talking about," the girl retorted, failing to understand.

Ned quickly asked her to think hard. Suddenly Sadie said:

"Oh, yes, I remember. And what did you say your name is?"

"Drawoh."

After a moment's reflection, the girl said, "I guess I don't know you."

"No," said Ned. "But tell me, have you had any recent communications asking you for money?"

"One came today, but I threw it away," Sadie replied. "I'm not giving any more of my money to those folks. I have to go now."

Sadie hung up.

"Good work, Nancy!" Ned declared as he rejoined her. "Apparently that trick séance brought Sadie to her senses."

"For a few days, anyhow," Nancy agreed. "The job isn't over, though, until these swindlers are behind bars! They still have great influence over Lola and Mrs. Putney and goodness knows how many other people.

"I can easily understand how a person like Sadie would be so gullible, but it's almost unthinkable that Mrs. Putney would fall for that stuff," Ned said.

While the two friends were talking, Hannah Gruen called Nancy to the telephone. The message was from the clerk at the Claymore Hotel. The late-morning mail had brought two more letters addressed to Mrs. Egan.

"Isn't that wonderful, Ned?" Nancy cried. "I'll have to go over to the hotel right away."

"I'll take you there," Ned offered.

He drove Nancy to the hotel and waited in the car while she went inside. The girl was gone several minutes. When she returned, her face was downcast, and she looked very disturbed.

"What's the matter?" Ned demanded. "Didn't you get the letters?"

Nancy shook her head. "The regular clerk went to lunch," she explained. "In his absence, another clerk gave the letters to someone else!"

CHAPTER XIV

The Cabin in the Woods

"A YOUNG woman picked up the letters," Nancy told Ned. "Mrs. Egan must have discovered our scheme and sent a messenger. She was lucky enough, or else she planned it that way, to have the letters called for when my friend was off duty."

"Maybe Mrs. Egan's back in town," Ned suggested.

"Yes, that's possible. The police were never able to trace her. According to word Dad received, she left the plane at one of the stops between here and Chicago."

Ned whistled softly. "Wow! If she's back here, she'll be in your hair, Nancy!"

"She hasn't registered at the Claymore. I found that out. But that doesn't prove she isn't in River Heights. Ned, something's got to break in this case soon. We know that there are several people in the racket and it may be that Brex is the mastermind behind everything. Blackwood Hall evidently had been used as headquarters until we got too interested for their comfort. All of the supernatural hocus-pocus was used not only to fleece gullible victims, but also to scare us off the scent. I feel that there will be a showdown within the next few days."

"Well, I want to be there when that happens, Nancy," said Ned.

Later that day, Nancy called George and Bess and asked them to go with her to Blackwood Hall. The drive to the river road was uneventful. They parked their car some distance away and all three trekked through the walnut woods in the direction of the historic mansion.

"But, Nancy, what *do* you expect to find this time?" asked Bess.

"I realized when I was reviewing the case with Ned today that we never had checked those wheelbarrow tracks from Blackwood Hall. They may lead us to the spot where the gang is now making its headquarters."

The old house looked completely abandoned as the girls approached.

Suddenly George cried, "The wheelbarrow tracks lead away from the house and right into the woods."

For some distance the girls tramped on, stopping now and then to examine footprints where the ground was soft. Suddenly, in the flickering sunlight ahead, they caught sight of a cabin in a clearing among the trees. Approaching cautiously they noted that all the windows were covered with black cloths on the inside. The wheelbarrow tracks led to what obviously was the back door.

"That must be the place!" Nancy whispered excitedly. "See! A road leads right up to the front door just as Mrs. Putney told me!"

Bess began to back away, tugging at George's sleeve. "Let the troopers find out!" she pleaded.

Nancy and George moved stealthily forward without her. After circling and seeing no signs of life around the place, George boldly knocked several times on the front door.

"Deserted," she observed. "We may as well leave."

Nancy gazed curiously at the curving road which led from the cabin. Only a short stretch was visible before it lost itself in the walnut woods.

"Let's follow the road," she proposed. "I'm curious to learn where it comes out."

Bess, however, would have no part of the plan. She pointed out that already they were over a mile from Nancy's car.

"And if we don't get back soon, it may be stolen, just as your father's was," she added.

This remark persuaded Nancy reluctantly to give up her plan. The girls trudged back through the woods to the other road. The car was where they had left it.

"I have an idea!" Nancy declared as they started off. "Why don't we try to drive to the cabin?"

Nancy was convinced that by following the main road they might come to a side lane which would lead them to the cabin. Accordingly, they drove along the designated highway, carefully scrutinizing the sides for any private road whose entrance might have been camouflaged.

"I see a side road!" Bess suddenly cried out.

Nancy, who had noticed the narrow dirt road at the same instant, turned into it.

"Wait!" George directed. "Another one branches off just a few yards ahead on the highway we were following. That may be the one instead of this."

Uncertain, Nancy stopped the car and idled the engine. Before the girls could decide which road to follow, an automobile sped past on the highway they had left only a moment before. Nancy and the others caught a fleeting glimpse of a heavily veiled woman at the wheel. On the rear seat they thought they saw a reclining figure.

The car turned into the next narrow road, and then disappeared.

"Was that Mrs. Putney on the back seat?" George asked, highly excited.

"I didn't get a good enough look to be sure," Nancy replied. "I got the car license number, though. Let me write it down before I forget."

"Hurry!" George urged as Nancy wrote the

numbers on a pad from her purse. "We have to follow that car!"

"But not too close," Nancy replied. "We'd make them suspicious."

The girls waited three minutes before backing out into the main highway and then turning into the adjacent road. Though the automobile ahead had disappeared, tire prints were plainly visible.

The road twisted through a stretch of woodland. When finally the tire prints turned off into a heavily wooded narrow lane, Nancy was sure they were not far from the cabin. She parked among some trees and they went forward on foot.

"There it is!" whispered Nancy, recognizing the chimney. "Bess, I want you to take my car, drive to River Heights, and look up the name of the owner of the car we just saw. Here's the license number.

"After you've been to the Motor Vehicle Bureau, please phone Mrs. Putney's house. If she answers, we'll know it wasn't she we saw in the car. Then get hold of Dad or Ned, and bring one of them here as fast as you can. We may need help. Got it straight?"

"I—I—g-guess so," Bess answered.

"Hurry back! No telling what may happen while you're away."

The two watched as Nancy's car rounded a bend and was lost to view.

Then Nancy and George walked swiftly through the woods toward the cabin. Approaching the building, Nancy and George were amazed to find that no car was parked on the road in front.

"How do you figure it?" George whispered as the girls crouched behind bushes. "We certainly saw tire marks leading into this road!"

"Yes, but the car that passed may have gone on without stopping. Possibly the driver saw us and changed her plans. Wait here, and watch the cabin while I check the tire marks out at the end of the road."

"All right. But hurry. If anything breaks here, I don't want to be alone."

From the bushes George saw Nancy hurry down the road and out of sight around a bend.

For some time everything was quiet. Suddenly George's attention was drawn to a wisp of smoke from the wide stone chimney.

"There's someone in there, that's sure," she concluded. "Somebody's lighted a fire."

Overpowering curiosity urged George to find out what was going on inside the cabin. She could see nothing through the black-draped windows. Trying to decide whether to wait for Nancy or to make some move of her own, she noticed smoke seeping through the cracks around the door!

"The place must be on fire!" George exclaimed. When still no sound came from inside, she could stand the strain no longer. "I'm going to break in!" she decided.

She flung herself against the locked door, but it scarcely budged. Looking about, she found a rock the size of a baseball. She let it fly at the window nearest the door. The glass splintered and the stone carried with it the black curtain that had covered the window. With a stick she poked out the jagged bits of glass that still clung to the pane. When the smoke had cleared, George stuck her head through the opening.

The one-room interior was deserted, and *there was no fire,* not even in the big stone fireplace! A few wisps of smoke remained. But it did not smell like wood smoke.

"I didn't dream up that smoke," George thought, growing more uneasy all the time. "But the door was locked and I saw no one leave."

Time dragged on, and still Nancy did not return. Finally, after an hour had elapsed, George, alarmed, tramped back to the road where they had taken leave of Bess.

She was about to start for River Heights on foot when the convertible came into view around a bend. Bess pulled alongside.

"Do you know anything about Nancy?" George asked quickly.

"Why, no."

Her cousin related the strange story of the

George hurled a rock at the window

cabin and Nancy's disappearance. Bess, too, was greatly concerned.

"And I didn't bring anyone along, either," she wailed. "Mr. Drew was called out of town unexpectedly, and I couldn't find Ned."

"Just when we need them so desperately! Did you find the car owner's name?"

"Yes, it belongs to Mrs. Putney! But what are we going to do about Nancy?"

"I think Mr. Drew should be notified if we can possibly get word to him. Hannah may know where to reach him by telephone," said George.

The girls made a hurried trip to the Drew home. The housekeeper told them that the lawyer had departed in great haste and was to send word later where he could be reached.

"I really don't know what to do," Hannah Gruen said anxiously. "The Claymore Hotel has been trying to get in touch with Nancy, too. The chief clerk there wants to see her right away. We'd better notify the police. I dislike doing it, though, until we've tried everything else."

No one had paid the slightest attention to Togo, who was lying on his own special rug in the living room. Now, as if understanding the housekeeper's remark, he began to whine.

"What's the matter, old boy?" George asked, stooping to pat the dog. "Are you trying to tell us something about Nancy?"

Togo gave two sharp yips.

"Say! Do you suppose Togo could pick up Nancy's trail and lead us to her?" George asked.

"When she's around the neighborhood, he finds her in a flash," Hannah Gruen said. "Nancy can scarcely go a block without his running after her, if he can get loose."

"Then why don't we give him a chance now?" Bess urged. "Maybe if you get something of Nancy's, a shoe, perhaps, he might pick up the scent—"

"It's worth trying," the housekeeper said, starting for the stairway.

She returned in a few moments with one of Nancy's tennis shoes, and announced she was going along on the search. Taking the eager Togo with them, the group drove back to the spot where Nancy was going to investigate the tire marks. George dropped the shoe in the dust.

"Go find Nancy, Togo!" Bess urged. "Find her!"

Togo whined and sniffed at the shoe. Then, picking it up in his teeth, he ran down the road.

"Oh, he thinks we are playing a game," Mrs. Gruen said in disappointment. "This isn't going to work."

"No, Togo knows what he is doing," George insisted, for in a moment he was back.

Dropping the shoe, the dog began to sniff the

ground excitedly. Then he trotted across the road and into the woods, the others following. Reaching a big walnut tree, he circled it and began to bark.

"But Nancy isn't here!" quavered Bess.

Suddenly the little dog struck off for some underbrush and began barking excitedly.

CHAPTER XV

Two Disappearances

"TOGO's found something!" Bess exclaimed, following George, who was parting the bushes that separated them from the dog.

George uttered a startled exclamation as she came upon Nancy stretched out on the ground only a few feet away. Togo was licking his mistress's face as if begging her to regain consciousness.

Just as Hannah Gruen reached the spot, Nancy stirred and sat up. Seeing her dog, she reached over in a dazed sort of way to pat him.

"Hello, Togo," she mumbled. "Who— *How* did you get here? Where am I?" Then, seeing her friends, she smiled wanly.

Observing that she had no serious injuries, they pressed her for an explanation.

"I don't know what happened," Nancy admitted.

On the ground near the spot where the cabin road crossed another dirt road, she had found the familiar Three Branch insigne.

This time, a tiny arrow had been added. Without stopping to summon George, Nancy had hurried along the trail until she came upon another arrow.

A series of arrows had led her deeper into the woods. Finally she had come to a walnut tree nearly as large as the famous Humphrey Walnut.

The tree had a small hollow space in its trunk. It contained no message, however. She had been about to turn back when a piece of paper on the ground had caught her eye. Examination had revealed that it was a half sheet torn from a catalog.

"It matched that scrap of paper I found in the clearing near the Humphrey Walnut," Nancy said.

Obviously the sheet had been ripped from the catalog of a supply house for magicians' equipment. One advertisement offered spirit smoke for sale.

While Nancy had been reading, she had heard footsteps and looked up. Through the woods, some distance up the path, she had seen a young woman approaching. Hastily Nancy stepped back, intending to hide behind the walnut tree.

At that moment something had struck her from behind.

"That's the last I remember," she added ruefully.

"Who would do such a wicked thing?" Mrs. Gruen demanded in horror.

"It's easy to guess," Nancy replied. "The tree must be another place where the members of the gang collect money from their victims. I probably had the bad luck to arrive here at the moment a client was expected.

"You mean the same fellow who had the reaching rod hit you to get you out of the way?" Bess asked. "Oh," she added nervously, "he still may be around!"

"I doubt it," Nancy said. "He probably took the money that girl left, and ran."

"I'm going to inform the police!" Hannah Gruen announced in a determined voice.

Nancy tried to dissuade her, but for once her arguments had no effect. On the way home with the girls, Mrs. Gruen herself stopped at the office of the State Police. She revealed all she knew of the attack upon Nancy.

As a result, troopers searched the woods thoroughly; but, exactly as Nancy had foreseen, not a trace was found of her assailant. However, when they searched the interior of the cabin, they found evidence pointing to the fact that its recent residents were interested in magic.

When they reached home, Mrs. Gruen told Nancy about the telephone call from a clerk at the

Claymore Hotel. She went to see him at once, and was given a letter addressed to Mrs. Egan. It was signed by Mrs. Putney!

The note merely said that the services of Mrs. Egan would no longer be required. The spirit of Mrs. Putney's departed husband was again making visitations to his former home to advise her.

Taking the letter with her, Nancy mulled over the matter for some time.

The next morning, she decided to pay Mrs. Putney a visit, hoping she would be able to see her this time. But Mrs. Putney was not there, and a neighbor in the next house told Nancy she had been gone all morning.

"Doesn't Mrs. Putney ever drive her car?" Nancy asked, seeing it through a garage window.

"Not since her husband died."

"Does she have someone else drive her?"

"Oh, no! She won't let a soul touch the car."

Nancy was puzzled. Someone must have taken the car without Mrs. Putney's permission.

"If that woman we saw in the back seat was Mrs. Putney, maybe she didn't know where she was or what she was doing, any more than poor Lola did when she walked into the river!" Nancy told herself.

Nancy thanked the woman and withdrew. She hurried back to the garage to look for evidence that the car had been used recently. Fortunately the door was not locked. She examined the car carefully. It was covered with a film of dust and the rear axle was mounted on jacks. It had obviously not been driven for some time.

Something else struck Nancy as peculiar. The license plate bore a number that was different from the one registered as Mrs. Putney's.

"Hers must have been stolen and someone else's plate put on her car!" the young detective thought excitedly. "Maybe this number belongs to one of the racketeers and he used Mrs. Putney's to keep people from tracing him!"

Nancy dashed off in her convertible to the Motor Vehicle Bureau office. There she learned that the license on the widow's car had been issued to a Jack Sampson in Winchester, fifty miles from River Heights. But this revelation was mild in comparison with what the clerk told her next.

"Jack Sampson died a few months ago. His car was kept in a public garage. The executor of the estate reported that the license plate had been stolen."

As soon as Nancy recovered from her astonishment, she thanked the clerk for the information. Telephone calls to Winchester brought out the fact that the deceased man's reputation had been above reproach. He could not have been one of the racketeers. Nancy decided that before telling the police where the stolen license plates could be found, she would give Mrs. Putney a chance to tell what she knew about it all.

Hurrying back, she was just in time to see the widow coming up the street with several packages. Nancy hastened to her side and offered to take them. Although Mrs. Putney allowed her to carry them, she did not invite Nancy into the house. Therefore, Nancy told her story of the license plate as they stood on the front porch.

"I wasn't in that car you saw, and you must be mistaken about the license plate," Mrs. Putney told her flatly.

"Come, I'll show you," Nancy urged, leading the way to the garage and opening the door. "Why—why—" she gasped in utter bewilderment.

The correct license number was back on the car!

"You see why I have come to doubt your ability to help me," Mrs. Putney said coldly. "I no longer need your assistance, Nancy. As a matter of fact, I have every expectation of getting my stolen jewelry back very soon. My husband's spirit has been visiting me right here at home as he used to do, and he assures me that everything will turn out satisfactorily."

Leaving Nancy distressed and more concerned than ever, Mrs. Putney walked into the house without even saying good-by. As Nancy started away, she decided that further protection for the widow would have to come from the police.

Next, she drove to police headquarters to see her old friend Captain McGinnis. Nancy explained that she knew someone had appropriated the Putney license plate, and probably would do so again.

"Mrs. Putney has told me some things that make me think someone prowls around there late at night or early in the morning," Nancy told him. "I'm afraid she may be in danger."

Nancy kept to herself the idea that a member of the ring of fake mediums might be playing the role of Mr. Putney's spirit. She had noticed that two windows of Mrs. Putney's bedroom opened onto the roof of a porch. It would be very easy for an agile man to climb up there and perform as the late Mr. Putney.

The officer agreed to keep men on duty to watch the house night and day. Nancy was so hopeful of rapid developments, now, that every time the telephone rang, she was sure it was word that the police had caught one or more of the gang.

But when she had received no word for a whole day, she went to see Captain McGinnis. He told her that plainclothesmen had kept faithful watch of the Putney home, but reported that no one had been found trying to break in; in fact, Captain

McGinnis said he was thinking of taking the detectives off the case because the house was now unoccupied.

"You mean Mrs. Putney has gone away?" Nancy asked incredulously.

"Yes, just this morning," the officer replied. "Bag and baggage. Probably gone on a vacation."

Nancy was amazed to hear this, and also chagrined. She had not expected such a turn of events!

"I'm certain Mrs. Putney isn't on vacation," Nancy told herself grimly. "It's more likely that she received a spirit message advising her to leave.

Recalling the widow's mention of getting back the stolen jewelry, Nancy surmised that Mrs. Putney might have gone off on some ill-advised errand to recover it. Thoroughly discouraged, Nancy had yet another disappointment to face. Scarcely had she reached home, when an urgent telephone call came from Mrs. White.

"Oh, Nancy! The very worst has happened!" the woman revealed tearfully. "Lola's gone!"

"Gone? Where, Mrs. White?"

"I don't know," Lola's mother wailed. "She left a note saying she was leaving home. Oh, Nancy, you must help me find her!"

CHAPTER XVI

A Well-Baited Trap

WORRIED over the news about Lola, Nancy went without delay to see Mrs. White. She learned that the girl had departed very suddenly. Mrs. White was convinced her daughter had been kidnapped or had met with foul play.

"Have no fear on that score," Nancy said reassuringly. She told Mrs. White of her idea that a group of clever thieves might be mesmerizing or threatening their victims in order to get their money. "They're too interested in Lola's earnings to let anything happen to her," she finished.

After telling Mrs. White she was sure her daughter would realize her mistake and return home, Nancy left. She decided to walk in the park and thrash matters out in her own mind. Presently she seated herself on a bench and absently watched two swans in a nearby pond.

She scarcely noticed when a thin woman in

black sat down beside her. But when the stranger took out a handkerchief and wiped away tears, Nancy suddenly became attentive.

"Are you troubled?" she inquired kindly.

"Yes," the woman answered. Eager to confide in someone, she began to pour out her story.

"It's my daughter." The stranger sighed. "She's causing me so much worry. Nellie works and makes good money, but lately all she does is complain she hasn't a penny. She must be frittering it away on worthless amusements."

Nancy listened attentively, made a few queries, and then suggested to the woman that she ask her daughter if she made a practice of leaving money in a certain black walnut tree.

"In a walnut tree!" exclaimed the woman.

"Also, find out if she sends money through the mail, and if so, to whom," Nancy instructed. "Ask her if she ever visits a medium or is helping support orphans at a place called Three Branch Home. Find out if you can whether or not spirits mysteriously appear to her at night."

"My goodness!" the woman cried in amazement. "You must be a policewoman!"

Nancy scribbled her father's unlisted telephone number on a scrap of paper and gave it to the stranger. "If you need help or have any information, call me here at once," she added.

The woman pocketed the telephone number

and quickly rose from the bench. "Thank you, miss. Thank you kindly," she murmured.

Only after the stranger had disappeared, did it occur to Nancy that she might have been unwise in offering advice so freely.

Definitely annoyed at herself, Nancy returned home, where she found a telegram from her father. It said that private detectives working for him in Chicago had traced some of Mrs. Putney's stolen jewelry to a pawnshop there. But the ring belonging to her husband and her pearl necklace were still missing.

Her father's mention of the Putney jewels caused Nancy to wonder anxiously what had become of the widow and of Lola White. Could there be any connection in their simultaneous disappearance? A panicky thought struck the young detective. Perhaps they were being held prisoners at some hideout of the racketeers.

Almost at once Nancy put this idea out of her mind. These people were too clever to resort to kidnapping. Since they knew that Blackwood Hall was under surveillance, it was logical to assume that the gang was operating in new surroundings. If she could discover where Mrs. Putney had gone, then perhaps she would be able to locate the men who were seeking to separate the gullible woman from her money.

From Mrs. Putney's next-door neighbor Nancy

learned that her late husband had owned a hunting lodge on Lake Jasper, across the state line,
where he had spent a great deal of time each summer.

So far as anyone knew, his widow had not visited the place since his death. Nancy thought
there was a good possibility that Mrs. Putney
might be at the lodge now. Moreover, Lake Jasper
was the place where Mr. Drew's stolen car had
been found!

Hannah Gruen did not entirely approve of
Nancy's making a trip to Lake Jasper, preferring
that she wait until her father returned. In the end,
the housekeeper agreed to the plan but only after
the parents of Bess and George had consented to
having their daughters accompany Nancy.

"If for any reason you decide to stay more than
one night, telephone me at once," Hannah
begged.

Taking only light luggage, the girls started off
early the next morning. During the drive, Nancy
confided to her friends that she suspected Lola
had run away from home and did not intend to
return.

"Those people who seem to have her in their
control have probably found her a job in another
town. I must do everything I can to trace her, as
soon as I find out about Mrs. Putney."

Lake Jasper was situated in the heart of pine
woods country, and was one of a dozen beautiful

small lakes in the area. Not knowing Mrs. Putney's address, the girls obtained directions at the post office. They learned that the hunting lodge was at the head of the lake, in an isolated spot.

"No sense going there until we've had lunch," remarked Bess. "It's after one o'clock now, and I'm faint from hunger."

At an attractive tearoom nearby, the girls enjoyed a delicious lake-trout dinner. Later, as they walked toward the car, Nancy suddenly halted.

"Girls," she said, "do my eyes deceive me, or is that Lola White walking ahead of us?"

The person Nancy pointed out was some distance down the street, her back to the three girls.

"It's Lola all right!" Bess agreed. "What do you suppose she's doing at Lake Jasper?"

"My guess is she's here with Mrs. Putney," Nancy replied grimly.

"But I'm sure they don't know each other," Bess said.

"Perhaps the gang arranged for her to come up here with Mrs. Putney," Nancy suggested.

The girls drove half a block ahead of Lola. Satisfied that they had made no mistake in identifying the girl, they alighted and walked directly toward her.

At an intersection the four met. Lola gazed at them, but her face was expressionless. She passed the trio without a sign of recognition.

"Well, of all things!" said Bess as the three

friends halted to stare after Lola. "She certainly was pretending she didn't know us."

"Maybe she didn't," Nancy replied. "Lola acted as she did the time Ned and I found her wading out into the river. I suggest we follow her. Maybe she'll lead us to the Putney Lodge."

The girls waited until Lola was nearly out of sight and then followed in the car. Leaving the village, Lola struck out through the woods. Nancy parked and they continued on foot. A mile from town, near the waterfront, they saw a cabin constructed of peeled logs. An inconspicuous sign tacked to a tree read *Putney Lodge*.

"Your hunch was right, Nancy," Bess whispered as they saw Lola enter by a rear door.

Nancy hesitated. "Seeing Lola here complicates things," she said. "I'm afraid there's more to this than appears on the surface."

Just then Mrs. Putney came out on the porch. The girls remained in hiding. After she went indoors, Nancy said:

"Lola may be completely under the spell of those who have been getting money from Mrs. Putney. They may be using her services here."

"You think Lola, in a hypnotized state, is expected to steal from Mrs. Putney!" Bess gasped.

"Either that, or she may have been instructed to assist a member of the gang. I'd like to do a little scouting around before we let them know we're here."

When the girls reached town, Nancy stopped at the bank. Unfortunately it was closed for the day, but by making inquiries she located the home of the bank's president, Henry Lathrop. Nancy introduced herself and learned that her father once had brought a case to a successful conclusion for Mr. Lathrop.

"And what can I do for you?" the man inquired.

Nancy asked him if Mrs. Henry Putney had a safe-deposit box at the bank in which she might be keeping stocks, bonds, or cash.

"Her husband had a large safe-deposit box, and she has retained it."

Nancy's pulse quickened as she learned Mrs. Putney had spoken to the banker early that morning. The widow had been carrying an unusually large handbag. She had taken her box into a private room and been there some time.

"Something up?" Mr. Lathrop asked.

"I'm afraid so," Nancy answered. "I hope I'm not too late. You see, Mr. Lathrop, a gang of thieves has made away with her jewels, and I suspect that they are now after her inheritance. I've been trying to catch up with these people—"

"If what you say is true, the police should be called in to protect Mrs. Putney," the banker said.

"I agree," Nancy replied. "I have a feeling that the people who are after Mrs. Putney's money may show their hand tonight."

Later, when Nancy related her story to George and Bess, they wanted to know what she was planning.

"A call on the State Police. The next job needs strong men!"

At headquarters Nancy gave the police all the details of the case. The mob was obviously ready to strike and make a quick getaway. It was time that the law stepped in. The young detective made such an impressive presentation of the facts that she was promised that a cordon of troops would be assigned to the lake area that night.

Nancy and her friends obtained a large room at the Lake Jasper Hotel, where the police promised to notify them at once should anything develop. Nancy awoke several times during the night, wondering what might be taking place at the Putney Lodge. She had just opened her eyes again as it was beginning to grow light, when the telephone on the stand by the bed jingled.

Nancy snatched it up. She listened attentively a moment, then turned excitedly to call her friends who were still asleep.

"Girls!" she cried. "The troopers have a prisoner!"

CHAPTER XVII

Breaking a Spell

AT headquarters Nancy, Bess, and George learned that a man had been caught entering the Putney Lodge shortly after midnight. He had refused to give his name or answer any questions.

"Will you take a look at the fellow through our peephole and see if you recognize him?" the officer in charge asked. "He's in the center cell."

The three girls were led to a dark inner room. One by one they peered through a sliding wooden window which looked out upon the cell block. None of them had ever seen the prisoner in question, who was pacing the floor nervously.

"Maybe he'll break down this morning," the officer said. "Suppose you come back later."

As they left police headquarters, Nancy proposed that the girls go to the Putney cabin. When they arrived, the lodge showed signs of considerable activity. Mrs. Putney was in the living room, hurriedly packing. She made no effort to hide her displeasure at seeing the three girls.

"How did you know I was here?" she asked.

"It's a long story," Nancy replied. "But please answer one question: Do you still have your stocks and bonds safe in your handbag?"

This question evidently came as a complete surprise. The woman stammered for a moment and then sat down.

"Nancy Drew, I can't face you! You're uncanny. Not a soul in this world knew—"

"Mrs. Putney, please don't be upset," Nancy pleaded. "When you refused to take me into your confidence any longer, and left River Heights, I simply had to use my common sense as any detective would do. I'm trying to protect you against your own generous nature. You have never believed me when I told you that you are the victim of an unscrupulous gang. When I learned that you had opened your safe-deposit box I had to inform the police. It was they who caught your burglar."

The widow finally raised her head. "Yes, my securities are safe. So you—you know about the thief?"

"Very little. Tell me about him."

"It was so upsetting," the widow replied nervously. "My maid and I were sleeping soundly in our bedrooms."

So Lola was working as a maid!

"Suddenly we heard a shot fired," Mrs. Putney went on, "and there was a dreadful commotion. Several State Police officers were pounding on the door. I slipped on a dressing gown and went to see what they wanted. They asked me if I could identify the man they had caught trying to get in through a window."

"Was he anyone you knew?" asked Nancy.

"No, I never saw him before in my life. But I'm frightened. That's why I'm going home."

"And your maid?"

"I haven't told Violet yet."

Nancy quietly revealed that "Violet" was Lola White, that they had met her in the village, and were afraid she was under the influence of the same gang to which the night marauder belonged.

Mrs. Putney became more and more trusting as the conversation progressed. She was ready to admit that she had been foolish to act without advice.

"I suppose you received a spirit message to take your valuables from the bank and hold them until the spirit gave you further instructions," Nancy stated.

"Yes. My late husband contacted me."

"Will you please put them back in your safe-deposit box and not touch them again until—" Nancy hardly knew how to go on to compete with the spirit's advice—"until you have consulted Mr. Lathrop," she ended her request.

"I'll think about it," Mrs. Putney conceded. "Thank you, anyway, for all your help."

Bess spoke up, asking how Lola White happened to be working for her. Mrs. Putney said that the spirit had told her the girl would come to her at the lodge seeking employment and that she was to engage her.

"She had no luggage and told me her name was Violet Gleason," Mrs. Putney added. "She seems very nice, though odd. But if she's acting under some sort of mesmeric spell as you believe, then I don't want her around!"

"Maybe we can bring Lola out of it," Nancy suggested. "Then she'll want to go home, I'm sure. Let's go and talk to her."

Lola was sitting on the dock. As they approached her, she continued to stare at the girls without showing any sign of recognition. She was not unfriendly, however, and Nancy endeavored to bring her out of her trance by mentioning her mother, the school she had attended, a motion-picture house in River Heights, and several other familiar names. Lola merely shook her head in a bewildered way.

"Is her condition permanent?" Bess asked anxiously as the group returned to the lodge.

"I'd like to try one more thing before we take her home," Nancy said. "I don't want Mrs. White to see her this way. Mrs. Putney," she added, turn-

ing to the widow, "you will have to help us perform an experiment."

Mrs. Putney agreed to do anything to assist.
However, when Nancy explained that her idea
was to conduct a fake séance which would bring
Lola to her senses, Mrs. Putney hesitated. Finally
she said:

"I suppose it's only fair to give it a trial. And I
must admit you've been right many times, Nancy.
Yes, I'll help you."

While Bess and George stayed with Lola,
Nancy and Mrs. Putney went to the village. The
widow returned her stocks, bonds, and cash to the
bank. Then they drove to Winchester, where
Nancy purchased materials needed for the experiment.

At midnight the three girls posted themselves
on the side porch of the lodge. Through a window
they could see Mrs. Putney and Lola seated in the
candle-lighted living room beside a dying log fire,
as had been planned.

"Now, if only Mrs. Putney doesn't lose her
nerve and give us away!" Nancy said.

"I hope we don't fumble *our* act!" Bess said,
nervously adjusting her long veil and gown.

"We won't," replied Nancy. "Shall we start?"

Without showing herself, she flung wide the
double doors leading from the porch into the living room. George, out of sight, waved a huge fan.

The resulting gust of wind extinguished the candles and caused the dying embers on the hearth to burst into flames.

George, hidden by darkness, reached in and uncorked a bottle of phosphorus and oil. At once a faint green light glowed spookily in the room.

Working from behind the door, Nancy, by means of a magician's reaching rod, made a large piece of cardboard appear to float in mid-air.

At the same time Bess, the long veil over her face, glided in and seated herself beside the trembling Lola. The girl half arose, then sank back, her eyes riveted on the moving cardboard.

With a quick toss of her wrist, Nancy flung it from the reaching rod, directly at Lola's feet. Plainly visible in glowing phosphorous characters was the Three Branch insigne.

Lola gasped, and even Mrs. Putney, who knew the séance was a fake, recoiled as if from a physical blow. A voice intoned:

"Lola! Lola! Give no more of your money to the orphans. They are not real, and their spirits do not need your help. Lola, do you hear me?"

There followed a moment of complete silence. Then the girl sprang to her feet, muttering:

"Yes, yes, I hear! I will obey!"

She reached out as if to grasp the arm of the figure who was veiled, and then toppled over in a faint. As Bess rejoined the other girls on the porch, Nancy closed the doors. Mrs. Putney

flooded the room with light. The séance was at an
end.

"Shouldn't we show ourselves now and help
bring Lola out of her faint?" Bess asked anxiously
as they watched through the window.

"That might give everything away," Nancy
said. "I think Mrs. Putney is capable of handling
things now. Let's look on from here."

To the relief of the trio, Lola soon revived.

"How are you feeling?" they heard the widow
inquire solicitously.

"Sort of funny," the girl answered, rubbing her
head. "Where am I?"

"At my lodge, Lola. You are employed here as a
maid."

"How can that be?" the bewildered girl asked.
"I work in a factory. I must get back to my job! My
mother needs my help. I've been giving away too
much money."

When Nancy, Bess, and George heard this, they
knew the séance had been a success. Not only had
Lola regained her normal thought processes, but
the idea of refusing to give funds to unworthy
causes also had taken firm root.

"Our work here is done," Nancy whispered to
her friends. "Let's return to the hotel."

"I'm so relieved for Lola's sake," said George.

The next morning the girls decided to leave
Lake Jasper without seeing Mrs. Putney again.

"I'm sure the poor woman is aware now that

she was being cheated by those people," Nancy said. "After she's had time to think matters over, she'll probably call me."

Before leaving Lake Jasper, Nancy went to the police station to see if the prisoner had revealed his identity and admitted his attempted crime.

"No, but we've sent his fingerprints to Washington to find out if he has a record," the officer said.

Nancy asked to look at him again through the peephole. This time, she felt that there was something vaguely familiar about him.

"We know by his accent he's from the South," the police officer told Nancy, "but he won't admit it, nor answer questions about his identity."

The officer turned on a tape recorder and Nancy listened to the prisoner's conversation with a guard. Only when the girls were en route home did it dawn upon Nancy that the man's voice resembled that of the New Orleans photographer!

"Girls!" she exclaimed. "Perhaps he and the prisoner are related! What was that photographer's name? Oh, yes, Towner."

Stopping at a gas station, she telephoned the police station and suggested they try out the name Towner on the prisoner, and mention New Orleans as a possible residence. In a few minutes word came back that the man had denied any connection with either one.

Nancy shrugged. "That photographer naturally

would be connected with this racket under an assumed name," she remarked.

During the drive to River Heights, the girls discussed the mystery from every angle. George and Bess were sure that the whole case soon would be solved and they praised Nancy for what she had done to prevent the gang from fleecing Mrs. Putney.

Nancy, however, pointed out that the original case involving the stolen Putney jewels still remained unsolved.

"The most valuable pieces—the pearl necklace and her husband's ring—haven't been recovered," she said. "Howard Brex, the man I suspected, hasn't been located for questioning yet. Until that has been accomplished, my work isn't done."

Upon her arrival home, pleasant news awaited Nancy. During her absence at Lake Jasper, Mr. Drew had returned.

"I've had a long trip," he remarked, a twinkle in his eye. "Traveling to New Orleans took me several hundred miles out of my way!"

Nancy's eyes opened wide. "New Orleans!" she exclaimed. "Dad, what did you learn?"

Instead of answering, the lawyer handed his daughter a small envelope.

CHAPTER XVIII

Startling Developments

NANCY opened the envelope with great excitement. Inside was a photograph of a thin-lipped, rather arrogant-looking man in his early thirties.

"Who is he?"

"Howard Brex!"

Mr. Drew explained that he had obtained the picture from the New Orleans police. Officers there still were trying to discover where he had gone since his release from prison. Nancy studied the picture and exclaimed suddenly:

"He bears a slight resemblance to the New Orleans photographer! And here's something else, Dad."

Excitedly she related the events that had taken place during his absence. In conclusion, she told about the capture of the Lake Jasper housebreaker, whose voice was very much like that of the photographer.

"Perhaps they're all related!" she speculated.

Mr. Drew offered to wire the New Orleans police for more information.

Then a telephone call confirmed the fact that Mrs. Putney had returned from Lake Jasper. Nancy hurried over to show her the photograph of Howard Brex. The widow received her graciously, but when shown the picture she insisted that she had never seen the man. Nancy had great difficulty in concealing her disappointment.

Upon returning home Nancy telephoned the Lake Jasper police for news of their prisoner. He still refused to talk, but the report from Washington on his fingerprints revealed that he had no criminal record.

No reply came to Mr. Drew's telegram, either that day or the next. But on the second day Nancy received a disturbing letter. It was signed "Mrs. Egan."

Written on cheap paper, the message was brief and threatening. It warned Nancy to give up her sleuthing activities or "suffer the consequences."

Nancy was worried. "This comes of talking to that strange woman in the park!" she thought. "But she certainly didn't look like the kind of person who would serve as a lookout for the gang."

In the hope of seeing the stranger again, Nancy watched the park most of that day. In the late afternoon she saw the woman walking rapidly toward her, carrying several packages.

Nancy stepped behind a bush until the middle-aged woman had passed. Then she followed her to a rooming house.

The woman entered an old-fashioned brick structure. Nancy waited on the stoop for a moment and then rapped on the door, which was opened by the woman she had followed. She greeted Nancy with such evident pleasure that the latter's suspicions vanished.

"Do come in. I lost the telephone number you gave me, and I've been trying for days to find out how to get in touch with you."

Nancy quickly asked a few questions to be sure she was not being misled. The woman was Mrs. Hopkins. Her daughter Nellie, she said, was at work, but should be home soon.

"After talking to you, I asked Nellie those questions you suggested!" Mrs. Hopkins revealed. "She broke down and told me everything!"

Nellie, she added, had disclosed that unknown persons frequently got in contact with her by telephone. Usually it was a woman.

"Each time this stranger called she claimed that she had received a spirit message for Nellie," Mrs. Hopkins continued. "My daughter was asked to give money to the Three Branch Home, the earthly headquarters of the spirits. Orphans are brought there and trained as mediums to carry on the work of maintaining contact with the spiritual world."

"There is no such place as Three Branch Home, Mrs. Hopkins," said Nancy. "It was just a scheme of those thieves to get money for themselves!"

"Nellie realizes that now, I think. Anyhow, she was instructed to leave her contributions on a certain day each week in the hollows of various walnut trees. The places were marked by the Three Branch sign."

"Did she do so, Mrs. Hopkins?"

"The last time Nellie went to the place, she was frightened away. She heard a sound as though someone had been struck, then she heard a moan."

Nancy was convinced that Nellie was the girl she had seen coming toward the big walnut tree where she had been struck unconscious, but she said nothing.

She continued to ask Mrs. Hopkins a few more questions. Nancy did not realize how time had flown by until a young woman, apparently returning from work, entered the room. After Nancy was introduced, Nellie Hopkins grasped the young detective's hand fervently.

"Oh, I never can thank you enough for saving me," she said gratefully. "I don't know why I let myself be taken in by those—those crooked people, except that they said good luck would come to me if I obeyed, and bad luck if I refused."

Nancy replied that she was glad to have been of

service, then she took the picture of Howard Brex from her purse. "Ever see this man?" she asked.

"You don't mean that *he* is a racketeer?" asked Nellie. "I saw him only once. He was tall and slender, and he seemed so nice," she added.

Nellie went on to say that she had met the man in the photograph when she had sat next to him on a bus. She admitted talking to him about her job and her family. She had even told him where she lived. Nellie had never seen him again, and did not even know his name, but she was sure, now, he had used her information to his own advantage. It probably was he who had turned over her address to Mrs. Egan.

Mrs. Hopkins' eyebrows raised, but she did not chide her daughter. The girl would not be so unwise again, she knew.

Nancy went home pleased to know that at last she had found a witness who could place Howard Brex with the group whose activities were connected with the disappearance of Mrs. Putney's jewels. All during the case the tall, thin man, the onetime designer of exquisite jewelry, had figured in her deductions. Just what was the part he played in the mystery? Her father, smiling broadly, opened the door.

"Time you're getting here!" he said teasingly. "I have some news."

"From New Orleans?" she asked eagerly.

"Yes, a wire came this afternoon. Your hunch

was right. The real name of that photographer you saw in New Orleans is Joe Brex. He's the brother of Howard.

"In fact, Howard has two brothers. The other one is John. Their mother was a medium in Alabama, years ago," Mr. Drew continued. "She disappeared after being exposed as a faker."

"But her sons learned her tricks!" Nancy declared. "And maybe she runs that séance place in New Orleans. Oh, Dad, thanks ever so much. We've now placed Howard and Joe Brex as members of our racketeers. I've still got to tie them up with the hocus-pocus that persuaded Mrs. Putney to bury her jewels at the designated spot, and with all of the goings-on at Blackwood Hall. But we're getting places, Dad!"

"The three brothers probably run the extortion racket together, with the woman you saw on the plane to help them," Mr. Drew said grimly.

"We must go back to Lake Jasper and talk to that prisoner tomorrow!" Nancy urged.

During the evening Mr. Drew made a call to the New Orleans police, suggesting they shadow the photographer, Joe Brex, and raid one of the services at the Church of Eternal Harmony.

Nancy's father went on to tell their suspicions concerning Joe's brothers, and to hazard the opinion that the photographer might be in league with them.

"If you can get a lead on whether Joe has been

disposing of any jewelry or other stolen articles, it might be the breaking point in our case."

"We'll see what information we can get for you," the officer told Mr. Drew.

"While I think of it," the lawyer finished, "if you can locate a picture of John Brex, will you send it to me at once?"

"Glad to do it," the officer replied.

The next morning, while Nancy was packing a change of clothes in case she and her father should stay overnight at Lake Jasper, Hannah Gruen brought in a telegram to Mr. Drew. Since he received many such messages, his daughter thought little about this one until she heard him utter an exclamation of surprise in the next room. Running to him, she asked what the wire said.

"Joe Brex recently left New Orleans in a hurry! His whereabouts is not known. The Church of Eternal Harmony was found locked, and the medium gone. The police couldn't locate a picture of John Brex, they say."

Before Nancy could comment, Hannah summoned her to the telephone. "Lake Jasper police calling."

The officer on the wire was brief. "Miss Drew, I'd like your help," he said. "That prisoner who wouldn't talk broke jail last night under very mysterious circumstances! The guard says there was a ghost in his cell!"

CHAPTER XIX

Trapped!

THE story that the Lake Jasper police told Nancy was a startling one.

On the previous night, the cell block had been guarded by an easygoing, elderly man who served as relief during the late hours of the night.

According to his story, he had been making a routine check tour of the cell block, when suddenly a pale-green, ghostly figure appeared to be flitting through the air inside the center cell. A sepulchral voice called him by name and said: "I am the spirit of your dear wife Hattie. Is all well with you? If you will unlock the cell, and come in where I am waiting to speak to you, I will tell you about our Johnny who was drowned and of Allan who was killed in the war."

In fear and trembling, the guard had obeyed. No sooner had he entered the cell when a damp cloth was pressed against his nostrils, and his keys

seized from his belt. Just before he lost consciousness he heard the cell door clang shut.

"The same old trick!" exclaimed Nancy.

She told the officer on the telephone the latest
information Mr. Drew had received, and their
conclusion that the three Brex brothers were re-
sponsible for the spirit racket.

"We think your prisoner was John Brex. One
of his confederates must have supplied him with
the information about the guard. But how could
anyone get inside the jail to deliver the spirit para-
phernalia to the man in the cell?" asked Nancy.

"Well, a woman came to the office and told us
that she understood we were holding an unidenti-
fied burglar. She asked if she might visit the prisoner. One of our men took her to the cell and
stayed with her in the corridor."

"Was the guard with her all the time she was
inside the cell block?" Nancy asked.

"Yes, he was," the officer at the other end of the
telephone replied. "Wait a minute," he added
quickly. "He left her when she fainted."

"Fainted?" repeated Nancy.

"Well, the woman looked at the prisoner for a
long time without a word. Then suddenly she fell
to the floor. Our man ran to get some spirits of
ammonia. When he got back she was still out, but
came around in a jiffy when he applied the smell-
ing salts to her nose."

"There's your answer," said Nancy. "She was a

member of the Brex setup and passed the robe and other things through the bars while the guard was out of the corridor. Where is she now?"

"Gone," replied the officer. "When we took her back to the office she told us that she had thought the man in the cell was her brother she hadn't seen in fifteen years, but decided he wasn't. We had to let her go."

"Well, I think when you catch up with Brex and his fainting visitor you will find them to be confederates," Nancy said.

The officer thanked Nancy for the explanation, and said a nation-wide alarm would be sent out on the escaped prisoner.

"Wherever those gangsters are, I'm sure they didn't have time to take all their loot with them," Nancy remarked to Ned the next afternoon as they sat together in his car in front of the Drew home. "They must have hidden it somewhere around here. Let's try to think where they would be most apt to cache it until things blow over and it becomes safe for them to collect it."

"Some bank vault?" Ned suggested.

"I doubt it. My hunch would be Blackwood Hall."

"But the troopers searched the place."

Nancy reminded him that although the police had been skeptical about her story, she was sure a live "ghost" had come out of one wall and gone through another in the old mansion.

"And those creaking sounds—" Suddenly she snapped her fingers. "There must be some way of getting from the underground room to the upstairs floors without using the stairs."

"Gosh, you could be right! How about hidden stairs between the walls?" Ned asked.

"I'm more inclined to think it may be a secret elevator—one you can operate by pulling ropes to raise and lower it," said Nancy.

"Let's go!" said Ned.

"Wait just a minute while I run into the house. I want to tell Hannah where we're going."

Nancy returned in a moment, and they set out for Blackwood Hall.

"So much about the place hasn't been explained," Nancy said thoughtfully. "Those sliding panels, for instance. They may be entrances to secret rooms as well as to an old elevator!"

In case they should run into trouble, Ned stopped at home and got his short-wave radio sending set.

When they reached Blackwood Hall, Nancy suggested that they separate, and he keep watch outside, in case any of the racketeers should show up. Ned agreed to the plan.

"Yell if you find anything, and I'll come running," he declared.

Nancy took a small tool kit from the car. Once in the house, working inch by inch, she made an inspection by flashlight of the second- and third-floor hallways of the dwelling. There was no evidence of any spring or contrivance that could move the carved walnut panels.

"The panel on the third floor must open from the outside," Nancy said aloud, "for I distinctly saw the "ghost" emerge from the wall on the second floor and disappear *into* the wall in the third-floor hallway. I'll have a look at the basement room and then come back here with a hatchet."

The main part of the basement, entered from the kitchen, revealed nothing to indicate the existence of a hidden elevator.

"If there is one, it must be in that secret room after all," Nancy decided.

Using the hidden door in the organ room, she slowly descended the steps. Her flashlight cut a circular pattern on the cracked walls of the tunnel as she played the light from side to side.

Finally Nancy reached the walnut door. To her amazement it now was bolted on the inner side, but with the tools from the car she managed to let herself in.

All was quiet inside the pitch-dark room. From the doorway, Nancy played her flashlight quickly around the four sides of the room. Satisfied that it was empty, she entered cautiously.

The door behind her creaked softly. Nancy

whirled around. There was no draft, yet the heavy walnut door seemed to move several inches. The door must be improperly hung, she thought.

Then, inch by inch, she began to inspect the paneled walls. At the far end of the room, she came upon a section which she found, upon minute examination, was not in a true line with the rest of the woodwork.

"This may be something!" Nancy thought, her pulse pounding.

She tugged and pushed at the paneling. Suddenly it began to move. It slid back all the way to reveal, just as Nancy had expected, a small, old-fashioned elevator, consisting of a wooden platform suspended on ropes, with another rope extending through a hole in the floor.

But her first thrill of discovery gave way to a cry of horror. Facing her in the elevator were two men—Howard Brex and his brother John, the escaped prisoner from Lake Jasper!

Confronted by the pair, Nancy backed away and tried to flee through the walnut doorway. Howard Brex seized her arm while the other man, holding a flashlight, blocked the exit.

"No, you don't!" Howard warned. "You've made enough trouble for us."

"I'm not afraid of you or your brother!" Nancy stated defiantly. "The police will be here any minute."

"Yes?" the man mocked. "If you're depending

"Nancy Drew, you've made enough trouble!" Howard
Brex rasped

on your boy friend to rescue you, guess again. We'll take care of him as soon as we dispose of you."

Nancy was dismayed to hear that the man knew Ned was awaiting her outside. She realized that if she screamed for help, it would only draw him into the trap.

"What do you plan to do with me?" she demanded.

"We'll take care of you, so you'll never bother us again," Howard Brex replied as he shoved her roughly toward the elevator. "Fact is, we've decided, since you have such a fondness for ghosts, to let you spend the remainder of your life with the ghost of Blackwood Hall!"

"You had plenty of warning," Howard went on. "But would you mind your own business? No! Not even after I knocked you out in the woods one day when you were spying on one of my clients."

Nancy knew she must keep them talking. As soon as Ned became concerned about her long absence he would radio for help. "So you admit you've cheated innocent people with your fake séances," she remarked.

"Sure, and don't think it isn't a good racket!" John Brex boasted.

"How many people have you fleeced?"

"So many that we'll be able to take a long vacation," his brother bragged.

"You sold some of Mrs. Putney's jewelry. But you still have her most valuable pieces!" Nancy accused him.

"Sure," Howard agreed. "We'll wait until the hubbub dies down. We'll sell the necklace and her husband's ring after we skip the country."

"You climbed along the roof outside of Mrs. Putney's bedroom window at night and spoke to her as if you were her husband's spirit," Nancy went on accusingly.

"You're a smart kid," John Brex mocked.

"You do know a lot," said Howard. "Even more than I thought. Well, the sooner we get this job over with, John, the better for us."

"I suppose your mother helped with the racket," Nancy remarked, hoping to gain time. "She ran those fake séances in New Orleans, and pretended to be the portrait of Amurah coming to life."

"It was a good trick," Howard said boastfully.

"She had a double wall built in the house so she could hide there?" Nancy asked.

"Sure, and she did the rapping back there, too."

"Was the old man at the Church of Eternal Harmony your brother Joe?"

"Yes, in disguise. The whole family's in the racket. John's wife has been helping us, and her friend, too."

"The friend is the one who drives the car, isn't she?" Nancy queried.

"Wouldn't you like to know?" John sneered.

"And she hypnotizes people?"

"No!" growled Howard. "She just gives them a whiff that makes them drowsy. *I* do the hypnotizing. Whenever any of my clients get out of line, I produce the beckoning hand."

"One of your luminous wax hands," declared Nancy. "And you must be a ventriloquist as well. Lola White nearly lost her life walking into the river because you hypnotized her," she accused him.

"That was your fault," the man replied. "You came snooping around here before I had a chance to get her out of it."

"Did you do your hypnotizing near the walnut trees that were used as hiding places for money and letters?" Nancy asked. "Or at the cabin where you held the fake séances?"

"Both places."

"I imagine the Three Branch symbol represented you three clever brothers."

"That'll be enough from you, young lady," snarled John. "I'm getting fed up with this dame's wisecracks, Howie!"

"You even played the organ," Nancy said coolly, turning to Howard. "And when you didn't have to use the dummy ghost, you dressed like one yourself."

John interrupted roughly, "This has gone far enough."

Before Nancy could ask another question, the men thrust her into the elevator. Her flashlight and car tools were taken from her.

"Nancy Drew, you're about to take your last ride!" Howard told her brutally. "In a few moments, young lady, you will join the ghost of Blackwood Hall!"

CHAPTER XX

A Hidden Discovery

THE secret panel closed in Nancy's face. A few moments later she felt the rope beside her moving and the lift began to rise slowly upward with a creaking, groaning sound.

What were John and Howard Brex going to do now? Move out their loot? Capture Ned?

With a jerk, the elevator suddenly halted. Nancy tugged at the rope. It would not move!

At the same moment, Nancy saw a faint, greenish glow arising from one corner of her prison. Presently she became aware of an unpleasant odor rapidly growing stronger. Then Nancy understood.

"Those fiends uncorked a bottle of phosphorus and oil in this elevator, and they've probably added a deadly sleeping potion for me to inhale," she thought, breaking out in cold perspiration. "That's what they meant by saying that in a few moments I would join the ghost of Blackwood Hall. They meant Jonathan Humphrey, who died in the duel. I'll die at Blackwood Hall too!"

For an instant Nancy nearly gave way to panic. Then reason reasserted itself.

From her pocket she took a handkerchief. Covering her nose and mouth with it, she groped about frantically on the floor of the dark elevator. Guided by the greenish glow, she found a small bottle in one corner.

Already weak and dizzy, Nancy had no time to search further for the stopper. Instead, she pulled off her suit jacket and jammed part of the sleeve into the opening of the bottle.

Immediately the light was extinguished. But Nancy by now felt so drowsy that she was forced to sit down.

Sleep overcame her. She had no idea of how much later it was when she awoke. But now she felt stronger. The sickening odor was gone. She could think clearly.

She pounded against the wooden sides of the elevator shaft. Three of the walls seemed to be as solid as stone. Only the fourth seemed thin. Could this be the panel of the third-floor hallway?

The old house was as still as death itself. Nancy was certain Howard and John Brex had fled, and no doubt they had captured Ned too. As time dragged on and still no one came, she became convinced that her friend had met with disaster.

"I told Hannah that Ned and I were coming here," Nancy thought. "She'll be worried about our long absence and send help."

Then a harrowing thought came to her. Maybe her friends had come and gone while she was asleep! By the luminous hands of her wrist watch, Nancy knew she had been in the elevator over two hours.

"It's no use!" she despaired. Then instantly she added, "I *mustn't* give up hope!"

Nancy sat down again on the floor, trying to figure out some means of escape. But scarcely had she closed her eyes to concentrate than she became aware of sounds.

Pressing an ear against the crack between the elevator floor and the wall, Nancy listened intently. With a thrill of joy she recognized Bess's high-pitched voice. Then she heard others speaking: her father, Hannah Gruen, and George Fayne.

Nancy began to shout and pound on the elevator door. Attracted by the noise, her friends came running up the stairway. Nancy kept shouting directions, until finally they were able to locate the wall panel behind which she was imprisoned.

"Nancy!" her father called. "Are you all right?"

"Yes, Dad, but I'm in an elevator and can't get out. I can't even move it."

"We'll soon find a way. If we can't open this panel, we'll tear the wall down!"

"Is Ned safe?" Nancy asked anxiously.

"Haven't seen him," her father replied. "Hannah got worried after you'd been gone so long, and told us you had come here. Ned isn't with you?"

"No," Nancy replied in a discouraged voice, then added, "Please go down to the ghost room and see if you can find out how to move this elevator."

Several minutes passed, then Mr. Drew reported no success.

"It's a very old-fashioned hand type and works by pulling a rope," he said. "Evidently they have locked the wheel over which the rope passes at the top. Well, here goes the wall!"

Nancy heard a thud, then the sound of splintering wood. A moment later light beamed through a small hole.

"Hand me the flashlight," said Nancy. "Maybe I can find out how the panel opens."

In a few moments Nancy located a lock. Releasing it, she pushed up the section of wall and tumbled into her father's arms.

"Thank goodness you're safe!" Hannah cried, hugging her in turn. "When you didn't come home, I knew something had happened!"

"Bless you, Hannah, for bringing help!" Nancy exclaimed.

From the yard came the sharp yipping of a dog. "Why, that sounds like Togo!" Nancy exclaimed.

"We left him in the car," her father explained. "Something must have excited him."

Hastening downstairs, the party reached the front porch just as several state troopers, surrounding two women and two men, emerged from the woods. Nancy was overjoyed to see Ned leading the procession!

"They've captured Howard and John Brex!" she cried. "And that first woman with them—she's the one we met on the plane. The other must be the veiled chauffeur!"

Ned ran to Nancy's side. Breathlessly he explained that upon seeing the two men leaving Blackwood Hall, he had hurriedly summoned state troopers by means of the short-wave set.

"Then I trailed the Brex brothers and kept sending my location to the police. What a chase!"

"You did a swell job, fellow," complimented one of the troopers. "We sure had a hard time trying to keep up with you."

"We caught the men and the women at a little hotel down the river," Ned added. "They were packing their duds, intending to make a getaway."

"Good work, Ned!" Nancy congratulated him. "This practically winds up the case, except for capturing Joe Brex."

"Don't worry about that," Mr. Drew interposed. "The police will run him in before forty-eight hours have elapsed."

The four prisoners refused to talk when confronted by Nancy and her party. Though they would not admit that they had any loot hidden at Blackwood Hall or elsewhere, their arrogance was completely gone. Howard Brex looked completely crestfallen when Nancy repeated to the troopers all the damaging evidence he had boastfully revealed to her a few hours earlier.

When Ned heard how they had put her in the elevator to die, he was filled with remorse. Having no idea anything more had happened than Nancy had smoked out the gangsters, he had felt it all right to leave her and go after them.

"I'll never do that again!" he vowed.

Tearfully, John Brex's wife, the woman they had seen on the plane, admitted her identity. She acknowledged having trailed the three girls to New Orleans after learning that Mrs. Putney had engaged Nancy to find the stolen jewelry. When they threw her off the scent, and she saw them coming out of the Church of Eternal Harmony and heading for the photographer's, she hastened to warn Joe. John happened to be there, and the three concocted the scheme of putting the warning on the plate and carrying Nancy away in a car to an empty house in order to frighten her off the case.

Mrs. Brex's friend also admitted her guilt. She had adopted clever disguises for the sole purpose of deceiving Nancy, as well as the people the group sought to cheat. It was she who had picked up the Egan letters at the hotel.

"Don't say another word!" John shouted. "You've said too much already!"

Here George interrupted to address Howard Brex. "After you had abandoned having séances at Blackwood Hall and moved your equipment by wheelbarrow to the cabin, we tracked you there and found smoke—acrid smoke, not wood smoke, coming out the chimney and from under the door."

Howard sneered. "Had you guessing, eh? All I was doing was trying out a new brand of spirit powder. I ducked out a back window when I heard someone trying to break into the place."

After the prisoners were taken off to jail, Nancy suggested that a trooper remain at Blackwood Hall with her and the others to investigate the paneled walls of the rambling old house.

"I want you all to take an elevator ride with me!" Nancy said gaily, "and see if we can locate the gangsters' loot."

The wall panel on the third floor still stood open. Nancy swung a flashlight around the elevator. In a moment she found what she was looking for: the mechanism to run the car. It was high up in the shaft under the roof. An iron bar was thrust through the wooden wheel over which the rope ran.

In a moment the wheel again was free. Using the rope, Nancy lowered the elevator platform to the level of the second floor. There she examined carefully each wall of the elevator shaft. To her joy she located the spring that operated the panel from the inside. It rolled back exposing the second-floor hall.

Then she turned her attention to the opposite wall of the elevator shaft. It, too, seemed to be a panel, and she went over every inch of it for a catch. When she found it, she pressed the release and the panel slid noiselessly upward.

"A secret room!" she cried.

The others crowded around her. Before them stood a manikin dressed in flimsy white, as well as reaching rods, bottles of phosphorus, oil, and several books on hypnotism.

Besides these, the searchers found box upon box of envelopes stuffed with bills. But most important was a notebook containing the names and addresses of people who had been swindled by the spirit racket.

"This money will help repay all those people who have been robbed," Nancy declared.

Under the eaves Nancy came upon a large chest which proved to contain a complete set of craftsmen's tools such as a jeweler would use—Howard Brex's outfit.

"I suppose those clever imitations which Mr. Freeman detected when Mrs. Putney took them to be cleaned were fashioned right here in Black-wood Hall," Mr. Drew said thoughtfully.

"But where are Mrs. Putney's missing gems?" Nancy asked.

"Right here in this envelope!" George spoke up. "Now your work on the case is really complete." Turning to the officer, she said, "Nancy got into this thing trying to trace Mrs. Putney's stolen jewelry. Whoever would have thought that all this could happen before the thieves were caught?"

The following day, events occurred very rapidly. Joe Brex and his mother were arrested in Chicago. Joe acknowledged he had built up a good business in spirit photography.

He and the others finally confessed their full part in the sordid Three Branch swindle, and admitted that they first cajoled, then threatened their victims when they did not yield to the suggestions of the spirits. The men also admitted having stolen Mr. Drew's car to move out some of their props.

To celebrate the successful conclusion of the mystery, Hannah Gruen planned a surprise dinner and invited all of Nancy's closest friends, and also Mrs. Putney.

"Oh, my dear," the widow said, tears in her eyes, "I was so unfair to you in my thoughts. At times I felt you lacked all understanding of my case. But you've made me realize how utterly stupid I was to be fooled into thinking my husband's spirit was giving me messages. Now, dear, I know you won't accept money as a reward for the work you have done in my behalf, but I hope you will take as an expression of my everlasting gratitude this cameo ring which belonged to my husband's mother. It is one of the jewels you helped me to recover."

"Oh, Mrs. Putney, I couldn't," protested Nancy.

"Nonsense," Mrs. Putney interrupted. "I have no one to inherit my lovely things when I go. I want you to have it as a memento of a case you solved in which many innocent people were saved from serious loss."

"You are very generous, Mrs. Putney. I would love to wear it. I enjoyed every moment I was working on the mystery—except the quagmire and the elevator incident," Nancy declared. "Dad," she said, turning to Mr. Drew, "I would never have done it without all the help you gave me."

"Ridiculous," Mr. Drew objected.

"I'll bet you could tackle your next case single-handed," Mrs. Putney insisted.

That exciting mystery, *The Clue of the Leaning Chimney,* was to come as a baffling surprise to the girl detective.

"Say," said George, laughing, "we learned enough about magicians' tricks to go into the ghost business ourselves. How about fitting up a studio at Blackwood Hall and running séances?"

Bess shivered. "No, thanks. We've just learned that it never pays to flimflam the public."

"Anyway, it's much more fun to catch the people who try to do the flimflamming!" Nancy said, smiling.

THE CLUE OF THE LEANING CHIMNEY

AS a result of an encounter with a sinister stranger on a lonely country road, Nancy Drew and her friend Bess Marvin discover that a rare and valuable Chinese vase has been stolen from the pottery shop of Dick Milton, a cousin of Bess.

Dick had borrowed the vase from his Chinese friend, elderly Mr. Soong. He is determined to repay Mr. Soong for the loss and tells Nancy that if he can find "the leaning chimney," he feels he will be on the track of a discovery which will solve his financial problems.

Nancy finds the leaning chimney, but it only leads her into more puzzles. Can there be any connection between the vase theft—one of a number of similar crimes—and the strange disappearance of the pottery expert Eng Moy and his daughter Lei?

Join Nancy and her friends in their exciting adventures as they unravel all the twisted strands of this intriguing mystery.

*A man was stepping through a panel in the
rear of the closet*

The Clue
of the
Leaning Chimney

BY CAROLYN KEENE

PUBLISHERS   *Grosset & Dunlap*   NEW YORK

Contents

The Clue
of the
Leaning Chimney

CHAPTER I

The Mysterious Stranger

"Oh, Nancy, this road is so lonely! And here we are with all this money. It'd be awful if it were stolen!"

Bess Marvin gripped the handbag in her lap a bit more tightly and peered nervously through the windshield of the convertible.

A dark forest flowed past the car on either side of the road. Black clouds were gathering in the night sky, and the wind whispered dismally through the swaying trees.

The pretty, somewhat plump girl shivered slightly.

"Cheer up, Bess," comforted the slim, titian-haired driver. "We'll soon be home."

Nancy Drew spoke with more confidence than she felt. As she deftly steered the car around a turn in Three Bridges Road, her blue eyes mirrored a slight uneasiness in her own thoughts. She glanced at the handbag in Bess's lap. It contained three hundred and forty-two dollars and sixty-three cents, the proceeds of a charity rummage sale the two eighteen-year-old girls had run that evening in Masonville.

Nancy, who was treasurer of the group, had the responsibility of depositing the money in a River Heights bank. Studying the dark, deserted road ahead, she wondered if she had not made a mistake in taking the lonely short cut. The attractive girl tucked a stray wisp of hair into place and put the thought firmly out of her mind.

"Don't be a ninny," she chided herself. "Just because there's no traffic, that's no reason to start imagining things."

"Nancy, can't you drive faster?" Bess asked.

Stealing a look at her nervous companion, Nancy smiled with affection. Bess was one of her closest friends.

There was a sudden flash of lightning, followed by a clap of thunder. A few drops of rain spattered against the windshield.

"Oh dear!" wailed Bess. "More trouble."

Nancy did not comment. The car was approaching a series of sharp, twisting curves in the road just this side of Hunter's Bridge. Driving safely around them required all her attention.

As they rounded the final turn, the headlights suddenly focused on a man. He was bending over something in the road, directly in the path of the car! He was unaware of Nancy's car!

The man was unaware of Nancy's car!

Bess screamed. Nancy twisted the steering wheel frantically, at the same time jamming her wrist against the horn and stepping on the brake. There was a screech of tires as the car swerved past the man and came to a stop thirty feet beyond.

"D-did we—?" Bess stuttered, unable to speak the awful thought that they had hit the man.

Nancy quickly took a flashlight from the front compartment and got out of the car. The man was lying in the middle of the road!

"Oh, Bess!" she cried fearfully. "He's hurt!"

But even as she hurried toward him, the man stumbled to his feet and began looking around him in the road as if he had lost something.

"Are you all right? I didn't hurt you?" Nancy asked.

To her astonishment he growled, "Go away!"

The brim of his battered felt hat was pulled low over his forehead and the turned-up collar of his topcoat concealed his mouth and chin. But Nancy got a quick glimpse of a pair of piercing, black eyes. Abruptly the man ran across the road and ducked behind some bushes.

"Is this what you're looking for?" Nancy called, picking up a bundle which had rolled off to one side.

"Put that bundle down and get out of here!" he ordered sharply.

"But I want to help," Nancy protested. "You may be hurt—"

"Listen, sister, I'm okay," his rough voice cut in. "But if you don't go now, *you'll* get hurt!"

As if to emphasize the threat, a rock, hurled out of the darkness, struck the road a scant six inches away and bounded into the ditch.

Bess, who had come up behind Nancy, tugged at her friend's sleeve. "Come on!" she whispered nervously. "He means it!"

But Nancy, her suspicions aroused, turned over the bundle she was holding. As she stared through a large tear in the paper, another rock, well aimed this time, smashed Nancy's flashlight. It also shattered Nancy's chance of getting a better look at the stranger's bundle.

Bess uttered a squeak of fear. "Oh, Nancy, hurry! Put that thing down and come on!"

This time Nancy obeyed the warning and hurried back to the car. Rain was falling in large drops as she started the motor. Nancy looked back, but neither the man nor the bundle was in sight.

"Whew!" said Bess as they drove through the downpour. "Next time you stop to talk to a man on a deserted road, count me out!"

Nancy laughed. "He certainly was nasty," she agreed. "Too bad we couldn't get a good look at him."

"What do you suppose was in that old bundle that made him act so funny?" Bess asked.

"A vase," Nancy told her. "At least, from what I could see, it looked like one. Green porcelain with an enormous red claw."

"Green porcelain with a red claw?" Bess repeated. "That's odd."

"Why?"

"Well, it sounds an awful lot like a vase on display in the window of Dick Milton's pottery shop," Bess went on. "Dick's vase is green, too, and it has a black Chinese dragon with red claws!"

Dick Milton was a cousin of Bess's. He had a small shop on Bedford Street in River Heights where he made and sold pottery. The young man also held classes in ceramics, one of which Bess was attending.

"The vase is beautiful," Bess went on. "Dick didn't make it—somebody lent it to him, I think."

Bess babbled on, explaining the perfection of the vase with the enthusiasm of one who has just learned how various pottery pieces are made.

"You ought to join our class," she said. "It's lots of fun."

Nancy found her attention wandering. Her thoughts went back to the man in the road. What was he doing in such a deserted place so late at night? Obviously he had not wanted to be seen. Her car, suddenly rounding a curve, had caught him unawares. And why had he behaved so strangely about the vase? Could it, by any chance, be the one from Dick Milton's shop?

"Why, Nancy, you're not even listening!" Bess's voice broke in accusingly.

"I'm sorry, Bess," she apologized. "I was thinking of that man and how suspiciously he acted."

"I know what that means," Bess declared. "You're itching for a new mystery to solve!"

Nancy, the daughter of a prominent criminal lawyer, was well known for her ability as an amateur detective. People who were in trouble frequently came to her for assistance.

The rain had ceased and a few stars began to flicker as Nancy drove through River Heights. When she turned into Bedford Street, Bess noted their new direction with surprise.

"This is the way to Dick's shop!"

"I know," said Nancy. "I want to look at his window."

Soon she eased the convertible to a stop under a street lamp in front of the pottery shop. The two girls got out and hurried to the plate-glass window.

Nancy frowned with anxiety as she peered at the clay dishes and bowls displayed on a black velvet background. There was no vase. Nancy tried the door. It was locked.

"The dragon vase has been stolen!" Bess whispered.

"Let's not jump to conclusions," said Nancy as she tried to quell her own fears. "Perhaps Dick put the vase somewhere else for the night. I'll phone him to make sure."

They walked quickly down the street to a corner drugstore. Nancy slipped into a telephone booth and dialed Dick's number. A sleepy hello answered.

"Dick Milton?" asked Nancy. "This is Nancy Drew. I'm sorry to call you so late, but it's urgent."

"What's the matter?" Dick asked excitedly.

"It's about the dragon vase in your store window," replied Nancy. "It isn't there now. Did you remove it?"

"The dragon vase? No!" Dick Milton's voice trembled with emotion. "It was there when I closed the shop. You say it isn't there now? This is terrible!"

"I'll get the police," Nancy offered.

"Tell them," Dick gasped, "the vase doesn't belong to me—and it's worth thousands of dollars!"

CHAPTER II

A Double Theft

DICK said he would come right down. He arrived as a police car pulled up to the curb and two officers stepped out. Nodding to the girls and the police, the young proprietor unlocked the shop door and entered. He switched on the light.

"You say a vase has been stolen?" queried Officer Murphy.

"What kind of vase?" his partner put in quickly.

"A Chinese vase," Dick replied dejectedly. "A rare Ming piece over two thousand years old."

"Whew!" exclaimed Murphy. "Let's see where the thief entered. It's evident it wasn't by the front door."

"Then we'd better check the back," the other officer said.

The two policemen hurried to the rear of the building, followed by Dick, Nancy, and Bess.

"Look!" Murphy exclaimed, pointing to an open window in the back of the shop. Marks of a jimmy were visible on the sill.

"Don't touch anything," Officer Reilly said to Dick, who reached up to close the window. "We'll take fingerprints."

Quickly he opened his kit and dusted the sill and a nearby chair which the thief might have touched as he entered. But not a print was to be found.

"The thief must have worn gloves," Nancy whispered to Dick.

"No doubt he left footprints outside," declared Murphy.

Nancy hurried out the back door with the officers, who beamed their flashlights on the earth beneath the window. Big, oval prints indicated the thief's feet had been covered with something to keep them from making shoe prints.

"What's your guess, Miss Drew?" Murphy asked.

"The thief tied burlap bags over his shoes."

"And I think you're right."

Suddenly they were startled by a cry from Dick, who had gone back to the shop. They ran inside.

"What's the matter?" Nancy asked.

"The small, green jade elephant!" he exclaimed. "It's gone, too!"

"Oh dear!" Bess cried out. "Was that loaned to you, too?"

"Yes," moaned Dick. "It was another of Mr. Soong's pieces. How can I ever repay him!"

"Who's Mr. Soong?" asked Reilly.

"He's a retired Chinese importer who lent me the vase and the elephant," explained Dick. "Business hasn't been so good, so Mr. Soong let me display his pieces, hoping they would attract customers to the shop."

"They attracted more than customers," put in Murphy. "And not a clue to the thief."

"Maybe I have a clue," Nancy spoke up.

Often she stumbled upon a mystery as she had this one. The first case the young sleuth had solved was *The Secret of the Old Clock*. Recently she had unraveled a mystery involving *The Ghost of Blackwood Hall*.

Nancy told the police about the man and the green vase with the large red claw she had seen at Hunter's Bridge.

"He just might be our thief," said Murphy. "Come on, Reilly. Let's try to track him down. Thanks for the tip, Miss Drew."

After the officers had gone, Bess asked Dick when he was going to tell Mr. Soong about the loss.

Dick groaned. "That, Bess, will be the hardest part. And after all Mr. Soong has done for me!"

With leaden feet he walked to the telephone and dialed. The shop was strangely quiet as the three waited for someone to answer at the other end of the line.

"I guess Mr. Soong is either out or asleep," said Dick. "I'll phone him first thing tomorrow morning. Well, it's late," he added. "You girls had better go home."

"If the police don't catch the thief," said Nancy as Dick locked the pottery shop, "I'd like to help you solve the mystery. I'll drop in to see you tomorrow."

The next morning, when Nancy went down to breakfast, her head was still full of the stolen vase mystery. Hannah Gruen, the Drews' middle-aged housekeeper, noticed Nancy's preoccupation as she came from the kitchen carrying a breakfast tray. Mrs. Gruen put the food in front of Nancy, but the girl didn't seem to see it. She sat as if in a trance.

"Wake up, Nancy," the housekeeper said, laughing.

"Oh, Hannah," Nancy said with a smile. "I was just thinking about dragons." She went on to relate the previous night's adventure.

"How strange!" Mrs. Gruen remarked. "But please eat, dear."

Nancy's mother had died many years ago, and the housekeeper had run the Drew household for so long she was regarded as one of the family.

Mrs. Gruen was proud of the young detective's accomplishments, but she always worried when Nancy was working on a case.

Nancy ate quickly and rose from the table. "I must go to Dick Milton's right away," she announced.

On the way, Nancy deposited the rummage-sale money at the bank. When she arrived at the pottery shop, she found the young man in better spirits.

"I told Mr. Soong about the theft first thing this morning," he said. "He was very calm about it all and said that unfortunately the loss was only partly covered by insurance. Of course money can't replace such a rare, old piece. I must somehow repay the part not covered by insurance."

"Any report from the police?" Nancy asked.

"No trace of the thief," Dick answered. "I guess you'd better join in the hunt. But first, will you please do me a favor, Nancy?"

"Surely."

"I want you to take this piece of jewelry back to Mr. Soong. I've explained to him who you are."

Nancy inspected the sea-green jade pendant that Dick held in his palm.

"It's lovely," said Nancy. "May I hold it?"

Dick placed the pendant in her hand. "It's the last piece from Mr. Soong in the shop," Dick explained. "I don't want this to be stolen, too!"

"Oh, I'd be thrilled to take it to Mr. Soong. I've heard his home is like a museum," replied Nancy. "I'd love to meet Mr. Soong, too, and have him tell me about the vase and the elephant. Then, if I ever see his prize possessions, I'll be able to recognize them."

Dick placed the jade on top of a fluff of cotton in a tiny white box, wrapped it, and gave the package to Nancy. Ten minutes later she arrived at the address Dick had given her and parked her car in front of the attractive Colonial house.

She went up the walk, and lifting the brass knocker, rapped on the door. It was opened by a short, inscrutable-looking Chinese servant wearing a black alpaca jacket. He regarded Nancy silently.

"Is Mr. Soong at home?" she inquired.

He bowed slightly and stepped back to let her pass. Nancy waited in the foyer while he closed the door, then he showed her into a study and motioned for her to be seated.

Nancy sat down on a nearby couch and turned to thank the servant, but he had silently disappeared. Her eyes wandered over the study.

As she gazed at the fireplace, her attention became fixed on a square piece of tapestry hung over the mantel. Nancy rose and studied the tapestry more closely. It was richly woven, with a Chinese dragon embroidered in black and red against a background of jade green.

"Do you like it?" a soft voice behind her inquired.

Nancy whirled sharply. Standing in the doorway was a short, gentle-faced Chinese with spectacles and a tiny goatee. He wore a richly brocaded mandarin coat and beautifully embroidered Chinese slippers. His eyes twinkled, and his slippers shuffled softly as he advanced into the study.

"I hope I did not frighten you."

Nancy smiled. "I'm afraid you did, just for a moment! You're Mr. Soong?"

"Yes."

"I'm Nancy Drew, a friend of Dick Milton's."

"Oh yes, the illustrious Drew family. I've heard of you and your father. Please sit down."

After giving him the package, Nancy mentioned last night's robbery. She told Mr. Soong about the strange man on the road. Mr. Soong showed intense interest when she mentioned the dragon's-foot design on the vase.

"This tapestry you found so fascinating," he said, indicating the cloth over the mantel, "bears the identical design that is glazed on the vase."

He rose and went to the fireplace. "The dragon you see here was an emperor's emblem. It has five claws. Only the emperor and his sons and Chinese princes of the first and second rank were allowed to have emblems showing dragons with five claws. Lesser princes had to be content with four-clawed dragons."

"How interesting!" Nancy murmured.

Soong fixed his gentle eyes on Nancy. "Did you notice the number of claws on the vase?"

"No, I didn't," Nancy admitted. She stood up. "I must go now. I'll let you know if I find another clue."

Mr. Soong nodded and smiled. "It was good of you to come," he said in his soft, musical voice. "I have heard much about your detective abilities and I am flattered that one so charming and capable should wish to help me recover the vase." He paused. "Perhaps you can aid me in still another matter, Miss Drew—you and your father."

"What sort of matter is it, Mr. Soong? I'd like to be of service in any way I can, but if it's a legal problem Dad will know how to solve it better than I."

Mr. Soong hesitated. "To tell the truth, I am not certain at this moment what kind of problem it is, although it has legal aspects. Suppose I call on Mr. Drew and tell him about it." His eyes twinkled. "With the condition, of course, that he repeat the story to you."

Nancy laughed. "That's the kind of condition I like!"

Mr. Soong tinkled a tiny Chinese bell and the servant silently appeared.

"Ching will show you out," the elderly Chinese gentleman said. "Good-by."

Nancy returned to Dick's shop and told him

of her visit. "Mr. Soong's a fine person," she added.

"He certainly is," Dick replied, stroking his chin thoughtfully. "That's why I want to repay him as soon as possible. It probably will take a long time," he commented forlornly. "The vase and elephant were worth an awful lot of money."

"I'm going to hunt for them," Nancy said with determination.

"But if you don't find them, I'll pay Mr. Soong back somehow," Dick declared. "I must! And I'm sure I could do it if only—"

His fist hit the top of the counter so hard that the little clay dishes jumped. "If only I could find the leaning chimney!" he exclaimed.

"The leaning chimney?" Nancy asked quizzically. "What's that?"

"I wish I knew." Dick frowned. "It's a clue to some valuable clay. The leaning chimney may be part of a house, part of a factory—or it may exist only in someone's imagination.

"I learned of it by accident. I was in a phone booth one day when I overheard a man talking in the adjoining booth. I didn't pay any attention until I heard 'unusual China clay,' then 'Masonville' and 'leaning chimney.' I tried to hurry my call so I could ask him about the clay, but when I hung up he had disappeared."

Dick sighed. "I've hunted for such a chimney in what little time I could take away from the shop, but all the chimneys I've seen are as straight as a flagpole!"

Nancy laughed, then grew serious once more. "China clay is the main ingredient for making fine pottery, isn't it, Dick?"

"It's the best there is!" he replied. "Why, if I could locate a valuable deposit of China clay nearby, I might buy it cheap, and make the finest of porcelains like the ancient Chinese! Then I could repay Mr. Soong!"

Dick's eyes glowed at the prospect and the worried frown vanished from his face. Seeing the change in him, Nancy determined to do everything in her power to locate the valuable pit.

"Maybe I can help you find the clay, Dick," she said. "I'll try, anyway."

He stared at her in surprise for a moment, then his mouth broke into a wide grin. "Would you?" he exclaimed. "That's mighty swell of you!"

"If what you overheard the man say is true," said Nancy, "the chimney must be somewhere in or around Masonville."

"If it only were!" There was a dreamlike look in Dick's eyes. "I'd enlarge my place, install extra kilns, and do a thriving business. I can just visualize it all—Dick Milton, Inc., Fine Potteries."

Then he smiled. "Please forgive me for such silly daydreaming. But, you see, I would like my wife and baby daughter to be proud of me."

"A little girl? How nice," Nancy said with a smile. "How old is she?"

With a fatherly air of authority he said, beaming, "Susan's her name and she's fifteen months. I'd like you to see her, and meet my wife Connie, too, sometime."

"I'd love to," said Nancy. "But, right now, before I start for Masonville to look for the leaning chimney and the China clay, I'd like to learn more about how you make pottery."

Dick led Nancy into the workroom back of the shop, where the thief had jimmied the window.

In the center of the room stood two long benches crowded with plaster of Paris molds, unfinished clay pieces, a potter's wheel and various jars and cans. Stacked in a corner were huge, round crocks. Dick explained that these contained ordinary moist clay which he had prepared for his classes.

"But one can get much finer results with China clay," he remarked.

"What are those big black boxes?" Nancy asked, pointing to three square, ovenlike vaults on benches to one side of the room.

"Oh, they're my electric kilns for baking." Dick smiled. "I'm firing a piece now. I'll let you have a preview."

He led Nancy over to one kiln. Through a small peephole, she could see a bright-red glow.

Inside was a small pyramid-shaped object and beyond that was a vase about seven inches high.

"This is the biscuit stage," Dick informed her.
"When that little cone which you see in front of
the vase starts to bend, I'll know my piece is
finished and turn off the heat. After the vase is
completely cool, I'll put on a coat of glaze and
refire it. Then it will be ready for sale."

As Nancy and Dick returned to the front of
the shop, she thanked him for his instructive
demonstration.

"Bess wants me to join your class," Nancy remarked. "Maybe I will—after I find the leaning
chimney!"

At that moment a customer entered the store,
and Nancy said good-by.

"Keep me posted," Dick called as she went
out.

Nancy walked to her car and started off. As it
rolled along the road toward Masonville, she
tried to figure out what a leaning chimney would
have to do with a clay pit. Perhaps the man whom
Dick had overheard was talking about two different things. Maybe there was no link at all between them!

"I may be on a wild-goose chase," Nancy
thought. "But it's worth the try."

Almost without realizing it, she found herself
on the back road which she and Bess had taken
the night before from Masonville. Nearing Hun-

ter's Bridge, she slowed down, then stopped at the side of the road.

"I'll look around," she decided. "Maybe I'll find some kind of clue to the thief's identity."

Sliding across the seat of the convertible, she stepped onto the soft dirt shoulder of the road. The earth was still slightly damp after the rain. Various sizes of heavy shoe marks here and there indicated to Nancy that the police had made an investigation.

Nancy walked into the underbrush a few feet, searching carefully for anything the officers might have overlooked. As she ducked under a bush, a large drop of water slid from its leafy cup and dripped onto her neck. Nancy hunched her shoulders as a chill ran down her back.

Suddenly she heard a faint rustling. Behind the shrubbery a thorny bush with long, prickly branches was quivering violently, as if a moment before someone had brushed against it.

Her breath coming quickly, Nancy glanced at the damp ground behind the bush. Clearly imprinted in the soft earth were a man's footprints!

Was she about to come face to face with the thief who had stolen the vase?

CHAPTER III

The Secret Panel

NANCY advanced a few steps, then stopped to listen. She might hear the thief, she figured, if he were lurking in the woods. But the only sound in the ominously silent thicket was the sudden, chirping of a robin.

"I must be careful," Nancy thought. "I'd be foolish to try tracking the thief alone. But if I don't follow him, I may lose a valuable clue."

As she pondered, her thoughts were jarred by the screech of brakes, accompanied by the skidding of tires on pavement.

Nancy's heart skipped a beat. A sickening thought flashed through her mind. Maybe someone was coming to meet the man in the woods!

"I may be trapped!" she chided herself. "What a goose I was to walk right into it!"

She hastened toward the road, carefully concealing herself from the newcomer. When Nancy saw the other car she gave a sigh of relief. In it

were Bess and another girl, with the boyish name
of George Fayne.

"Hi!" George called gaily. "What's the idea of
going sleuthing without us?"

George, as well as Bess, had shared many of
Nancy's exciting adventures. George, athletic
and outspoken, was a striking contrast to her
mild-mannered cousin Bess.

Nancy did not answer her dark-haired friend.
She motioned for the two girls to get out of the
car quickly and follow her.

"I think I'm on the trail of the person who
stole the vase," she explained, starting off.

Bess locked her car and followed the others.
Footprints were clearly visible in the woods. But
fifty feet farther on they vanished in the thick
undergrowth. There was no sign of the man.

"Oh dear!" Nancy said, disappointed.

George grinned. "What did you expect—that
he was going to wait for you?"

Reluctantly Nancy turned back. "I know one
thing about the man who was here," she said,
"whether he's the vase thief or not. He's not very
tall."

"How do you know?" Bess asked.

"By the small footprint and the short stride.
Also, he wears lifts in his shoes," Nancy replied.

"Hypers!" said George, using one of her pet
expressions. "You slay me!"

"Tell me about the shoes," Bess demanded.

Nancy explained. "These imprints are deeper than the usual footprints, and here's the trademark, anyway." She pointed to the heelprint. "I just happened to read an ad yesterday about this make of elevator shoes."

"Nancy, what are you up to?" asked George. "Bess told me about the stolen vase and elephant. Is that why you came here?"

"Not exactly. I was on my way to Masonville to look for a leaning chimney."

"A what?" George demanded.

Nancy explained about the clue to the China clay pit, and that it might be in Masonville.

"That's where we're going," said Bess. "To that darling dress shop next to the inn. How about having lunch with us?"

"Love to," Nancy replied. "Meet you at the inn at one o'clock."

Bess and George hopped into their car and followed Nancy. Entering the outskirts of Masonville, Nancy slowed her car and motioned she would leave the girls and start her sleuthing.

She drove around the city slowly in ever-narrowing circles, her keen eyes alert for a chimney that leaned, bent, curved, or was anything but perpendicular. At the end of half an hour, she was convinced she had never seen so many smokestacks in her life.

Then suddenly she saw it. A chimney that clearly leaned at an angle of several degrees!

"This is luck!" she told herself elatedly.

The chimney was on a house next to the corner dwelling in a row of old-fashioned, red-brick homes. The chimney was the only feature that distinguished the house from the others. The adjoining corner house was boarded up.

Nancy parked the car at the curb in front of the house with the leaning chimney. As she climbed the creaking steps to the porch and rang the bell, she saw a sign in the front window: ROOMS FOR RENT.

After a short interval, a white-haired, elderly woman came to the door, wiping her hands on an apron. She adjusted her spectacles and looked at Nancy inquiringly. The young detective smiled and said a trifle self-consciously:

"I know this sounds a little silly, but I've been looking for a leaning chimney and the first one I've found is yours. I've been told the chimney may have some connection with China clay."

The woman looked puzzled. "China clay?" she repeated slowly. "What do you mean?"

"Perhaps I'd better introduce myself," said Nancy. "My name is Nancy Drew—"

"Nancy Drew!" the woman interposed with surprise. "From River Heights?" When Nancy nodded, she added, "Is Mrs. Gruen your housekeeper?"

It was Nancy's turn to show surprise. "Yes, do you know Hannah?"

The white-haired old lady chuckled. "Land sakes, yes! I helped Hannah's mother take care of her when she was a little girl." She opened the door wider and stepped aside. "Come in and sit for a while. I'm Mrs. Wendell."

"Oh, I've heard Hannah speak of you." Nancy smiled. "I've wanted to meet you."

Nancy went into the neat, old-fashioned living room and sat down. Hastily removing her apron, Mrs. Wendell settled herself in a rocker.

"How is Hannah? I haven't seen her in so long."

"Oh, she's fine," Nancy answered politely. Then she steered the conversation back to China clay.

Mrs. Wendell was thoughtful for a moment, then she said:

"I've been living in this house for several years, Nancy, and never saw nor heard of a pit of China clay anywhere in the neighborhood. But—now let me see," she added, moving gently back and forth in the rocker. "I have something that may help you.

"There's an old trunk in the attic room. It belonged to Mr. Petersen, who sold me the house. He's dead now. The trunk's got some old papers and maps in it. I've been hankering to read them, but somehow never got around to it. Getting old, I guess. No curiosity left."

Nancy laughed.

"Seems to me if the leaning chimney's got anything to do with the China clay you're looking for," continued Mrs. Wendell, "the papers might mention it."

Nancy listened with mounting interest. "I'd like to look at them," she told Mrs. Wendell.

"All right," the woman agreed. "I'll fetch my keys."

She went to the kitchen, then returned and they started slowly up the long, narrow stairs. Arriving at the third floor, Mrs. Wendell knocked gently on a door.

"I'm sure Mr. Manning, who rents this room, isn't home," she said. "He hardly ever is around during the day."

When there was no answer, she turned a key in the lock. Just then the front doorbell rang.

"Seems every time I come upstairs the bell rings!" Mrs. Wendell sighed. "You go along inside. The trunk is in the closet."

Nancy entered the small, one-windowed room. It was simply furnished with an iron bedstead, a chest of drawers, and two straight-backed chairs. A washbasin sat on a wooden stand under a mirror next to a closet door. She walked across the room and opened the door.

"Oh!" Nancy gasped.

A man was just stepping through a panel in the rear of the closet!

Quick as a flash he stepped back. The panel slid across the space and a lock clicked into place.

"Mrs. Wendell! Come here!" Nancy cried at the top of her lungs.

Nancy quickly thrust aside a couple of suits that dangled on a rack and tried to open the panel. It would not budge. She examined the faint cracks in the closet wall that outlined the panel. They might easily go unnoticed in the subdued light. Then she turned to see the startled landlady.

"A man just sneaked through a panel in the back of this closet," said Nancy.

"Well, I never—!" Mrs. Wendell exclaimed in astonishment, then she began to tremble nervously.

Nancy dashed to the window and looked out to see if anyone would leave the adjoining vacant building. Glimpsing no one, she raced downstairs and looked on the street. The intruder did not appear.

"He must be hiding back of the panel," Nancy decided, and reported this to Mrs. Wendell. "Shall we break through?"

"If you think we should," the woman said shakily. "There's a hatchet in the basement."

Nancy got it and returned to the attic.

"Stand back, Mrs. Wendell," she warned, raising the hatchet.

Nancy gave the secret panel several hard whacks. The partition sagged. Then a final bang sent it flying into the space beyond.

She stepped through the narrow opening. After a second's hesitation, Mrs. Wendell followed. They stood in the attic of the corner house. The room was empty. Whoever had closed the secret panel had disappeared!

Nancy went to the door. It was locked, but the key was on the inside. Apparently the thief had not gone out that way.

She investigated a closet, Mrs. Wendell holding her breath in fear. No one was inside the cobwebby space.

Puzzled as to where the man had gone, Nancy noticed that the room's single, dirty window was half open. Lifting it all the way, she looked out just in time to see a man's hand grip the top of the high back-yard fence, then disappear!

Pursuit, Nancy figured, would be useless. The man had too much of a head start.

"We'd better call the police," she suggested.

"Oh dear!" said Mrs. Wendell. "I never thought I'd get mixed up with the police."

"I wonder how he got down," Nancy mused. She leaned out the window. The answer to the riddle was apparent. A foot away was a rainspout, entwined with heavy vines. It would be a simple matter for someone to cling to the vines and climb down to the ground.

As Nancy turned around, Mrs. Wendell gave a loud sneeze. The sound echoed through the musty attic.

"Such dust!" she said. "Nancy, what do you make of all this?"

"I don't like it."

Glancing about the room, Nancy saw several packages on the floor. They were wrapped with newspapers and tied with string. She bent over one of them and examined it closely. The newspaper was printed in Chinese!

Quickly untying the string, Nancy opened the bundle. It contained a beautiful Chinese vase decorated with lotus blossoms!

She untied a second bundle, then a third. They, too, held exquisite Oriental vases.

Mrs. Wendell stared at the porcelains in amazement. "My lands!" she burst out. "Where did *they* come from?"

Nancy had a hunch about that. But she decided to say nothing of her suspicions for the present.

"Don't be worried," Nancy begged. "Everything will come out all right."

Mrs. Wendell went downstairs. She waited a moment for one of her roomers to leave, then called police headquarters.

Meanwhile, Nancy unwrapped the remainder of the bundles. Each one contained a beautiful Oriental vase. She had hoped Mr. Soong's Ming piece and the jade elephant would be among them, but she was disappointed.

The Chinese newspapers intrigued her. After

carefully unfolding one of them she stuck part of it in her handbag.

Two Masonville policemen arrived, and Mrs. Wendell at once told them of Nancy's prowess as a detective. Nancy smiled and explained what had happened.

"What was the fellow like?" asked one of the officers, named McCann.

Nancy said she regretted not having had a better look at the intruder so that she might identify him, but the man had his head down as he was stepping through the opening.

"Looks like you discovered something big, Miss Drew," said Officer McCann as he picked up the vase patterned with lotus blossoms.

"This one fits the description of a vase stolen from the Masonville Museum last week," Officer McCann declared. He turned to Mrs. Wendell. "What do you know about all this stuff, ma'am?"

Mrs. Wendell was flustered, but Nancy put her arm reassuringly around the woman's shoulder as she spoke up falteringly:

"I don't know anything about it, Officer."

"Who lives in this room?" he asked, stepping back into the attic room.

Mrs. Wendell told of having rented it to a John Manning six months before. He had asked to be left alone because he was working very hard "writing a book" and did not want to be disturbed. The secret panel mystified her, she said. She was sure it had not been there before Manning rented the room.

"Manning probably installed it while you and the other tenants were away from the house," Officer McCann declared. "What does he look like?"

"Why, he's medium tall," the woman reflected, "with black hair and sort of olive skin. He . . . he spoke very nice, not like a rough thief. Seemed to me like he'd traveled a great deal."

"Um." The officer pondered, as if mentally reviewing the rogues' gallery.

"Oh, and he has piercing black eyes," Mrs. Wendell added quickly.

At once Nancy recalled the piercing black eyes of the strange-acting man she and Bess had encountered the previous night. Her gaze wandered around the floor of the room and the closet. "Mrs. Wendell," she asked, "did you ever notice anything unusual about the height of Mr. Manning's shoes?"

"Why, no," she said, somewhat surprised.

Nancy told the policeman about the unusual footprints she had found at Hunter's Bridge. He agreed that the prints might well have been made by the thief, and that the thief might be the man known as John Manning.

While the three had been talking, the other policeman had been examining the attics in both houses, searching for additional loot. Finding none, he wrapped up several of Manning's personal belongings to study later for fingerprints and compare them with those on the vases. Finally the two officers gathered together the pieces of pottery and started down the stairs.

"If you ever want a job on the Masonville force, let us know!" one of them said to Nancy.

"I really only stumbled on this," Nancy said modestly. "I came here looking for a leaning chimney and found an attic full of loot."

The policemen glanced at each other incredulously. "A leaning chimney?" echoed McCann. "And that led you to discover a crook?"

The other officer cocked his head. "I guess that's what they call woman's intuition. I wish I had some of it!"

After the police officers had descended the stairs, accompanied by Mrs. Wendell, Nancy looked about Manning's room. What a sight! Dresser drawers were pulled out, the mattress overturned, the rug rolled back, the contents of the trunk scattered over the floor. Even the cardboard backing had been removed from the pictures. Manning's suits had been examined also. The pockets had been turned inside out and their linings inspected.

"I wonder if there could be anything the police missed," Nancy mused as she surveyed the room.

True, they had found plenty of loot, but they

had not uncovered a single thing that might be a clue to the identity of the thief.

"The floor!" Nancy said half-aloud. The police hadn't examined the floorboards.

Getting to her knees, the young detective scrutinized the rough-hewn planks. Perhaps a loose one might have served as a hiding place for Manning's mail. But every board was secured by big, broad nails used by carpenters sixty years before.

"Nothing there," sighed Nancy, rising to her feet.

Then a thought flashed through her mind. "The window shade!"

Nancy had a sudden vision of letters falling from the tightly rolled-up shade when she pulled it down. Going to the window, she tugged the cord. The shade came halfway down, but no letters fluttered to her feet.

Nancy made a discovery, however. The sun, streaming through the window, faintly outlined some dark squares on the shade. Excitedly Nancy removed the shade from its little brass fixtures and laid it on the bed.

"This *is* a find!" she mused in puzzled delight.

Taped to the outside of the shade were four pages torn from an art magazine. They were full-color photographs of rare old Chinese vases!

Attached slightly above them were two yellow sheets of paper listing the museums and homes where the vases could be found!

CHAPTER IV

The Blinding Glare

"THAT'S pretty conclusive proof Manning's the thief," Nancy told herself. "I'll take these papers to the police."

It was easy to understand how they had overlooked the papers Manning had concealed so cunningly in the shade. She unrolled it another foot. More papers were attached. Each contained Chinese writing done in bold brush strokes with black ink.

"I wonder what they mean," Nancy thought. "They must have something to do with the vases."

Just then she glanced at her watch. Less than half an hour to meet Bess and George! She had not even looked through the contents of the old trunk for a clue to the China clay pit!

Carefully Nancy removed the papers from their hiding place and put them in her handbag. While she was restoring the shade to the window, Mrs.

Wendell returned. She said the police would send a man to watch the house, but they doubted that Manning would return.

"And I got a carpenter comin' right away to board up that hole into the other house," Mrs. Wendell reported.

Nancy told of her new find, then looked over the contents of the trunk. Scattered among old clothes were a lot of yellowed letters. Nancy scanned the correspondence. Much of it was personal, so she read only enough to convince herself there was no mention of China clay.

"Mrs. Wendell," she said, "did Mr. Manning ever say anything about this trunk?"

The woman looked startled. "Yes, he talked quite a bit about it. He said it wouldn't bother him in the room and insisted I leave it here. Why did you ask?"

"I believe he might have come here on purpose to look for something in it; something that belonged to Mr. Petersen."

"Oh, gracious!" said Mrs. Wendell. "This gets more complicated every minute."

"Don't worry any more about it." Nancy patted the woman's arm. "Just forget the whole thing."

Nancy said good-by and went to her car. She drove as rapidly as she dared in order to keep her date with Bess and George at the Masonville Inn. But when she reached it, she was minutes late.

"Well," said George when Nancy had parked, "I hope you don't keep Ned Nickerson waiting like this!"

Nancy blushed, thinking of Ned, a student at Emerson College. Nancy enjoyed his company, and had attended many parties and dances with him.

"I just couldn't get here any sooner," Nancy replied. "Wait till you hear about the secret panel!"

At lunch Nancy told her friends what had happened. Bess's eyes grew wide with astonishment and George said, "Gosh!" and "Hypers!" several times.

After Nancy had finished eating, she showed the girls the photographs of the vases, then copied the Chinese symbols in a notebook.

"We'd better go," said Bess. "I said I'd be home by four."

"Oh, heck!" George complained. "That dress I bought won't be ready for an hour." She explained that it was being altered slightly.

"I bought two dresses, Nancy," said Bess. "They're positively yummy."

"Um." Nancy smiled. Then, pretending to be envious, she said, "I'll be at Helen Townsend's birthday dinner tonight in just an old pink sheath. Tell you what. Suppose you go on home, Bess, and I'll wait for George. I want to stop at police headquarters with these papers."

The arrangement suited Bess, who drove off at once. She took a longer but more traveled road back to River Heights than the one where the suspected thief had been.

An hour later Nancy and George followed but took the short cut. Nancy braked as the convertible went around the series of twisting curves approaching Hunter's Bridge.

"Do you think the man you saw here was Manning?" George asked. She leaned forward, looking alertly ahead, as if she expected the man to jump out at them any moment.

"Either Manning or a pal," Nancy answered. "Mr. Soong's vase wasn't in that attic."

"But it would have reached there eventually if you hadn't spoiled Manning's plans," said George. "I wonder where Mr. Soong's vase is."

Nancy was about to reply when suddenly both girls were blinded by a stabbing glare. Nancy threw up her left hand to shield her eyes. Then, as quickly as the glare had come, it disappeared.

"What was that?" George asked.

Nancy stopped and got out. "I don't know," she said. "But I intend to find out."

"Not without me," George declared.

Together the girls walked to the sparse woods from which the flash had come. In a few seconds Nancy and George came upon a car. It was a maroon coupé with a badly dented right rear fender. The car was empty.

Attached to the outside frame was a side-view mirror. It had been tilted, possibly by the jarring trip off the road. On a hunch, Nancy adjusted the mirror. As she did so, she was struck by the same stabbing glare that had blinded her in the convertible. A ray of sunlight had been reflected from it to the road!

"Funny place to leave a car," George commented.

"This may be a meeting place for Manning and his friends." Nancy circled the coupé, then jotted down the license number in her notebook.

As if confirming her deduction, Nancy and George heard the murmur of men's voices deeper in the woods. The girls started forward.

Taking care not to make a sound, they stepped cautiously as the voices grew more distinct. Presently the girls saw two men. Their backs were turned, and they seemed to be bending over something on a log. Unable to hear what they were saying, Nancy and George crept forward.

Nancy's attention was so fixed on the men that she did not notice a dry twig in her path. The next moment, there was a sharp crack as she stepped on the twig.

The girls heard a startled exclamation, followed by a hollow crash, as if something had dropped and broken. Without looking back, the men scooted into the brush and disappeared.

"George, I'll see what they dropped," Nancy

whispered, running quickly toward the log.

"Be right back!" called George, and raced off in the direction of the disappearing men.

Hoping that they would be heading for their car, George plunged into the dense underbrush. She had to get a look at them!

Beside the log, Nancy found part of a wrinkled newspaper. On it lay fragments of what had been a small Oriental bowl. Nancy glanced at the newspaper. It was Chinese!

She bent over to pick up the paper and the broken pieces. They might prove to be a valuable clue. But hardly had she put the last fragment in her bag when a bloodcurdling scream rent the woods.

It came from George!

Nancy raced pell-mell toward the sound, which had come from the direction of the car. Her worst fears aroused, she fairly flew, heedless of the brambles that tore at her dress. Finally she came in sight of the coupé standing exactly where she had seen it.

George was not there!

As Nancy stood uncertain under a low-hanging limb, a shadowy figure suddenly leaped at her. She felt a stinging pain and collapsed to the ground!

CHAPTER V

A Chinese Puzzle

NANCY recovered her senses in a few minutes and got up. There was a dull throbbing in her forehead, but her memory cleared at once.

Her first thought was of George. There was no sign of her. The maroon coupé was gone, and for an instant Nancy was fearful her friend might have been kidnapped. But she discarded the horrible thought at once.

"More than likely George was knocked out too," she reasoned.

Picking up her handbag, which lay on the ground, she began calling George's name. To Nancy's relief, the shout was answered.

"I'm over here! Blindfolded! My hands are tied!"

Nancy traced the sound. George stood with her back to a tree, rubbing her wrists against the bark to tear off the belt of her dress with which they were bound. Nancy quickly freed her and removed the blindfold. George's story differed only slightly from Nancy's.

"It all happened so fast!" George said. She took a deep breath. "I thought I'd lost the men. When I turned around to go back to you, one of them jumped out of the bushes and tied my scarf over my eyes. I screamed and tried to tear it off. But another man bound my hands and told me to keep still!"

"Did you see either of them?" Nancy asked.

"Not enough of their faces to identify them."

Nancy led the way out of the woods to the road. The girls, disappointed and chagrined, but thankful nothing harmful had happened, climbed into Nancy's car and headed for home.

Suddenly George shook off the mood and grinned. "Those fellows were pretty dumb," she said. "You have their license number."

"And they left some other evidence." Nancy told of the pieces of the bowl still in her purse. "One of the men might have been Manning."

Some time later Nancy stopped in front of George's house, and her friend got out. "See you tonight at Helen's birthday party."

"You bet. I wouldn't miss it for anything!"

Nancy drove to the motor-vehicle office to learn the name of the owner of the maroon coupé, if possible. The man in charge knew her, and after hearing her story, obligingly telephoned state headquarters for the information.

"You just got here in time," he said, while holding the telephone. "We're about to close."

He found that the license plates had been issued to a Paul Scott of Masonville, and that the coupé had been reported stolen that very afternoon!

"I'll bet those men planned to hide the car in the woods until they could paint it another color and put different license plates on it," Nancy said to the man. "May I call the police?"

"Sure thing. Use my desk phone."

After Nancy had talked to Police Chief McGinnis, she drove to Dick Milton's shop and told him about the leaning chimney in Masonville. Dick was disappointed that the clue had not led to a China clay pit. Then Nancy left him and headed for Mr. Drew's office. She had promised to pick up her father at six o'clock.

Fortunately an automobile pulled away from the curb in front of the building where Carson Drew had his law office. Nancy skillfully guided the convertible into the vacant spot. As she was about to get out, she saw a short Chinese gentleman with spectacles and a tiny goatee emerge from the building.

"Mr. Soong!" she called.

The Chinese smiled and came over to her.

"You're just the person I want to see!" Nancy greeted him. "Can you spare a minute?"

Mr. Soong nodded. He looked very natty in a gray felt hat and a blue pin-striped suit. He carried a handsome Malacca cane. Nancy opened the door and he seated himself beside her.

"May I drive you home?" she asked.

"That would be very kind. I must hurry to keep an engagement."

On the way, she told Mr. Soong of her day's adventures. The Oriental gentleman's face reflected his amazement. He could not identify John Manning, but he begged Nancy to be extremely careful in further investigations.

When Nancy pulled up at Mr. Soong's home, she opened her bag and took out the wrinkled newspaper which held the broken fragments of a Chinese bowl. But first she showed Mr. Soong the symbols she had copied.

"I hope they're not as mystifying to you as they are to me," Nancy remarked.

"It is no mystery what they mean," he replied.

He translated the first set of symbols on the sheet, pointing his finger at each character as he spoke. "Made in the studio of deep peace."

Nancy looked at him, perplexed, but he went on to the second group of characters. "Made for the hall of fragrant virtue," he translated.

Mr. Soong smiled at Nancy's puzzled expression. "Each set of symbols is a sort of Chinese

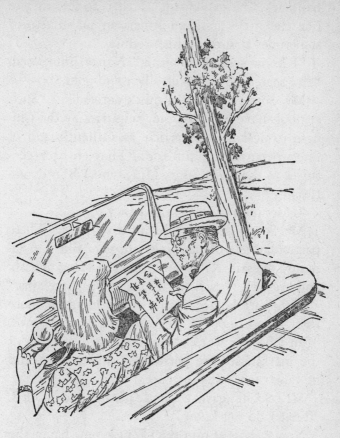

"It is no mystery what the symbols mean,"
Mr. Soong replied

hallmark," he explained. "That is to say, they're like the little mark an American manufacturer sometimes stamps on his products."

"I know what you mean," Nancy interposed. "I've seen such marks on silver and gold."

Mr. Soong nodded in quick agreement. "Such symbols have been used for centuries by the Chinese to designate an article as authentic and of fine workmanship," he said. "They go back centuries to the great Sung, Ming, and Ch'in dynasties."

"How interesting!" said Nancy.

Mr. Soong peered again at the symbols. "These particular sets of markings are very old and famous," he said. "They are from the Ming dynasty and are well known to all experts on porcelains."

"Oh!" exclaimed Nancy. "I'm learning more than I had hoped!" Her brow knit in a frown. "But what use would Manning have for copies of the markings?" she persisted. "And why should he take such pains to conceal them?"

Mr. Soong gave a gentle shrug and smiled. "That I do not know."

Nancy showed him the Chinese newspaper she had taken from the attic in Masonville. It was a Chinese daily published in New York, Mr. Soong told her.

"This Mr. Manning may work with Chinese in New York," he suggested.

Next, Nancy opened the wrinkled newspaper

which held the fragments of the broken bowl. The paper, Nancy saw, was the same as the other.

Mr. Soong examined the pieces with interest, but they were so small he could tell only that the bowl had been made of excellent clay. He looked at Nancy inquiringly, as if to ask for more information. But she shook her head with a sigh.

"They're all the leads I have—this time!" she replied.

Mr. Soong stepped from the car and gravely shook Nancy's hand.

"You have done very well, Miss Drew," he said softly. "With the help of both members of your illustrious family, I am confident that my unworthy problems will soon be solved."

The Chinese bowed slightly, then turned and went up the walk to his front door. Nancy looked after him, puzzled. "Now, what did he mean by that?" she asked herself.

Nancy hurried back to her father's office building. While she was trying to squeeze into a parking space, a familiar voice said:

"Mind if I take you home?"

Nancy looked around swiftly. "Dad!" she cried.

She planted a kiss on his cheek as he got in. Carson Drew was a tall, handsome man of middle age, with alert blue eyes like those of his daughter. Like Nancy's, too, they twinkled when his sense of humor was aroused.

The relationship between Nancy and her father

was warm and companionable. No matter how busy Mr. Drew was with his own criminal cases, he always found time to discuss Nancy's cases.

Now, driving home, the distinguished-looking attorney and his attractive daughter talked about her latest adventures. As Nancy swung the convertible into the driveway of the Drew home, she suddenly remembered Mr. Soong's parting words. Nancy repeated them to her father and asked if he knew what they meant.

"You bet I do. Mr. Soong paid me a visit today. He wants you and me to undertake a search."

"A search?"

"That's right. A Chinese puzzle that goes back five years!"

He got out of the car and Nancy quickly followed him.

"Dad, stop keeping me in suspense!" she begged. "What's it all about?"

"I'll tell when we get inside," he promised, mounting the steps to the porch. "It's the story of the missing Engs!"

CHAPTER VI

The Vanishing Vase

"WHAT are the missing Engs?" Nancy inquired when she and her father were seated in his study. "Some valuable jewels?"

Mr. Drew laughed. "You're not even warm! The Engs are Chinese friends of Mr. Soong's; Eng Moy and his daughter Eng Lei. As you know," he added, "Chinese last names come first!"

Carson Drew paused for a moment.

"Go on, Dad," Nancy begged impatiently.

"Five years ago Eng Moy wrote to Mr. Soong from China. He said he and his daughter were leaving on a trip to the United States and hoped to visit him. According to Mr. Soong, Eng Moy was a well-known maker of porcelains in China. The purpose of his trip was to study American pottery methods."

"Did Eng Lei make pottery, too?" Nancy asked.

Her father shook his head. "Not at the time

the Engs left China, at any rate. She was only twelve years old then. That means she's about seventeen now."

"When did they disappear?" Nancy asked, interested at once in hearing about a girl so close to her own age.

"That's coming. Eng Moy continued to write to Mr. Soong," Mr. Drew explained. "Eng described tours they had taken through pottery plants in several cities in the United States. Each succeeding letter was postmarked a little closer to River Heights. Finally Mr. Soong received a letter saying they would visit him the following week."

The lawyer paused.

"And they didn't come?" Nancy asked.

"No. That was four and a half years ago. Mr. Soong hasn't heard from the Engs since!"

"Maybe something happened so they couldn't write."

"That's what Mr. Soong would like to find out," Mr. Drew replied. "He came to my office today because he had received a letter from a relative in China. Mr. Soong supposed the Engs had returned to the Orient without paying him the promised visit. He had been a bit perplexed when his letters to China were never acknowledged."

"Sounds very strange," said Nancy.

"He learned something from the letter he received today," said Mr. Drew. "The relative wrote that the Engs never had returned to China and the United States immigration authorities could not account for it."

"Then the Engs are probably still in this country," Nancy reasoned.

"Seems that way," her father agreed. "Mr. Soong fears his friends have met with—well, let's call it foul play."

"What do *you* suspect happened to them?" Nancy asked.

"I don't suspect anything yet," Mr. Drew replied. "But there are several reasons why some aliens want United States authorities to lose track of them. Espionage is one. Receiving and selling smuggled goods is another."

"Not a friend of Mr. Soong's!" said Nancy, shocked.

Her father smiled dryly, "You're probably right, but that doesn't solve the mystery."

Nancy looked at her father searchingly, then asked how she might help on the case.

Mr. Drew smiled affectionately. "As soon as I get a clue, I'll put you to work on it."

"Thanks, Dad." Nancy looked at her watch and gave a start. "My goodness, I must run or I'll be late for Helen's birthday dinner!"

She dashed upstairs to dress. A few minutes later Nancy hurried down, blew a kiss to her father, and waved good-by to Mrs. Gruen.

"Wait a moment," the housekeeper said. "You

worry me, Nancy," she said. "It will be late when you leave the Townsend house and I don't like your coming home alone."

"I'll soon settle this," Mr. Drew declared. "Hannah, I'll drive my daughter and her friends to Helen's and go back for them."

Twenty minutes later he dropped Bess, George, and Nancy across town. Mr. Townsend teased the girls with a "Glad you made it. I'd begun to think I'd have to eat four pieces of birthday cake!"

Helen smiled and said, "If I know Nancy, she probably was tracking down some villain."

"That's right." Nancy laughed. "A new way to say 'Happy Birthday.'"

Helen took the girls' coats and handbags up-stairs to her room.

In a few minutes Mrs. Townsend called every-one into the dining room. As Nancy was about to follow, she noticed an exquisite vase on the desk near a window. She lifted the vase carefully and examined the porcelain.

It was in a lovely shade of brown, showing a peach tree at the edge of a sparkling blue lake. An ancient Chinese, attired in a richly brocaded robe, sat under the tree beside a deer.

Nancy studied the bottom of the base. Painted with small, black brush strokes were several Chi-nese symbols. They seemed to be the same as one set of characters she had copied from the sheets in Manning's room!

Nancy ran upstairs and got her clutch bag. Then, seating herself at the living-room desk, she took a pen from its ornate holder and quickly copied the symbols. She dried the ink on a small blotter which lay on the desk and slipped the paper into her bag.

She was about to go into the dining room when she spotted two strange marks cunningly worked into the leaves of the peach tree. Nancy stared at the small, barely visible markings. The more she looked the more puzzled she became. Before she could copy the little symbols, Mrs. Townsend hurried into the room.

"Nancy, come on!" she coaxed.

"I'm sorry," Nancy apologized. "This vase—"

"Like it?" Helen's mother asked.

"Love it!" Nancy replied. "It's one of the finest I've ever seen."

"It's a Ming vase. My husband gave it to me for an anniversary present," Mrs. Townsend said, leading the way into the dining room.

Nancy followed. As she ate, the young detective kept thinking about what she had just discovered. After the birthday cake had been served, Helen began to unwrap her gifts. "Ohs" and "Ahs" greeted each gaily wrapped package. Besides several pieces of beautiful lingerie, she received an attractive figurine Bess had made in Dick Milton's pottery class.

"Oh, it's lovely!" she exclaimed. "Thanks heaps, Bess."

There was a roar of laughter as a baseball glove from George was opened. But this was something Helen had said she wanted, months before, and no one would give it to her!

Nancy's gift was the surprise of the evening. She had prearranged with Mrs. Townsend that it would be brought in last. Cuddled on a cushion in a little pink basket was a fluffy white kitten.

"Nancy, you darling!" Helen burst out. "You remembered I've been meaning to get one."

The girls gathered around to admire the kitten. Then, as the hands of the clock moved toward ten-thirty, the guests said they must leave.

Nancy, Bess, and George went upstairs for their coats. When Nancy came down carrying her coat, she went to the desk to get her bag. She stopped short in surprise. The bag was gone!

When Mrs. Townsend and the others came downstairs Nancy asked them if they had seen her bag. But none of them knew anything about it.

"What could have become of it?" Mr. Townsend asked, joining the search.

Nancy noticed that the window near the desk was partly open. Could someone have reached in and taken the bag?

"May I have a flashlight?" she asked.

Obtaining one from Mr. Townsend, she dashed

out the front door and went around to the side
of the house, followed by the others. Under the
partly opened window was a flower bed. In it
were footprints!

At that moment she heard Mrs. Townsend call,
"Isn't this yours, Nancy?"

Nancy turned. Helen's mother was holding out
the familiar blue bag.

"Yes, that's mine," Nancy said. "Thank you.
Where did you find it?"

"It was lying here in the grass," Mrs. Townsend explained.

"Oh, I hope nothing's gone," said Helen.

Nancy opened the bag, feeling sure all the contents would be missing. At first glance it seemed
as if only the money in it was gone. Then she
realized that the paper on which she had copied
the Chinese symbols from the vase was also missing.

Suddenly Nancy was struck by a dismaying
thought. Without a word, she darted into the
house. Her worst fears were confirmed.

The Townsends' beautiful, rare vase had vanished!

CHAPTER VII

Three on a Clue

NANCY stared in dismay at the vacant spot on the desk. Then she ran into the kitchen, snapped on the back-yard light, and dashed outside. Nobody was there.

By then Mr. and Mrs. Townsend and the girls had caught up to her. "What's the matter now, Nancy?" asked Mr. Townsend.

As she told them about the stolen vase, Nancy experienced a sudden twinge of guilt. If the thief had not observed her copying the symbols on the bottom, he might never have stolen the vase. But why was her copy of the symbols so important to him?

Suddenly Nancy thought she knew. She ran to the side of the house, fully expecting to see the same identifying footprints she had spotted at Hunter's Bridge; prints she believed were Manning's. But she was disappointed. These marks were short and wide.

When she told Bess and George the idea she had had about the footprints, George was inclined to think the thief was some pal of Manning's.

"He's probably one of those men in the woods," she added.

"And has been told to trail you, Nancy," Bess said fearfully.

"Hypers!" said George. "This puts such a damper on everything."

The other girls murmured in agreement. The Townsends insisted upon hearing about the case. Nancy told what she deemed necessary, then Mr. Townsend went to telephone the police. Two officers arrived, made a routine check indoors and out, then queried Nancy.

After they had gone, a thought suddenly flashed through Nancy's mind. She went to the desk and picked up the small blotter she had used to dry the ink on her notation of the Chinese characters. They were clearly reproduced in reverse.

"I'll take this home and compare the symbols with those on the paper there," she decided.

Nancy slipped the blotter into her bag and turned back to speak to Mr. Townsend. "Where did you buy the vase?"

"Why, let me see," he replied, reaching into his inside coat pocket. "I think I have the name of the shop right here in my wallet. Yes, here it is. Sen-yung's Oriental Gift Shop, Madison Avenue, New York."

Nancy made a mental note of the name.

Mr. Drew arrived shortly to take the girls home. Upon hearing of the theft, and the possibility that Nancy had been spied upon, he was glad he had escorted the girls to the party and back. Nancy, Bess, and George thanked their hostess for the lovely party, then left.

When the Drews reached home, they sat down for a few minutes to discuss the strange turn of events. Nancy took the blotter from her bag and handed it to her father. Then she went to her room to get a hand mirror and the sheet of paper containing the Chinese symbols found in Manning's room. Holding the blotter up to the mirror, she saw at a glance that the writing was the same as one set of characters on the sheet. It read:

"Made for the hall of fragrant virtue."

Nancy was thrilled at the new clue. But she was still puzzled over the thief's motive for stealing her copy of the symbols.

In the morning Nancy telephoned the Townsends to say again how lovely the birthday party had been, and to ask if there was any news of the thief.

"Not a speck," Helen replied. "Say, Nancy, maybe you could find the thief for us."

"If I get any clues, I'll let you know," Nancy promised, and hung up.

Since she could think of no way at the moment to trace the thief, Nancy decided to concentrate on finding the China clay pit. She went to the River Heights Public Library to scan books on local geology. But after poring over several volumes and maps, Nancy had found nothing.

She closed the books with a sigh and put them back on the shelf. Miss Carter, the librarian, had noticed Nancy's disappointed expression.

"Couldn't you find what you're looking for?" she inquired pleasantly.

Nancy shook her head and told the librarian the nature of her quest.

"Why don't you ask Miles Monroe?" Miss Carter suggested. "He's a retired professor of geology. If anyone knows of a clay deposit, he should. I'll give you his address."

"Thank you," Nancy said, smiling. "I'll go to see him at once."

The geologist lived in a small apartment. She pushed the buzzer under Miles Monroe's name card and in a moment a small peephole flew open. An eye stared at Nancy.

"If you're selling something," boomed a voice, "I don't want any of it!"

Nancy stifled a laugh. "I'm not a saleswoman. I came to see you about a geology problem!"

The eye stared a moment longer. Then the peephole snapped shut and the door flew open. A man stood in the doorway, looking Nancy up and down. He was tall and slightly stoop-shouldered, with a sharp, inquisitive face and a thatch of bristling red hair.

"Geology problem!" he snorted. "You're too pretty for such heavy thoughts. But come in!"

As Nancy followed the professor into the living room she noticed that he walked with a limp.

"Have a chair!" he said. Mr. Monroe seated himself, looking straight at Nancy. "Well, young lady," he asked, "what's on your mind?"

After Nancy introduced herself, she told of her search for a deposit of China clay. Monroe said he knew of none in the state.

"I've heard," Nancy went on, "that it may be identified in some way with a leaning chimney."

Miles Monroe scoffed. "First time I ever heard of using a chimney to find a vein of kaolin!"

"Kaolin?" repeated Nancy.

The professor replied, "That's what geologists call the fine white clay used in the manufacture of china and porcelain. The name comes from the Chinese *Kaoling*. It's a mountain in China which yielded the first kaolin."

Nancy eagerly absorbed this new knowledge as Miles Monroe added:

"Kaolin is formed by the weathering of granite

and other rocks. Then the clay is washed free of the quartz and mixed with feldspar, flint, and so forth to make porcelain." He smiled wryly. "You may as well know what it's all about if you're looking for the stuff."

"Of course," Nancy agreed. "But I had hoped you'd be able to tell me about a pit of China clay in this region. It's supposed to be near Masonville."

Professor Monroe rubbed his nose. "Don't know much about the land around Masonville," he replied. "Had to give up my field trips when I injured my leg in a fall six years ago. That's when I retired. Before that, I lived in Philadelphia."

"Well, I'm sorry to have bothered you," Nancy said, rising.

"Say, wait a minute!" Miles Monroe burst out suddenly. "There's one section I had an interest in and was always going to get to. It's a stretch of woods several miles out of River Heights toward Masonville."

He gave her directions for reaching it.

"There's an abandoned Civil War iron mine and smelter out there, I was told. It may have a leaning chimney. If you find a China clay pit, I would like to know about it."

Nancy thanked him for the information. She was glad to have the lead, slim as it was.

Professor Monroe walked to the door with her,

and she went down to her car. Then she drove to George's home.

Her friend was mowing the front lawn. Seated on the ground was Bess, clipping a hedge.

Nancy tooted her horn. The two girls looked up and ran to the car.

"I'm going for a short drive in the country. Just got a new lead on the leaning chimney," Nancy told them. "Want to come along?"

Bess eyed her friend suspiciously. "What do we have to do?" she asked.

"What difference does it make as long as it's fun!" scoffed George. She slid into the seat beside Nancy.

"Okay. I'll go tell your mother where we're going, George."

Bess returned in a moment and hopped into the convertible. Nancy headed for Three Bridges Road.

"Oh, my goodness!" Bess exclaimed as they neared Hunter's Bridge. "This awful place again!"

"But this time we're not stopping," Nancy reassured her, and Bess sighed in relief.

Shortly after crossing Hunter's Bridge they came to a narrow gravel road which veered to the right. Nancy turned the car onto it.

After traveling about eight miles from River Heights, she pulled up under a tree and stopped. The three girls got out and started through the woods to search for the abandoned mine.

They walked for nearly an hour among trees and through stony pastures, climbing old, rotted fences and slapping at insects. Bess's enthusiasm began to wane.

"I'm tired," she moaned. "Let's go back. I'll bet Professor Monroe doesn't know what he's talking about."

Even George and Nancy wondered whether the old mine really existed.

"Just a little farther," Nancy urged.

"We'll be in the next state," joked George. "But I'm willing."

The three trudged on, when suddenly a barrier loomed up ahead. It was a high, board fence, topped by strands of rusty barbed wire. The three girls stopped and stared in amazement.

"Why would anyone put up such a thing in this wilderness?" Bess asked.

The girls inspected the fence closely. It was about ten feet high. The boards adjoined one another so snugly that only the narrowest of cracks appeared between them. Nancy tried to peer through one to see what lay on the other side, but she could make out nothing.

"Hypers!" exclaimed George. "The fence must be five hundred feet long!"

"Come on," Nancy urged. "Let's try to find an opening we can see through."

The girls walked along the fence, their eyes probing for a gate or a wide crack.

"Here's the end of the fence," announced Nancy, who was in the lead.

Indeed, it looked like the end, but it was only the end of one side. The board barrier turned sharply at a right angle and continued another two hundred and fifty feet.

When the girls arrived at the middle of the second stretch of fence, Nancy's alert eyes spotted a small knothole.

"At last!" she exclaimed.

Stepping up eagerly, she closed one eye and peeked through the hole with the other. At first she was unable to see much because of a growth of trees and bushes. Then, shifting her gaze, Nancy saw an old, battered brick wall running parallel to the fence, a short distance back from it. The wall was about eight feet high and was topped by a sloping roof. Obviously it was part of a building. But within the range of her vision Nancy could see no windows.

"Find anything?" George asked impatiently.

"Only an old—" Nancy stopped speaking as she caught sight of something jutting from the roof of the building. Then she cried excitedly:

"Girls, it's a leaning chimney!"

CHAPTER VIII

Mystery in Manhattan

"LET me see!" George exclaimed excitedly.

Nancy stepped aside so the dark-haired girl could look through the knothole.

"Maybe it's the abandoned iron mine and smelter!" put in Bess.

"There are so many trees, it's hard to see just what's inside," George said.

"If this is *the* leaning chimney we're looking for," Nancy reasoned, "the China clay pit must be somewhere nearby. Possibly inside the fence."

"Let's go," she suggested, starting along the enclosure. "There *must* be an opening somewhere."

"You lose," retorted George as the trio rounded the edge of the fence.

No opening was in sight. Instead, the unbroken expanse of boards extended another five hundred feet.

When the girls reached the end of this, the

fence took another right angle turn. This time it stretched two hundred and fifty feet.

Bess groaned. "Oh, I'm so tired—and hungry."

"Perhaps," teased George, "there's a baseball park inside. If there is, we'll stop at the frankfurter stand."

"Think we'll need a helicopter to get inside," Nancy joked, examining the boards closely. "These planks are certainly fitted tight together."

As they walked on, she kept turning over in her mind several things that mystified her: the air of secrecy about the enclosure, the seeming lack of doors, and the apparent lack of activity.

"Since we can't get in," Nancy said, "I'm going to try looking inside to see if I can spot any clay pit."

Making her way to a nearby tree, she shinned up to the first branch, then swung herself into the crotch of the tree.

"Find anything?" George asked.

"I can't see much better from here," Nancy reported. "Too many trees inside."

Suddenly she was struck by something near the top of the leaning chimney. It was a rusted iron ornament fastened to the bricks.

"What does it look like?" asked George when Nancy reported her discovery.

"A lot of crisscross bars," Nancy replied. "Maybe the coat of arms of the old mine owner."

As she climbed down, Bess called from a distance, where she was standing on a little knoll. "I've got a good view of it from here."

George started for the spot when suddenly Bess let out a terrifying scream. Her two friends ran toward her. When they reached the knoll, Bess was trembling with fear.

"What happened?" Nancy demanded.

"Oh, N-Nancy," Bess said, pointing, "I saw a bony hand reach out of the chimney!"

Nancy and George looked. There was no sign of a hand. Bess said she had closed her eyes a moment to shut out the weird sight. When she had opened them again, the hand was gone.

"I think you're goofy," George scoffed. "A person sees things when he gets tired."

"I'm not that tired," Bess retorted. "I saw it. I know I did."

In panic she dashed through the woods toward Nancy's car. There was nothing for the other girls to do but follow her.

Nancy started the motor. Soon they were a good distance from the eerie spot.

"I never want to go there again," Bess declared.

"Not even to help your cousin Dick?" Nancy asked with a grin.

Bess finally conceded maybe she would get over her fright, and she did want Dick to acquire the special clay if possible.

After Nancy drove the girls to their homes, she decided to drop into Dick's shop and tell him of her latest discovery. She found a high school boy, who clerked for the young pottery maker after school, behind the counter.

"Would you like something, miss?" he asked.

"I'd like to see Mr. Milton."

"He's busy in the back of the shop right now," the boy answered. "But he'll be through in a minute. Will you wait?"

Nancy smiled. "He's a friend of mine," she said. "I'll go back and see him."

In the rear room Dick was engrossed at the potter's wheel, his sandy hair tumbling over his forehead. He was so busy he did not notice his caller.

Nancy watched while Dick deftly pressed a lump of clay on the center of the wheel, then allowed it to rise between his fingers in a spiral column before depressing it.

Once more the column spiraled. The young man again pushed it down, at the same time centering and truing the clay. Then he pressed his thumbs into the soft clay, rapidly forming a cylinder.

With one hand inside the cylinder and the other outside, Dick molded the clay into the thickness he desired. Nancy now saw the cylinder shape like magic into a large jar.

Dick snapped off a switch and the whirring wheel slowly stopped. As he turned around, a look of pleased surprise spread over his face.

"Nancy Drew! How did you get here?"

"Simple. That jar you just made is Aladdin's lamp. You rubbed it . . . and I appeared!"

Dick laughed, then grew sober. "I wish we could conjure up a genie to find that China clay pit," he said a bit ruefully.

"Maybe we don't need a genie," said Nancy.

"What do you mean?"

"We may have found the leaning chimney!" Nancy beamed.

Dick gasped. "Honestly?"

"I don't know yet." Nancy told Dick what she and her friends had discovered. "I'm going back soon to look more thoroughly."

A boyish smile of hope lit Dick's face as he escorted Nancy to the door.

"I'll keep you posted on further developments," Nancy promised.

After dinner that evening she accompanied her father to his study on the second floor.

"You're up to something, young lady," he said shrewdly. "What is it?"

Nancy told him of her visit to the strange enclosure. Mr. Drew frowned.

"I don't like the sound of it," he said. "Strikes me as a good place to stay away from."

"But, Dad!" Nancy protested, her blue eyes growing large with emphasis. "There may be a valuable pit of China clay around there. And if I don't go back, I'll never find out!"

"If it's inside the fence, the owner probably won't want to sell the clay, anyway," Mr. Drew reminded his daughter. "Well, look around if you wish. But be careful. Don't go there alone."

"All right," she promised.

Carson Drew took a paper from his pocket and said, "I have a clue, too. It's about the Engs."

"What is it?" Nancy asked eagerly.

"I received a phone call from San Francisco this afternoon," Mr. Drew explained, "and my secretary wrote down this report." He settled back in his chair and continued:

"It says that when the Engs arrived in San Francisco, on their trip to the United States, they were met at the dock by a man named David Carr.

"Carr was sales representative for the West Coast Trading Company, a San Francisco importing house," Mr. Drew went on. "He and Eng Moy apparently were acquainted as the result of business dealings. When the Engs left San Francisco on their tour of United States pottery plants, Carr went with them."

"Does the report mention what David Carr looks like?" Nancy asked.

"No. The report says there doesn't appear to be any photograph or description of him available. Even the officials of the importing company can't furnish any clues. It seems that Carr did practically all his work for them in China; contacted them by mail. Then, about the time he met the Engs in San Francisco, he dropped out of sight."

"Maybe Carr has something to do with the Engs' disappearance," Nancy speculated.

"Could be," her father agreed. He put the report away. "Anyway, it's a clue to work on."

As Nancy pondered, she glanced idly at a New York City newspaper which lay on her father's desk. Suddenly a small black headline caught her eye. She picked up the paper and scanned the story, then read it to her father.

It described a robbery that had taken place in New York. An ancient Chinese tea jar, dating from the Sung dynasty, had been stolen from the delivery truck of the Sen-yung Oriental Gift Shop on Madison Avenue.

"That's the place where Mr. Townsend bought the vase for his wife; the one stolen during the party!" Nancy exclaimed. "I'll bet there's some connection between the two robberies!"

She decided to put in a long-distance call to the gift shop the following morning and find out if the thief had been arrested.

"He may be the same person who stole Mrs. Townsend's vase!" Nancy cried excitedly.

Mr. Drew smiled. "Why not call the New York police tonight?" he suggested. "I'll do it for you if you like."

In a few minutes he had the desired information. The thief was still at large.

"How would you like to go to New York and talk to the owner of the gift shop yourself?" Mr. Drew suggested. "You'll get more information that way. Besides, you'll be able to spend a few days with Aunt Eloise."

"It's a deal!" exclaimed Nancy as she hugged her father. She had put off visiting her father's sister, Miss Eloise Drew, for far too long. "I'll catch the morning plane if I can get a reservation," she decided.

Fortunately, when she telephoned the airport, she was able to get a seat. Then she wired her aunt, telling of her time of arrival.

She slipped into bed with her head full of anticipation. New York always held a thrill for her!

Nancy was awakened the next morning by a small, cold nose sniffing her hand. She sat up to see Togo, her little fox terrier, squatting on her suitcase, his eyes fixed on her anxiously. His stubby tail began to wag while he whimpered pleadingly.

"No, Togo." Nancy yawned. "You can't come."

She rose and dressed quickly. Two hours later Nancy boarded the plane to New York. The trip was smooth and pleasant. A moment after the plane landed, Nancy saw her aunt, a tall, attractive woman of middle age.

Miss Drew, whom Nancy strikingly resembled,

possessed a charming grace which marked her as a woman of unusual intelligence.

Eloise Drew knew that Nancy was a lot like her, and secretly this gave her a thrill. Years before, when Nancy had lost her mother, Miss Drew had considered coming to live with her brother. But the private school where she taught, and in which she had a financial interest, needed her, too. When Hannah Gruen had proved so satisfactory, Miss Drew had decided to remain in New York. But she enjoyed her niece's visits immensely.

"You look wonderful, Nancy!" she said as they embraced. "And how's your father?"

"He's fine," Nancy replied, squeezing her aunt's hand.

The luncheon hour was made particularly exciting by the young detective's tale of the stolen potteries. At the end of the meal, Miss Drew readily agreed to Nancy's suggestion that they taxi to Sen-yung's Oriental Gift Shop.

Some time later their cab swung out of the heavy traffic on Madison Avenue and pulled up before the store. Nancy and her aunt stood outside a moment to admire the exotic and colorful Chinese potteries and jewelry, and odd pieces of Oriental bric-a-brac displayed in a large plate-glass window. Then they entered the shop.

Three men, one in deliveryman's uniform,

were talking at the rear of the store. One of them came forward as Nancy and her aunt entered.

Nancy hesitated. The name of the proprietor painted on the display window was Chinese, but the man who confronted her was not an Oriental.

"Is Mr. Sen-yung here?" she inquired.

The man shook his head regretfully. "Mr. Sen-yung has been at home ill for the past six weeks," he informed her. "Is there anything I can do for you? I'm John Tallow, Mr. Sen-yung's partner."

"I'm sure you can help." Nancy smiled. "Some time ago Mr. Townsend of River Heights purchased a lovely Ming vase here. I'd like to find out who sold you the vase."

"Mr. Townsend?" the man repeated slowly. "Just a moment. I'll look up the sale in my books."

He went into an office at the rear of the store. As Nancy and her aunt wandered about, examining the beautiful jewelry and porcelain, Nancy could plainly hear the other two men talking. She realized at once that one was a detective. It was evident from their conversation that the deliveryman was the driver of the truck from which the Sung tea jar had been stolen.

"I didn't get a good look at him," she heard the deliveryman say. "I'd just lifted the jar out of the truck to deliver it when I felt a gun at my back. Then a voice told me to get in the truck and drive away."

Nancy stepped forward. She apologized for the interruption and explained her interest in the case. The detective told her to ask as many questions as she wished, but there was little that the deliveryman could add to his story.

"The thief's hat was pulled down and his coat collar turned up," he said flatly. "I was too busy worrying about what he was going to do with the gun to look at him much. I did what he told me to do—left the jar on the sidewalk and scrammed!"

Nancy was disappointed not to learn more. At that moment she felt her aunt's hand on her sleeve.

"Do come and look at this vase," Miss Drew urged. "It sounds like the one you were talking about."

She led her niece to a glass cabinet off to one side of the shop. Nancy stared in amazement at the piece on display. Glazed on jade-green porcelain was a Chinese dragon in black and red.

The same design she had seen woven into the tapestry in Mr. Soong's home! The one he had said was on his stolen vase!

CHAPTER IX

Pursuit

NANCY hurried to the rear of the shop to find Mr. Tallow. Before she had a chance to ask about Mr. Soong's vase, he gave her some startling information.

"The Townsend vase," he told Nancy, "was sold to me by a Mr. David Carr."

Nancy stared at him in disbelief. David Carr! That was the name of the man her father had mentioned; the man who had vanished so mysteriously in company with the Engs!

"You're quite sure?"

"Quite." Mr. Tallow smiled pleasantly. "It's all written down in my ledger."

Nancy pointed out the dragon vase in the case. "Would you mind telling me where that came from?" she asked.

"Not at all," Mr. Tallow replied. "I bought that porcelain only yesterday from Mr. Carr."

Nancy caught her breath. She had been sure the dragon vase had been stolen from Dick's shop by John Manning. Were Carr and Manning the same person? Or had Manning sold the vase to Carr, who in turn had sold it to Sen-yung's Oriental Gift Shop?

"I'm sorry to have to tell you," Nancy said, "but this vase looks just like one that was stolen from a shop in River Heights."

Mr. Tallow's jaw dropped. "It can't be true!"

"The dragon design is exactly the same as the pattern on a Ming vase that belonged to a Mr. Soong," Nancy added.

"Mr. Soong!" the shopkeeper exclaimed. "I know him well! He is an old friend of Mr. Sen-yung! Oh, this is terrible!"

Mr. Tallow looked so worried that Nancy felt sorry for him and asked if she might examine the vase to see if it really were the same one.

"Of course, of course," he agreed.

He unlocked the cabinet door and handed the piece to Nancy. She laid the vase on its side and studied the bottom. Clearly painted on the base were several Chinese symbols. They appeared to be exactly like one set of the markings that she had found in Manning's room; the set Mr. Soong had said was on his vase.

Nancy translated the symbols. "Made in the studio of deep peace." She looked at Mr. Tallow. "Is that correct?"

He nodded nervously.

At that moment the door of the shop opened and a short, round-faced Chinese gentleman came in. He took off his hat, exposing a completely bald head, and fanned himself vigorously.

Mr. Tallow hurried toward him. "Mr. Sen-yung! Thank goodness you're back!"

After introducing his Chinese partner to Nancy, her aunt and the detective, Mr. Tallow repeated what Nancy had said about the dragon vase. Mr. Sen-yung's face became grave. Taking a magnifying glass from his pocket, he examined the pottery. Suddenly he straightened and turned to his partner.

"When did you buy this vase?" he asked sharply.

"Yesterday," Mr. Tallow replied.

"You should not have bought it without first consulting me!" Mr. Sen-yung told him heatedly.

"But you were ill!" his partner protested. "I didn't want to disturb you!" He looked at the vase, then back at the Chinese. "Is anything wrong?"

"Everything!" Mr. Sen-yung exclaimed. "This vase is a fake—an imitation!"

Mr. Tallow stared at him, dumbfounded.

"How can you tell, Mr. Sen-yung?" Nancy asked.

He showed her the barely perceptible but un-mistakable signs that had betrayed the vase to

"This vase is a fake—an imitation!"
Mr. Sen-yung exclaimed

him. Under the magnifying glass the colors showed no signs of having softened with the years, and there was a scent of newness about the porcelain. But most particularly the marks on the bottom stood out a trifle too clearly.

"It is a clever imitation," Mr. Sen-yung admitted. "Extremely expert."

Had this copy of Mr. Soong's vase been made in China and smuggled into the United States by David Carr?

Mr. Sen-yung asked his partner for the complete story of the purchase. Mr. Tallow said he had bought the dragon vase and also the one sold to Mr. Townsend from David Carr. The man had introduced himself as a sales representative of the West Coast Trading Company and shown credentials to prove his identity.

Knowing the fine reputation of the firm, Mr. Tallow had assumed the vases to be authentic. Now it seemed possible that the Townsend vase also was a fake.

"We must get the Townsend vase back at once," Mr. Sen-yung said. "If it, too, is a reproduction, we'll refund the money."

"It has been stolen," Nancy informed him. "That's really what brought me to New York." Then she asked Mr. Tallow, "What does David Carr look like?"

"He is medium height," the man replied, "with black hair and dark skin."

"Did you notice his eyes and his shoes?"

"Not his shoes," Mr. Tallow replied slowly. "But his dark eyes had a peculiar piercing stare."

"John Manning!" Nancy cried.

The two partners, Miss Eloise Drew, and the detective looked at Nancy in bewilderment. She quickly told them about the vase thief.

"Don't you see?" she finished. "Manning and Carr are probably the same man!"

"And he's the one who held up the delivery-man!" Mr. Tallow exclaimed. "I just remembered that Carr was here when I gave instructions as to when and where the jar was to be delivered."

"Did Carr say where he's staying?" Nancy asked.

"No, but I think I know where he may be," Mr. Tallow replied. "He dropped a piece of paper from his pocket. It was a letterhead from the Hotel Royalton."

Asking permission to use the office telephone, Nancy dialed the hotel. David Carr, she was told, was registered.

"If we hurry, we may catch him!"

The detective, who had been listening to Nancy's theories with great admiration, led Nancy, her aunt and Mr. Tallow to a police car in front of the store. Seconds later, they sped up Madison Avenue.

Side by side, Nancy and the detective hurried into the hotel lobby and went up to the desk.

The man showed his badge and asked for the number of David Carr's room.

The clerk looked surprised. "Mr. Carr? He just checked out."

"But I phoned only a few minutes ago," Nancy protested. "He was registered then."

"I'm sorry," the clerk told her. "He checked out right after you called."

"Did he leave any forwarding address?" she asked hopefully.

The clerk shook his head.

"Mind if we search his room?" the detective asked.

"Go ahead," the clerk replied. He took a key from the rack and gave it to the plainclothesman. "Room 414."

While Mr. Tallow waited in the lobby, to watch in case the thief should reappear, Nancy, her aunt and the detective proceeded to the room Carr had occupied.

The door was ajar. Inside, a maid was cleaning the room. The detective asked to see any scraps of paper she had picked up. The maid showed them to him. He and Nancy pored over the pieces, looking for a possible clue to Carr's whereabouts. But neither the maid's trash bag nor the room itself disclosed the slightest clue.

The detective grunted in disgust. "No use staying here. There isn't a ghost of a clue to where Carr went."

The maid stopped dusting and looked at them. "You mean the gentleman who was occupyin' this room?" she asked.

"Yes," Nancy said hopefully. "Can you tell us anything about him?"

"Well, I can tell you what I overheard," the woman replied. "Just as I came into the room to clean he was talkin' on the phone. Before he hung up, he said somethin' about meetin' somebody at the Oregon restaurant."

"Thanks!" cried Nancy.

She ran from the room, followed by her aunt and the detective. A few minutes later they joined Mr. Tallow in the lobby. Then all four taxied to the restaurant.

The Oregon was on a corner. Tingling with eagerness, Nancy almost dragged her aunt into the foyer of the narrow restaurant. The tables, she saw, were arranged along the two walls beyond a row of potted palms.

"Mr. Tallow, see if you can find Mr. Carr," she whispered. "Look through the palms."

Parting the fronds of one of the plants, he peered at the dining room. Not seeing the suspected thief, Mr. Tallow stepped into the entranceway for a better view.

"There he is!" he called excitedly.

There was a commotion at the rear of the room. Nancy saw a man spring from a chair and dash through the swinging door to the kitchen.

The detective ran in pursuit. Nancy, remembering the restaurant was situated on a corner, darted back toward the front entrance. If Carr should escape through a side door, she reasoned, he would come out around the corner.

Nancy's deduction was right. As she rounded the side of the building, Carr streaked from the restaurant's side entrance. Nancy was on his heels before the detective emerged.

The elusive Carr slipped in and out of the crowd. Pedestrians stared as Nancy raced after him.

At the corner she saw Carr dash into a subway entrance. He leaped down the steps three at a time, Nancy after him. Token in hand, he went through the turnstile like a streak of lightning.

Nancy had to pause a moment to buy a token. A train stood in the station. Carr ran forward alongside, slipping quickly into one of the forward cars.

The doors of the train were closing. Nancy leaped inside the nearest car just before the big door snapped shut. With a lurch, the crowded train started.

CHAPTER X

New Developments

NANCY was wedged tightly between the passengers as the train, with a roar, picked up speed. Reaching for a strap, she caught her breath and quickly planned her next move. She *must* push through the crowded train and find Carr!

Nancy gripped her handbag firmly and started to ease herself among the passengers. She excused herself frequently as she jostled men and women. Finally she reached the car into which the suspect had fled. Suddenly it dawned on her that she could not hold him alone. She must have help!

"I'll ask the conductor," Nancy decided, and stood on tiptoe to see if one were in sight.

As she craned her neck, she saw David Carr slouched in a seat near the far door. Near him stood the conductor. Excitedly Nancy moved forward once more.

At that moment the train started to slow for the next stop. In desperation, Nancy forged ahead. Suddenly, with a pitch that threw everybody off balance, the train jerked to an abrupt halt. The doors whipped open. Carr stepped out with the pressing crowd.

"Stop that man!" shouted Nancy. "The dark-haired one with the red tie!"

People around gaped, but no one went after him. Before Nancy herself could get to Carr, he had fled into the sea of humanity milling toward the exit.

When Nancy reached the top of the stairs, David Carr was out of sight. She searched in vain; then, disappointed, hailed a taxi to return to the Oregon restaurant.

"Nancy!" cried Miss Drew as her niece arrived. "Thank goodness you're safe. We feared Carr might have harmed you."

Nancy told her aunt and Mr. Tallow about the chase. As she finished, the detective hurried up to them. He said he had fallen over a stool that Carr had tossed at him in the kitchen. By the time he had reached the street, Carr had disappeared. Then he had searched the immediate area to no avail.

All four drove to police headquarters, where the detective made out a report on Carr. At Nancy's suggestion, they telephoned the West Coast Trading Company in San Francisco. As she had suspected, Carr had not been working for them recently.

"Your niece certainly has a good head on her shoulders," the police captain said to Miss Eloise Drew as she and Nancy left.

"They say I'm very much like my aunt," Nancy said with a smile. "But I'm sorry we didn't catch David Carr."

Reaching the sidewalk, the Drews took a taxi to the former teacher's apartment.

Next morning Nancy suggested to her aunt that they tour Chinatown. Recalling that the stolen vases discovered in Masonville had been wrapped in Chinese newspapers, Nancy wanted to go to the office of the *China Daily Times* and make some inquiries.

When the two reached Mott Street, they located the newspaper office and went inside. Nancy asked a pleasant man the names of subscribers in Masonville and River Heights. He willingly told her, but neither John Manning nor David Carr was among them.

"Nothing came of that hunch," Nancy told her aunt as they headed for a fine Chinese restaurant.

As they finished a delicious seven-course meal, Aunt Eloise gave her niece a worried look. "Wouldn't it be wise to give up the case and stay out of Carr's way, dear?" she suggested.

Nancy patted her aunt's hand reassuringly. "Don't worry about me, Aunt Eloise. I promise to be doubly careful. Anyway, I'm going home tomorrow and maybe he'll stay here."

Actually the young detective felt that if Carr and Manning were the same person, there was a good possibility he was already on his way back to the River Heights area. She would have to watch her step!

"You're going home?" her aunt repeated. "Oh, Nancy, I thought—"

"Sorry, darling," her niece said. "A friend of Ned's is being married. Ned's to be an usher. I promised to drive up to Emerson and get him day after tomorrow."

"I hate to have you leave," her aunt said wistfully. "But I bow to the younger generation! Now let's do some sightseeing."

The following day, on arriving home, she was welcomed by a smiling Hannah Gruen and a barking, tail-wagging Togo.

Ned telephoned just as Nancy started to unpack. Nancy plunged into a brief description of her activities.

"Wow!" he exclaimed when she finished. "You sound like a one-woman police force! Anyway, I'm glad you're back. I'd begun to think you'd forgotten about me."

"Not a chance!" she assured the youth. "I'll be at Emerson tomorrow by twelve o'clock."

"Okay."

Later, Nancy called Mr. Soong. The Chinese gentleman was shocked to hear that an imitation of his rare Ming vase had been sold to the Senyung Oriental Gift Shop. He congratulated Nancy on her brave attempt to capture Carr and expressed the hope that the man would be apprehended soon.

The next day when Nancy arrived at Ned's fraternity house she was immediately surrounded by the various members. Having attended many parties there, she was well known and well liked.

"Ned's not here," one teased. "Prof kept him after class. How about lunch with me?"

"Say, you big so-and-so," called a youth, clattering down the stairs. "Lay off!"

Ned appeared, grinning, turned Nancy around and marched her back to the car. They had lunch at an attractive inn, then started for Ned's home, a few miles out of River Heights. On the way, Nancy gave Ned all the details of her search for a China clay pit near the leaning chimney. While they were going through Masonville, she suddenly asked Ned to stop.

"What's up?" Ned asked.

They were in front of the courthouse.

"I've been wanting to find out who owns that fenced-in property in the woods," Nancy replied. "Let's go in to ask the Registrar of Deeds."

Ned followed her up the steps and into the

registrar's office. The clerk handed them a map and ledger. Together they flipped the pages until they came to the entry Nancy was seeking.

The records showed that a tract of land comprising some two hundred and fifty acres, including the abandoned Civil War mine, had been purchased by Miles Monroe of Philadelphia five years ago.

"Miles Monroe!" Nancy exclaimed in surprise. "That's where he said he came from!"

"Who's he?" Ned inquired.

"A geologist I went to see about the China clay pit. Now I know why Mr. Monroe asked me to let him know if I located it."

"Sounds phony to me," Ned declared. "Want to stop and see him?"

"If you have time."

"I'm not due at the bachelor dinner until seven-thirty. So let's go. I'd like to see this Mr. Monroe and ask him what he means by trying to put one over on the world's prettiest detective."

"Ned, stop it!" Nancy commanded.

They left the courthouse and drove to Miles Monroe's apartment in River Heights. As before, an eye stared through the peephole in answer to Nancy's ring. When the professor recognized Nancy, the door flew open.

"Glad you called," he said. "I have something to show you. But first, tell me why you came."

Nancy introduced Ned, then quickly got to the

problem on her mind. "We've found out your secret, Professor Monroe!"

"My secret?" he asked, perplexed.

"It's you who owns the old iron mine!"

"Me?" exclaimed the geologist. Then he burst out laughing. "I never owned a piece of land in my life!"

"The property is listed as being owned by Miles Monroe of Philadelphia," Nancy told him. "Who could this Miles Monroe be?"

The professor shook his head. "Search me!" he snorted. "To the best of my knowledge I was the only Miles Monroe in Philadelphia."

Nancy felt sure the man was telling the truth. Since he could tell her nothing more, she put the puzzling question aside for the moment.

"You said you had something to show me," she reminded him.

The geologist uncrossed his long, bony legs and limped over to the bookcase. He took out a thick volume that looked to be very old. Carefully he turned the pages to a place he had marked.

"After you told me you were searching for a China clay deposit," the professor said, "I came across a reference in this old book on geology."

With Ned looking on, Nancy read the paragraph the geologist had marked. It told of a fine white clay that had been found one mile southeast of a "crook in Huntsman's River" during the days of the early settlers.

"Huntsman's River?" Nancy said. "Why, that must be Hunter's Creek. That's the stream which runs under Hunter's Bridge."

"Exactly! And the clay the book describes is China clay, or I'm no geologist!"

"Thank you so much, Professor Monroe," said Nancy, rising to depart.

Ned shook hands with the geologist. "Nice to meet you, sir," he said. "This sounds like a good clue for Nancy."

When the couple reached the car, Ned suggested that they spend the next afternoon following the directions to the China clay pit.

"And how about Mrs. Gruen packing one of those super picnic lunches?" he added with a grin.

Nancy laughed. "It's a date."

At twelve the next day they started out. Nancy told Ned she had learned that no Miles Monroe was listed in the Philadelphia telephone directory. Her father had obtained this information.

"It's sure a mystery," declared Ned. "But maybe we'll soon clear it up."

Reaching Hunter's Bridge, Nancy showed him where to park and they locked the car. Taking the picnic basket, they started off, following the water upstream for a mile to a point where it swerved sharply.

"This must be the 'crook' the book mentioned," Ned said. "How about eating?"

Nancy nodded. She squinted at the position of

the sun, then pointed to the left. "And southeast should be in that direction."

Half an hour later the two explorers, their appetites well satisfied, set off once more. When they had gone exactly one mile, as the directions had indicated, Nancy stopped.

"The clay should be near here!"

"Say, what's this?" Ned exclaimed, bending down to examine a little gully. "Do you suppose this is part of the old clay pit?"

The two stepped into the depression, overgrown with weeds and brush. As they did, Ned kicked against a piece of flat, corroded iron.

"Probably part of an old forge," he remarked.

"Just what we need!" Nancy exclaimed. "We can use it as a shovel."

"For what?" Ned queried.

"To dig with," Nancy replied, pointing to the bottom of the gully.

Ned dug. Finally he said ruefully, "Nothing here but a lot of gravel. This isn't a China clay pit. It's only—"

He stopped speaking as a wild cry pierced the woods some distance ahead. It sounded like *bong*.

"Someone's in trouble!" Nancy exclaimed, starting to run.

A few moments later she and Ned emerged into a clearing. To Nancy's utter astonishment, the four-walled enclosure of boards confronted her!

CHAPTER XI

The Impostor

HAD the cry come from inside the mysterious enclosure? Nancy ran eagerly toward the fence and listened. There was not a sound.

"How do we get inside?" Ned asked, anxious to help the person in distress.

"There's no opening," Nancy told him. "I wish we could climb over."

"At least we can look over," said Ned, pointing to a stout tree limb lying on the ground. "If you'll help me, we can prop this against the fence for a ladder, Nancy."

Together they lugged the limb across the clearing and lifted it against the fence.

"You go up while I hold it," Ned suggested.

Nancy placed her hands around the bough and, monkey-fashion, started up.

"What do you see?" Ned asked as she reached the top.

"Not much. Trees. Lots of them." She scampered down. "But we're not far from the leaning chimney. Let's go over there and take a look."

Ned willingly dragged the tree limb the short distance and Nancy climbed up again. Below her was the rectangular enclosure, a stone wall, and the battered brick building she had seen some days before through a knothole.

Glancing up, Nancy was startled to find that the rusted ornament on the leaning chimney was gone. She looked at the ground below, thinking the symbol had dropped off. It was not there.

"Say, what's so interesting?" Ned called up.

"Come on up."

Nancy told him about the missing ornament, and also Bess's declaration that she had seen a hand sticking from the chimney. Maybe someone *had* climbed up inside, planning to remove the iron coat of arms, or whatever it was.

"This place gets more mysterious every day," Nancy remarked.

"It's funny there's no sign of life around, though," Ned commented. "You'd think somebody—"

He stopped speaking as they heard a far-off cry. Again it sounded like *bong,* and again it was impossible to tell whether the call of distress had come from inside the enclosure.

Almost simultaneously with the cry came the menacing crack of rotted wood.

"The tree limb!" Nancy cried. Nancy and Ned scurried down just as the old limb split.

Ned helped Nancy to her feet. "No more sleuthing today," he insisted. "Anyway, I can just about make that wedding rehearsal in time."

Nancy hated to leave so soon but said nothing. They trekked back to the car and Ned drove to his home in Mapleton, a suburb of River Heights.

"See you tomorrow afternoon at the wedding," he said, getting out. "And don't let any other usher take you up the aisle!"

Nancy laughingly promised. Then, as she drove on to River Heights, her thoughts turned again to the enclosure in the woods. Both leads which Miles Monroe had given her, the one to the old iron mine and the directions along Hunter's Creek, had led to the strange spot in the woods.

Was the China clay inside? Did the owner know about it? Nancy set her chin in determination. She would find out! And soon!

Hannah Gruen met her at the rear door of the Drew home, her kindly face lined with worry.

"What's wrong?" Nancy asked quickly.

"Oh, Nancy, Mr. Soong has been phoning you for the past half hour! He's terribly upset! He's at police headquarters!"

"What for?"

"I don't know," the housekeeper answered, "but I think he's in trouble."

Nancy ran down the porch steps to her car. She drove rapidly, wondering at every turn what the police could want with gentle Mr. Soong!

Nancy ran into police headquarters. The old Chinese gentleman was sitting dejectedly in Chief McGinnis's office. Nancy looked from Mr. Soong to the police officer, then back to Mr. Soong.

"What happened?" she asked.

Mr. Soong, his face lighting at the sight of the young detective, opened his mouth to speak. Chief McGinnis intervened quietly.

"Perhaps I'd better explain," he told Nancy. He picked up a paper from his desk. "I received this report today from the New York City police. A woman in New York, named Mrs. Marsden, has complained that a Chinese vase she bought is a fake. She claims it was sold to her by a Mr. Soong of River Heights. She mailed him money orders for five hundred dollars, which he cashed." The officer looked up, adding:

"We've checked with the postal clerk in Masonville. His description of the man who collected the money tallies exactly with that of Mr. Soong."

The Chinese turned despairing eyes on Nancy. "I know nothing about it," he said. "Surely you believe me?"

"Of course!" Nancy said emphatically. "Chief McGinnis, does the report give a description of the vase?"

The officer scanned the paper. "Yes, it does."

The young detective's pulse quickened with eagerness. She was playing a hunch. If it worked, everything would be straightened out!

"Does it say that the vase is brown," Nancy rushed on, "with a pattern showing an old Chinese sitting beside a deer under a peach tree at the edge of a blue lake?"

Chief McGinnis stared. "Why, yes!"

"And does it say the Chinese markings on the bottom of the vase mean 'Made for the hall of fragrant virtue'?"

The police officer's jaw dropped. "How did you know all that?" he demanded.

"Because that vase," Nancy replied evenly, "is the one stolen from the Townsends' home. I saw it there the night it was taken!"

"Well," Chief McGinnis said, "this is a new angle."

"What's more," Nancy continued, "Mr. Soong couldn't have been the thief because I measured the thief's footprints in the flower bed. They were short and wide. And as you can clearly see, Mr. Soong's feet are narrow!"

She paused for breath, and McGinnis wiped his forehead. He sat for a moment, considering, while Nancy watched him anxiously.

"That puts a different complexion on the case," the officer said at last. "But how do you explain the fact that the postal clerk's description of the man who cashed the money orders fits Mr. Soong?"

Nancy deliberated. "The thief probably wore a disguise so he could pass as Mr. Soong," she said finally. "It wouldn't be difficult—a pair of spectacles and a tiny goatee. He must have stolen some means of identification and forged Mr. Soong's signature to the money orders."

"You may possibly be right," the chief said, "but just the same I think I'll drive Mr. Soong over to Masonville, to see that postal clerk. Want to come, Nancy?"

"Yes, indeed."

"We'll go there in my car."

Late that afternoon Nancy, Mr. Soong, and the chief arrived at the Masonville post office. At Nancy's suggestion, the two men stayed out of sight while she went to the money-order window.

Nancy introduced herself to the clerk, then listened carefully as he described the man who had collected the money for the fake vase. His description corresponded exactly with that of Mr. Soong.

"You're quite sure you would recognize the man if you saw him again?" she asked.

"I'm positive!" the clerk told her confidently. "It isn't often that I cash orders for five hundred dollars, so I pay particular attention to anybody collecting that amount of money."

Nancy beckoned to Mr. Soong and had him stand facing the clerk. Chief McGinnis looked on approvingly.

"Is this the man?" she asked.

The clerk stared at the Chinese gentleman.

"That's the one, all right!" he declared. "I'd know him anywhere!"

Nancy thought quickly. There had to be *some* way in which she could prove to the clerk he was mistaken. She took a money-order application form and gave it to Mr. Soong, together with a pen.

"Please fill it out," she told her friend. Then she said to the clerk, "Perhaps you've overlooked something. Some small detail—"

She broke off as the clerk's eyes widened in watching Mr. Soong write.

"Hey, wait a minute, there is something wrong!" he said. "The Chinese I gave the money to signed his name with his right hand. This gentleman writes with his left hand."

"Then he can't be the same man!" Nancy stated triumphantly.

The clerk shook his head. "No, he can't," he admitted slowly. "In fact," he added, "this man speaks better English. I hadn't thought of that before. But the two of 'em look alike."

Chief McGinnis said he was sorry to have put Mr. Soong in such an embarrassing position.

They drove back to River Heights, and Nancy took the elderly Chinese home in her car.

"How can I ever repay you?" Mr. Soong said.

"By telling me more someday about your country's beautiful pottery," Nancy said, smiling.

He insisted she come inside at once to be presented with a little gift in token of his gratitude.

As she accompanied the Chinese toward his door, it suddenly swung open. In the entrance stood Mr. Soong's Chinese servant, Ching. His small, inscrutable eyes for once were wide with surprise. Then his lips parted in a toothy smile and he spoke rapidly in Chinese, gesticulating all the while.

Mr. Soong replied in the same tongue. Ching turned to Nancy, his smile growing bigger. Again he spoke.

"What is he saying?" she asked Mr. Soong.

"Ching is thanking you for delivering me from the hands of the police," he explained.

Mr. Soong chuckled. Then he disappeared for a moment, returning with a bottle of delicate wisteria perfume imported from China.

"It is little for me to do." He bowed when Nancy thanked him for the gift.

"I'll wear some of it to the wedding I'm going to tomorrow afternoon," she said.

"Miss Tyson's wedding?" the Chinese inquired. "Perhaps I shall see you there."

The next day, after the church ceremony,

Nancy and her friends drove to the reception at the bride's home. After wishing the couple every happiness and having punch and party sandwiches, Nancy and Ned went to admire the many lovely wedding gifts displayed in an upstairs room.

Mr. Soong walked in directly behind them. Almost at once, the man's eyes fell on a Chinese porcelain jewel box. He picked it up with a pleased exclamation.

"It's beautiful!" said Nancy.

The porcelain jewel case was decorated with plum blossoms. They were painted on a background of deep-blue water lightly coated with cracking ice.

As Mr. Soong started to replace the jewel box, his eyes suddenly bulged, and he exclaimed in Chinese.

"What is it?" Nancy asked quickly.

Mr. Soong pointed with a shaking finger to two Chinese symbols worked into the blossoms. They were the same strange symbols Nancy had seen concealed in the peach-tree pattern on the Townsends' vase!

She turned again to Mr. Soong. The elderly gentleman's lips were parted. He seemed unable to take his eyes from the symbols.

"What are they?" she asked.

"They are the marks of Eng Moy!" he whispered. "My missing friend Eng Moy!"

CHAPTER XII

A Jade Elephant

"Eng Moy!" Nancy gasped.

Mr. Soong nodded slowly, as if he still could not believe it himself. "I would know my friend's signature anywhere."

"But I don't understand," Nancy said. "If Eng Moy made the jewel box, why didn't he sign his name on the bottom? Why did he work it into the design where it can barely be seen?"

"That I myself do not understand."

Mr. Soong turned the box bottom up. Several Chinese characters were painted on the base.

"It is from the Wan Li period, the last great epoch of art in the Ming dynasty," Mr. Soong stated. "Eng Moy did not make the vase. So he could not have put his initials on it."

"There's no question that the box is authentic?" Nancy asked.

"Why do you ask?"

Nancy told the Chinese about the two symbols that were Eng Moy's signature concealed in the design of the Townsends' vase. "That piece—the one sold to Mrs. Marsden in New York City—was an imitation of an old vase," she added.

Mr. Soong stared at Nancy in hurt bewilderment. She decided to avoid offending him further. But she wanted to explore the possible link between Eng Moy and the swindler David Carr.

"Perhaps if I learn where this jewel box came from, it will help us find the Engs," she said.

Mr. Soong's face lit up. "A splendid idea!"

Nancy wandered about among the wedding guests until she found the bride's mother. Then she asked discreetly if she knew where the attractive old jewel box had come from.

"Why, Mrs. Dareff gave my daughter the box," the hostess said kindly. "It came from that lovely antique shop in Westville."

Nancy knew the store and its proprietor. She made a beeline for the telephone, Ned close by.

"A swell way to enjoy a reception!" he grumbled in mock disapproval as Nancy dialed.

"As soon as I finish this call," she promised, "we'll go have some more refreshments."

"You're on!" He grinned. "And furthermore, we're going from the reception direct to the country club. There's a dance tonight, and some of us have fixed up a little party."

"Fine," Nancy beamed. "Hello? . . . Mrs.

Lorimer? . . . This is Nancy Drew of River Heights."

She told the owner of the shop where she was, then asked about the jewel case.

"Isn't it lovely?" the woman effused. "Now let me see— Oh, yes, I purchased that piece several weeks ago from Mr. David Carr."

"Was he a man of medium height with rather piercing eyes? Is he from San Francisco?" Nancy asked.

"Why, yes. You know him?"

"I've heard of him. He's a thief, Mrs. Lorimer. If he should show up again, will you please tell the police right away?"

At that instant Bess Marvin rushed up to Nancy. "Come on! Quick!"

Nancy said good-by to Mrs. Lorimer and hung up.

"The bride's going to throw her bouquet," Bess said excitedly. "Don't *you* want to catch it?" she asked, glancing sidewise at Ned.

Nancy blushed and rushed away to where eager hands hoped to catch the symbolic "next to be married" bouquet. But she stayed in the background. The maid of honor caught the white roses.

While waiting for the bride to change to traveling clothes and come downstairs, Nancy noticed some guests she had not seen before. There were Dick Milton and his wife Connie. Joining the couple, she learned they had just arrived. Dick had not been able to get away from his shop, and Connie had had no one with whom to leave the baby.

"Sue's outside in her carriage," Connie explained, after being introduced.

"It's a shame you missed the wedding," Nancy declared. "Please let me know when you want to go out. I'll be glad to baby-sit for you."

"That's awfully sweet of you, Nancy. I hate to take you up on it right away, but are you free on the nineteenth?" Connie asked.

"Yes. I'll come over."

"I'd love to go to a luncheon party that day," Connie explained. "Dick's going out of town to see about some different kind of clay."

"Not China clay," Dick spoke up quietly. "You haven't had any luck, Nancy?"

She told him of her recent search and how both of Miles Monroe's clues to the China clay pit had led to the mysterious enclosure in the woods.

"The first chance I have I'll go out there."

"I hope you'll find the clay," Dick replied. "The sooner I repay Mr. Soong the better, and there's not much chance of my doing it unless something big comes my way."

"The bride's ready to leave!" an excited girl called out, and paper rose petals were tossed at the bride and groom as they hurried down the stairs and through the hall to the front porch. Then a car door banged, and the couple were off on their honeymoon.

Ned found Nancy, and after saying good-by to their host and hostess, they left for the country club with a group of friends.

Later, when the dance was over, Ned helped Nancy into the car and slid in behind the wheel to drive home.

"Let's take the Three Bridges Road," she said.

"Do you expect to find Manning-Carr at Hunter's Bridge?" he asked teasingly.

"Well, things seem to happen there," Nancy replied. "He may use it as a meeting place."

Ned swung the convertible onto Three Bridges Road and drove swiftly toward River Heights. When the car approached the twisting turns, Ned pressed on the brake and coasted. As they slowly rounded the final curve in the series of turns, Nancy stared intently at the underbrush a short distance back from the road. At the spot where she had previously seen a man's footprints, she now saw only the black shadows of the night.

Nancy turned her attention to the opposite side of the road, while the car continued slowly toward Hunter's Bridge.

Suddenly, behind some bushes at the edge of the creek where it curved under the bridge, Nancy saw the small white glow of a flashlight.

"Look!" She pointed excitedly, then took her own flashlight from the front compartment of the car. "Stop!" she told Ned. "Let's investigate!"

They got out and crept down the embankment toward the light Nancy had seen. The couple stepped carefully, avoiding twigs and stones that might make a sound and betray their presence.

As they neared the shrubs, the light went out. Nancy and Ned hardly dared to breathe, but they saw no one.

Finally Nancy beamed her flashlight ahead. The next moment she had kicked off her shoes and was wading into the water.

"What——!" Ned exclaimed.

Nancy was soon on the other side of the narrow, shallow stream. She swooped up something from the ground and played her flashlight beam on it.

"What is it?" Ned called.

She held up the object, a green jade elephant about three inches long and two inches high.

"How'd that get here?" Ned asked.

"Someone just dropped it," Nancy replied, "and I don't believe he meant to."

"I'll come over and help you find him," Ned offered. "Is the elephant any good?"

As Nancy was about to say she thought it was Mr. Soong's valuable jade piece, there came the roar of a motor.

"My car!" Nancy cried out, and ran back across the stream.

Slipping into her shoes, she dashed after Ned, who was already halfway up the embankment. Two feet from the top of the slope they knew the worst.

Nancy's convertible was speeding away into the night!

CHAPTER XIII

A Bold Plan

NANCY and Ned stood aghast as the car's tail-light finally disappeared.

"Well, if I'm not a nitwit!" Ned said. "If I had locked the car this wouldn't have happened. We'd better run to a telephone and notify the police," he added. "A state trooper can overtake your car."

Nancy smiled wanly. "I'm afraid we'll be too late, Ned," she replied. "The nearest phone is about two miles from here."

The youth frowned. "I guess our best chance is to thumb a ride," he said at last. "Maybe a driver will give us a lift to town in time to do some good."

But Nancy knew there was small chance of any-one driving through the lonely stretch of woods at that hour. She and Ned started hiking toward River Heights, Nancy clutching the jade elephant.

Ned looked very forlorn and incongruous in his formal clothes, with a white carnation on his lapel. Nancy's high-heeled shoes were uncomfortable on the rough road, and her stockings were still wet from her dash through the creek.

After trudging two miles, the couple came to a gas station, where Nancy telephoned the State Police. The officer said he would notify all patrol cars to be on the lookout. Then he promised to send a trooper to take Nancy and Ned to their homes.

Nancy said nothing about the jade elephant, wishing to present it to Mr. Soong or Dick herself.

"Nancy," Ned said as they reached her house, "I'm due to go back to college early tomorrow morning, but I think I'll stick around here and help hunt for your car."

"No, you go on back to Emerson," she insisted. "I have an idea the person who took my car will abandon it somewhere. It'll turn up."

But next morning Nancy learned that the police had not found the convertible. When she went into the dining room, her father was finishing his breakfast.

"Dad, I'm worried," she announced. "So far the police haven't found a single trace of my car. I guess it's gone for good!"

Togo frisked into the room and barked cheerfully at his mistress. Mr. Drew looked thoughtfully at his daughter as she absently scratched the terrier's ears.

"Any idea who took the car?" he asked at last.

"I'm almost certain Manning-Carr or someone he was going to meet is the thief," she answered.

The lawyer took a sip of coffee. "You're probably right," he agreed. "And I don't like the situation. I've done some more checking on Carr."

"Tell me about him," Nancy said, pushing her concern about the stolen car out of her mind.

"I learned from the authorities in Washington," Mr. Drew went on, "that he's wanted for smuggling and a dozen other offenses. Seems he's of mixed blood."

"Part Chinese?" Nancy interrupted.

"His mother was Chinese. He's American on his father's side. In appearance, Carr is supposed to resemble his father."

"Oh!" Nancy said excitedly. "Now I'm beginning to put two and two together."

"And that's not all the story," said her father. "Carr has a brother who's also reported to be a criminal. But he's too cunning for anything definite to be known about him. He may be in the Orient or he may be in the United States; the authorities aren't sure which."

"Does he look like Carr?" Nancy asked quickly.

"No," the lawyer replied, "he looks like a Chinese."

Nancy mulled over this information. She was

sure now the brother was working with Carr. That would account for the second set of footprints which had baffled her. It also would account for the person who had cashed the money orders made out to Mr. Soong.

"Carr's brother may be hiding in the enclosure in the woods," she said to herself after her father had left the house. "Even Carr may be there!"

Nancy determined that as soon as she returned the jade elephant, she would investigate the enclosure. She would ask if Bess or George could use the family automobile and drive her there. This time she was going to find out why the fence had been built!

Hannah Gruen insisted upon knowing what Nancy was planning. She thought it might be dangerous and felt it was her duty to warn Nancy.

"You may be trespassing on property that doesn't concern the mystery," she pointed out. "Innocent people may live there, and they would have a perfect right to guard their property from intrusion."

Nancy hugged the faithful housekeeper. "If something happens to me, I know you'll come to the rescue!"

As Nancy walked to the telephone, Mrs. Gruen smiled. She knew that the young detective was determined to solve the mystery, but that she would not do anything foolhardy.

Neither Mr. Soong nor his servant Ching answered the telephone, so Nancy dialed Dick Milton's shop.

"Hold everything, Dick!" she said. "I've found the stolen jade elephant."

"No fooling!"

She asked him if he wanted to return the article to Mr. Soong personally.

"You found the elephant. Please take it to Mr. Soong."

Nancy agreed and carefully concealed the piece in a drawer of the dressing table in her bedroom. She would take the jade piece to Mr. Soong later.

Humming cheerfully at the prospect of finding the key to the mystery of the enclosure in the woods, Nancy set out for Bess Marvin's house. Her plump friend and George were putting golf balls on the lawn. Nancy described the events of the night before and the girls listened with astonishment.

"So I'm looking for a driver to take me to the mystery enclosure," she said in conclusion.

"Again?" Bess gasped. "I don't like that place."

"Oh, don't be a ninny," George retorted.

"All right," Bess agreed reluctantly. "I'll ask Mother if we can take the car."

After a few minutes she reappeared and said she could have it late that afternoon. It was four o'clock when they started off. This time they tied a ladder to the top of the car.

Bess headed for Three Bridges Road. A short time later they parked the car and the three girls started off through the woods, carrying the ladder.

When they finally saw the familiar four-walled wooden enclosure in the clearing before them, they paused to rest. The mysterious compound was strangely silent.

Bess looked apprehensive. "Oh, Nancy, I don't like it!" she whispered. "Let's go back!"

"Don't be a silly!" George scolded her cousin.

Bess subsided uncomfortably, with nervous glances at the surrounding area. Nancy and George picked up the ladder and the three walked on. Passing the knoll near the leaning chimney, Nancy decided to take a look from there.

"Bess, maybe you were right!" Nancy exclaimed. "Maybe someone *did* reach a hand out of the chimney! There's a new symbol up there now!"

The cousins rushed to Nancy's side and stared in amazement. Nancy, puzzled, told them that the original iron ornament was missing when she and Ned had looked at the chimney.

"This new one," she said, taking a pencil and pad from her clutch bag, "is like the other one, only it has more crosspieces."

"Looks like an Oriental ornament of some sort," George remarked.

Nancy said nothing. She asked the others to help her prop the ladder against the fence, then nimbly climbed it.

The scene inside the enclosure was exactly the same as when she had viewed it with Ned. There was little to be seen because of trees and bushes.

Climbing down, Nancy suggested they move the ladder to a part of the fence over which she had not looked before. The girls carried it to the end of the enclosure opposite the leaning chimney.

Once more Nancy surveyed the grounds.

"See anything?" Bess demanded.

Nancy glanced down and shook her head.

"Maybe people just come here once in a while," George ventured.

"They go in and out all right," Nancy said, and added excitedly, "Girls, I see the entrance gate!"

"Where?" George asked.

"Not far from here. It's very cleverly constructed so it doesn't show from the outside."

She had barely uttered this statement, when Nancy's attention became fixed.

"Someone's coming!" she announced. "A strange-looking person!"

Coming toward Nancy among the trees of the wooden enclosure was a tall woman dressed in a flowing lavender robe. Over her head she wore a hood of the same color. Encircling her waist was a knotted rope, the ends of which dangled as far down as her sandaled feet. She stared at the girl perched on the ladder.

"Get down from there at once!" she ordered.

Going to the gate, she lifted the iron latch and pulled open the cleverly concealed gate. Nancy scrambled down the ladder just as the woman appeared outside the fence. She came rapidly toward the three girls.

"What are you doing here?" she demanded.

"We didn't mean any harm—" Bess stammered, but Nancy interrupted her.

"We're searching for something," she explained with a friendly smile. "We were looking to see if it might be on the other side of the fence."

"You have no right to spy on our grounds!" the woman retorted sharply. "Go away and never return!"

Bess tugged at Nancy's sleeve. "Come on!"

Nancy ignored her friend's suggestion.

"We'll leave as soon as we learn what we came to find out," she said.

The woman's eyes narrowed. "What do you want to know?" she asked after a moment.

"We're searching for a pit of China clay," Nancy told her. "We have reason to believe it's in this vicinity. Can you tell us anything about it?"

The woman's hands clenched below the long, wide sleeves of her robe.

"I know of no such thing. Heed my warning and never come back!"

George, who had been staring at her long, hooded robe, asked suddenly, "Are you a member of a religious sect?"

"I belong to the Lavender Sisters," the woman replied. "The gardens beyond that wall are sacred. Those who dare defy us and trespass will be tormented by evil spirits until the day they die!"

Bess turned to Nancy appealingly, but the detective was not yet ready to go.

"Do Oriental women live here with you?"

The Lavender Sister gave Nancy a searching look. "No. Why do you ask?"

"Because of the symbol on the chimney," Nancy replied.

"The symbol?" the woman asked, puzzled. Then she added quickly, "Oh, yes, the symbol. I had forgotten."

She gave no further explanation, and again ordered the girls away.

"Help me carry the ladder, George," Nancy said.

With Nancy carrying one end of the ladder and George the other, the girls started back through the woods. The woman watched them for a while, then she quickly re-entered the wooden enclosure and latched the gate behind her.

"What a strange place for a religious colony," Bess said, ducking under a low-hanging branch.

"Go away and never return!" the woman ordered

"I'm not convinced it *is* a religious colony," Nancy replied.

"Me neither!" George declared. "Most of the things the woman said sounded like a lot of mumbo jumbo! I think she's funny in the head!"

"You can't tell," Bess observed seriously. "I'm just as glad we're going away from the place."

"Say!" George exclaimed when they reached a dirt lane. "This isn't the way we came, but maybe it connects with the gravel road."

They had gone about two hundred feet when Nancy stopped short and stared fixedly at something directly ahead of them in a small clearing.

It was Nancy's car!

"Hypers!" George cried in disbelief.

The girls dropped the ladder and rushed forward. The convertible was undamaged.

Nancy opened the door and looked inside the car. Everything was just as she had left it, but the ignition switch was locked and the keys were missing. On the floor lay an old pair of elevator shoes.

Nancy turned and faced her friends.

"I don't know about you two," she declared, "but I'm going back to the enclosure and get inside! It's no coincidence that we've found my car and these shoes here. I'm sure the car was stolen by some friend of Manning-Carr, and I'll bet that enclosure is their hideout."

"That's why the Lavender Sister didn't want

us around," George added. "I'll go back with you, Nancy, and see what we can find out."

"But we mustn't get caught," Bess warned.

The sunlight was hidden by an overcast as the girls again emerged from among the trees and went toward the fence. Nancy placed the ladder in a different spot from where she had put it before and quickly climbed to the top.

"Keep watch!" she whispered. "I'll come out the gate."

It took only a moment to break the rusted strands of barbed wire. Then, taking a final look to make certain she was unobserved, the young sleuth carefully dropped the ten feet down inside the enclosure.

She crept cautiously to the edge of a clearing. To the right was the stone wall and the front of the old brick building with the leaning chimney.

Just as Nancy had decided to leave the concealment of the shrubs, she saw the Lavender Sister come through a small wooden door in the stone wall. At her side trotted a huge mastiff!

Nancy moved back farther into the bushes, hoping that her movements would go undetected in the failing light. The huge dog raised his head as if listening but did not look in her direction.

The woman with the mastiff strode toward the gate in the fence. As they came closer to Nancy, she saw that the dog was held by a long chain attached to his collar.

Nancy watched with sudden apprehension as the woman went up to the gate. Suppose she should leave the enclosure? She would surely see Bess and George waiting outside!

But luck favored the girls. Stepping to one side of the gate, the Lavender Sister hooked the leash to an iron ring attached to one of the boards. Leaving the mastiff to stand watch, she started back toward the brick building.

So relieved was Nancy at her friends' escape from detection, she had not given any thought to her own plight. But as her eyes returned to the mastiff, the truth struck her with sickening force.

She could neither do any investigating without attracting the dog's attention, nor could she leave the wooden enclosure by way of the gate!

Indeed, she dared not make the slightest sign or sound that would betray her presence to the mastiff and set him to baying an alarm.

She was trapped!

CHAPTER XIV

Mad Dash!

NANCY felt a wave of panic, but she swiftly steeled her nerves. Now was the time for cool reasoning, she told herself, not a surrender to sudden fears.

"If I go in the other direction, away from the dog, maybe he won't detect me," she decided. "I'll worry later about getting out of here."

Nancy tiptoed along, making her way to the old brick building. Not a sound could be heard from within. She tried the door. It was locked.

Suddenly lights sprang up behind some distant trees and spread a low white glow over the area. A moment later a red glare flared up briefly and Nancy could hear indistinct voices.

Presently there was a clink of metal, the rattle of a chain. Then an engine sputtered, coughed, and finally settled down to a steady chug-chug-chug.

"What's that for?" Nancy wondered. "It might

be a water pump, but why all the lights?"

Starting forward, she suddenly found her path blocked. Two Lavender Sisters came out of the shadows. One stood as if guarding the unseen operation. The other walked briskly toward the mastiff. Nancy recognized her as the woman she had encountered earlier.

The dog rose at her approach, and the woman placed a large tin pan heaped with raw meat in front of him. As the dog's jaws crunched into the meat, the Lavender Sister turned to go back. At that moment in a low but clearly audible voice from outside the high board fence came a call.

"Nancy!"

It was Bess's voice!

She called again, even more anxiously. "Nancy! Where are you?"

Nancy longed to reply, but more fervently than that she wished Bess would stop calling, because the woman was staring in the direction of the voice.

Hastily Nancy tiptoed nearer the fence. Taking a notebook from her bag, she quickly scribbled a warning:

"Hide!"

She tore off the page and wrapped it around a stone, which she tossed over the fence. She hoped Bess or George would see it. Then she looked again toward the woman.

The Lavender Sister seemed to be hesitating,

not certain whether to investigate or not. Then, with sudden decision, she walked to the gate and pushed up the latch.

"The ladder!" Nancy remembered wildly.

What if the girls had left it propped against the fence and the woman instigated a search of the grounds to see who had climbed over!

As the long-robed figure slipped outside the wooden enclosure, Nancy waited with bated breath for the outcome of the woman's search. Seconds dragged into minutes, but there was no sound. Finally the Lavender Sister reappeared inside the grounds and shut the gate behind her.

Nancy gave a sigh of relief. Taking the ladder with them, the girls had apparently hidden in the nearby woods.

Nancy's hope of seeing more of the grounds to learn if there were a China clay pit, or to locate Manning-Carr or his brother, faded as time went on. The two Lavender Sisters stood in stony silence, barring all chance to do this. Finally Nancy concluded she would have to give up and try to get out of the place.

"But that awful beast!" she told herself.

The mastiff uttered a low, throaty growl as if he sensed an alien presence. Nancy scribbled a second note to Bess and George, briefly describing her plight. After folding the paper around a stone, she tossed the note over the fence.

But neither a note nor the sound of a voice

came over the top of the wooden partition in reply.

Nancy was worried. "I hope they didn't run into any trouble."

This thought spurred her on to seek an escape from the enclosure and find out what had happened to them.

The dog stretched himself on the ground beside the gate, his massive head resting quietly but watchfully between his paws. Nancy looked at him and bit her lip in vexation.

"Guess there's only one thing to do," she reflected. "That's to wait until somebody comes and takes the brute away."

An hour passed, Nancy hoping against hope. Apparently the dog had been stationed beside the gate for the night.

A bold plan half formed in her mind, and she searched the ground along the fence until she found a rock beneath a shrub.

"It's dark enough now," she decided.

She stole stealthily among the trees and bushes in the direction of the dog. When about fifty feet from him, she stopped and took stock of her position. The ground that separated her from the dog was bare.

She weighed the small rock in her hand. Then she carefully approximated the length of the dog's leash.

"Here's hoping!" she murmured. Aiming at a

spot on the fence, Nancy let the rock fly with
unerring accuracy. The mastiff bounded to his
feet as the rock struck the boards with a loud
noise and ricocheted into some bushes. He stared
at the spot and bared his teeth in a low growl.
Then he trotted alertly toward the fence and
nosed among the foliage.

Nancy stood poised on the balls of her feet,
waiting until the dog had gone as far from the
gate as his leash would permit. Then she darted
forward, lifted the latch, and tugged at the gate.

The mastiff heard her and raced back with a
fierce snarl. For a frightening instant, Nancy
thought the gate would never open. Then it swung
in, and she ran outside the enclosure a split
second ahead of the dog!

Glancing over her shoulder, Nancy saw the dog
lunge and paw the air as he came to the end of
his leash. Angry barks filled the night. As Nancy
dashed among the trees, she heard excited
women's voices from the enclosure.

"Oh, I hope they don't let that beast loose!"
Nancy said fervently.

In the darkness she could not at once determine the direction she should take but dared not
pause.

"I must get away!" she told herself.

Running as rapidly as she could in the darkness, ducking under low-hanging branches, dodg-
ing around bushes, she suddenly stumbled onto a

narrow dirt lane. It appeared to be the same one Nancy and the two cousins had found earlier. Assuming it must lead to the gravel road, Nancy followed the path thankfully.

But her relief was short-lived! Bright white beams of light began to flash among the trees a distance behind her.

Her pursuers had picked up her trail! With the advantage of light, they began to gain on her. Her breath coming fast, Nancy went on around a bend in the lane. She stopped short.

Coming toward her along the winding path was a car. Its high beam lights blinded her temporarily. The driver surely had seen her. Now there certainly was no chance of escape!

Suddenly a wild thought came to Nancy. Maybe this was unexpected aid! Perhaps the girls had fled from the mysterious woods to summon help.

Nancy stared at the car tensely. With a gentle squeal of brakes, it rolled to a stop. Its lights dimmed.

Was she to be rescued or captured?

CHAPTER XV

Hot on the Trail

NANCY stood frozen to the spot. Not a sound permeated the woods from the direction of the car.

Then from somewhere behind her came a woman's voice: "That dog must have opened the gate! You know he did it once before. We may as well go back."

Nancy was jubilant. The Lavender Sisters did not know she had been inside the enclosure! But there was still uncertainty ahead. Courageously she stood her ground to see what would happen down the lane. A moment later a small figure bounded out of the darkness.

"Togo!" Nancy exclaimed joyously, and she hurried forward. In a few moments she was joined by Bess, George, Dick Milton, and Hannah Gruen.

"Nancy! Nancy, are you all right?" Hannah whispered hoarsely.

She stopped breathlessly in front of Nancy and hugged her.

"Yes, I'm all right. But I'm certainly glad to see you."

"Hypers!" said George. "You sure scared us!"

"What happened?" Bess demanded.

Nancy told her story. She ended by telling Dick that despite her efforts, she had learned nothing new about the China clay pit.

"The important thing is that you're safe!" Hannah Gruen declared. "Now let's get out of here. I'm sure your father will be terribly upset when he hears about this!"

"Where is Dad?" Nancy asked.

"He received an urgent telephone call from Washington," Mrs. Gruen explained, "and caught the afternoon plane. He doesn't know how long he'll be gone."

Nancy nodded. She wondered if the lawyer's trip to Washington concerned the Engs. Her thoughts were interrupted by Bess.

"George and I couldn't imagine what in the world had happened to you in that enclosure," Bess said as they walked toward her car. "We waited and waited. When you didn't answer after I called, George was all for going inside to find you! Then your note came over the fence, and we didn't know what to think!"

"But we hid in the woods," George said, "just as you warned us to do."

"And not a second too soon, I can tell you!" Bess went on. "We'd hardly jumped behind a tree when that Lavender Sister came outside."

"What about the ladder?" Nancy queried, still curious. "Couldn't she see it?"

"We took the ladder away and hid it right after you let yourself down inside, since you said you were coming out the gate," George replied.

"When the woman opened the gate," Bess took up the story, "we saw that awful mastiff chained right inside the gate." She gave a slight shudder. "So we knew you *couldn't* get out!"

After the Lavender Sister had re-entered the enclosure, the cousins explained, they had hurried through the woods to Bess's car and driven to Nancy's home to get her father. Upon learning that the lawyer had left for Washington, Bess had telephoned Dick Milton and asked him to return with them. Hannah Gruen, upset and anxious, had announced that she and Togo would go along too.

"It's a good thing we found the lane earlier," George declared, "or we couldn't have got here so fast."

"And a good thing I took it," Nancy said ruefully, "or you'd have missed me!"

They got into Bess's car, turned on the narrow lane, and drove off. The headlights focused on Nancy's convertible, still parked in the small clearing. Mrs. Gruen had brought the spare ignition key.

Easing into the driver's seat, Nancy turned on the motor and listened to its sound with evident satisfaction. Mrs. Gruen climbed in beside her. Whistling to Togo to join them, Nancy put the car in gear and followed Bess toward home.

Both cars pulled up at a corner a few blocks from Bess's home. "Thanks a million!" Nancy called to her friends.

She waved, then drove straight on while Bess turned off toward Dick's house. A few minutes later Nancy swung the car into her driveway.

"That's strange!" Mrs. Gruen spoke in amazement. "I left the lights on in the living room and hall when I went out."

The windows were completely dark. Suddenly the terrier began to bark excitedly.

"What is it, Togo?" Nancy asked quickly.

She opened the door of the car and the dog jumped out. He dashed up the front steps and scratched at the door.

"He acts as if someone were in the house!" Hannah Gruen exclaimed.

Nancy nodded. "Go around to the back of the house. I'll take the front. If there *is* a burglar inside, maybe we can trap him."

"All right. But be careful, Nancy."

"I will. And you, too."

She waited until the housekeeper got to the rear yard, then she went up the front steps.

Togo barked as she set foot on the porch. Turning her key in the lock, Nancy opened the door, snapped on the hall light, and looked inside. Togo sniffed the floor, racing from one room to another. Nancy followed him. No one was around, and apparently nothing had been disturbed.

In the front hall Nancy was joined by Mrs. Gruen. "I didn't see a soul—" she began, then broke off as Nancy's fingers tightened on her arm.

From the second floor of the house came soft distinct sounds!

"Come on!" Nancy whispered.

She flicked a switch to turn on the upper hall lights, then cautiously ascended the stairs, followed by Mrs. Gruen. Togo went ahead of them.

Nancy had just snapped on a light in her own bedroom when the dog began to bark wildly down the hall. As she turned to go after him, she glanced at her dressing table. The drawer had been lifted out and its contents strewn on the floor! One look told Nancy that Mr. Soong's jade elephant was gone!

As she turned to search the other rooms for the intruder, a scream came from a rear bedroom.

Recognizing the distressed voice as Hannah

Gruen's, Nancy ran to the back room. She found the housekeeper unhurt but staring wildly out the window.

"He went that way!" she cried, pointing toward the garden. "He jumped off the back-porch roof and disappeared over the hedge!"

Nancy ran downstairs with Togo in pursuit of the burglar. But her chase was fruitless. He had too much of a head start. Upon her return she asked the housekeeper what the man looked like.

"I'm afraid I didn't get a good look, Nancy," Mrs. Gruen confessed.

They searched the house. Nothing but the jade elephant was missing.

Nancy stood lost in thought. The man was no ordinary burglar or he would have stolen other things.

Who could the thief be? Manning-Carr?

Accompanied by Mrs. Gruen and Togo, Nancy went outside with a flashlight and examined the soft earth at the back porch.

She soon found the footprints she was seeking, deeply embedded in the ground from the force of the thief's jump. They looked like the same short, wide prints she had seen in the Townsends' flower bed after their vase had been stolen!

"I feel kind of fidgety," Mrs. Gruen remarked when they had returned to the house and made sure all the doors and windows were locked for the night.

Nancy called the police. She reported that she had recovered her car, then told of the theft of the jade elephant. As a routine matter they came and made an investigation. Then the young detective had a snack and wearily tumbled into bed.

Her waking thought was of Mr. Soong and she determined to go to his home at once to talk to him. Not only did she have the unpleasant task of telling him about the jade elephant, but she was eager to learn from him the meaning of the strange Oriental symbol she had copied from the leaning chimney.

As on previous visits, the door to Mr. Soong's house was opened by the servant Ching. His expressionless face spread into a smile when he saw Nancy and he made a deep bow.

"Is Mr. Soong at home?" Nancy asked.

The man shook his head.

Nancy deliberated a moment, then took a notebook from her purse and scribbled a short message asking Mr. Soong to call her at the house or after twelve-thirty at Dick Milton's home. This was the nineteenth, and she had promised to take care of Baby Sue.

She gave the message to Ching and he gesticulatingly promised to deliver it. Then he bowed smilingly and closed the door.

Nancy went back home to await Mr. Soong's call.

"I hope he hasn't gone out of town," she sighed. Just then the phone rang.

"Nancy Drew?" a voice boomed. "Come right over here!"

"Is this Mr. Monroe?" she asked.

"Sure is. And I believe I have a clue to the China clay pit to show you."

"What is it?"

The geologist refused to impart any further information over the telephone. Grabbing her handbag, Nancy explained her errand to Hannah Gruen, then drove off.

The tall, sharp-featured professor led Nancy into the living room in silence. Taking a package from his desk, he thrust it into her hands.

"What do you make of this?" he barked.

Nancy looked at the parcel. It had been sent from San Francisco and had obviously been unwrapped.

She studied the address. Painted in bold, black letters on gray paper were the words:

M. MONROE
GENERAL DELIVERY
RIVER HEIGHTS

Nancy looked questioningly at the geologist. "Open it!" he commanded.

She opened a white cardboard box inside the paper. Neatly packed in rows were several tubes of paint with Chinese markings.

"This is the kind of paint that potters use!" Nancy exclaimed in surprise as she recalled similar tubes of paint at Dick Milton's workshop.

"It is!" Professor Monroe snorted. "And these tubes must have been shipped from China. Their colors are among the finest and purest I've seen! Only thing is," he added dramatically, "I didn't order them!"

"Who did then?" Nancy asked.

"I'll let you guess," the geologist answered.

"This package must have been meant for the other Miles Monroe!" she exclaimed. "The man who owns the tract of land near Hunter's Creek!"

"Precisely!" the professor boomed, and his eyes sparkled. "And why would our mysterious friend have the paints sent to him unless he intended to use them on porcelain?"

Nancy tingled with rising excitement. She was convinced that the strange, fenced-in enclosure was near a pit of China clay. And someone was making pottery there!

"I'll take the package back to the post office," she told the geologist, "and stand watch until M. Monroe calls for it!"

"Good idea!" he barked. "Go to it!"

To herself Nancy said, "And I'll bet this other M. Monroe is Manning-Carr. Oh dear! I wish I hadn't promised I'd take care of Baby Sue today. There's no time to lose on this mystery."

But Nancy was a person of her word, and she

would not disappoint Connie Milton. She did decide, however, to call first Bess, then George, to ask them to help her out if something vital should develop. Using the geologist's telephone, she was told that both girls would be away until late afternoon.

"So I'm on my own this time," Nancy reflected, leaving the geologist's apartment.

When she arrived at the General Delivery window of the post office, she met with both disappointment and a surprise.

"M. Monroe was here only fifteen minutes ago!" the clerk informed Nancy as she handed him the parcel and explained the error. "He was plenty angry when I told him I had sent it to the professor!"

"Is Mr. Monroe an olive-skinned man with black hair and piercing black eyes?" she asked, giving the clerk a description of Manning-Carr.

The clerk shook his head decisively. "The man I talked to," he said, "was Chinese."

"Chinese!" she exclaimed. "What did he look like?"

The clerk stared at her helplessly. "Why, uh—like a Chinaman!" he replied.

Nancy bit her lip in vexation.

"Wait a minute, miss. I just remembered something! That Chinese said he was going to hunt up the other Miles Monroe and get his package!"

CHAPTER XVI

The Riddle Unravels

"THANKS a lot!" Nancy cried to the postal clerk.

She dashed off to a telephone booth in a nearby store. Within a few seconds she had the professor on the wire. Learning that no Chinese had been there, Nancy told him to be on guard.

Miles Monroe thanked her for warning him.

Feeling confident that the Oriental was probably the same one who had collected the money orders in Masonville under Mr. Soong's name, she put a call through to her friend Chief McGinnis.

Quickly the young detective voiced her suspicions. "And I'm sure he's Manning-Carr's brother."

The officer thought her clue a very important one. "I'll put a man on duty at the professor's place right away," he told her.

Nancy quickly hurried to her car. She was due at Connie Milton's. She hoped Mr. Soong had telephoned the Drew home by now and that Hannah Gruen had told him where he could reach her.

"Go onto the party and have a good time!" she told Connie when she arrived.

Connie thanked Nancy, and left. Nancy played with Sue for a few minutes, then placed the cooing infant in the carriage on the porch. Watching until she saw the baby's eyes slowly close, she tiptoed quietly into the house.

Nancy tried to read, but her mind was too full of the mystery. Finally she put aside the book and concentrated on her sketch of the iron ornament on the leaning chimney.

"Maybe the answer to the whole puzzle is in this," she mused.

When four o'clock came and she had not heard from Mr. Soong, Nancy could not check her mounting curiosity any longer. She went to the telephone and dialed his number. The call was answered immediately by the Chinese importer himself.

"I left a note for you to phone me!" Nancy told him.

"I'm afraid I don't understand."

"Didn't Ching give you my note?"

"Ching is not here," Mr. Soong replied. "He must have put the message in his pocket."

Nancy said that she had something important to show Mr. Soong, and he promised to hurry

over at once. When he arrived, Nancy told him
first of her recent experience inside the enclosure,
then showed him her sketch of the iron ornament.
Mr. Soong's eyebrows lifted in surprise.

"It is a Chinese symbol," he stated, confirming
Nancy's deduction. "It means 'help'!"

" 'Help'?" Nancy repeated.

"Yes." Mr. Soong took a pen from his pocket
and printed a word on the back of an envelope.
"If it could be written in English, the word would
be spelled like this."

"Phang?" Nancy said haltingly.

"That is just the way the word is spelled. It
is pronounced *bong*."

Nancy stared at him in sudden excitement.

"*Bong?* You mean that's a cry for help?"

Mr. Soong nodded.

"I heard such a sound come from near the enclosure!" Nancy announced triumphantly. "A
scream that sounded exactly like *bong!*"

Mr. Soong was so mystified Nancy hastily apprised him of everything she now suspected.

First, she said the enclosure was not merely a
religious retreat. With or without the knowledge
of the Lavender Sisters, the valuable clay was being dug up on the property.

"I heard a motor working last night," she
said. "They probably dig only when outsiders
aren't likely to be around."

Second, Nancy reviewed the double puzzle of

the stolen and faked potteries. The rare old pieces, including Mr. Soong's prized Ming vase which had been stolen by a thief known as John Manning; the clever imitations of valuable old potteries, which had been sold by a man named Carr; and the supposition that Manning and Carr were the same person, and used other aliases, perhaps Monroe among them.

Third, Nancy told the importer of finding her missing car near the enclosure. Since the car had been stolen by the person who had dropped the jade elephant by the stream, it looked as if he were associated with the pottery thieves.

Mr. Soong listened intently. "My dear," he said, "your powers of deduction contain the wisdom of a Chinese philosopher."

"I'm only putting two and two together," she replied modestly.

Then, last of all, Nancy brought up the subject of Eng Moy and his daughter Eng Lei. Both had vanished mysteriously in the company of a man known as David Carr. Eng Moy's signature had appeared on at least two of the pottery pieces, which were clever imitations.

"I believe," said Nancy, "that your friends are mixed up with this Carr in the fake pottery making. No doubt they are not willing partners. They may be the prisoners in that enclosure!"

Mr. Soong gave a start, then sat for a moment without speaking.

"I know how damaging the facts must appear. But when the truth is out, I believe in my heart that Eng Moy and Lei will be found to be innocent of any wrongdoing," he said with simple dignity.

Nancy leaned forward. "To save them from further harm, I believe we should notify the police at once," she said.

"Oh, no!" the Chinese cried out. "Please!"

"If that place in the woods contains criminals, it's our duty to notify the authorities."

The Chinese wrung his hands. "For the sake of my good friends," he pleaded, "don't tell the police now. Please give the Engs a chance to clear their names before they are arrested."

Then he hung his head. "If there were only some way—" He looked at Nancy. "Would you show me the path to the leaning chimney?" he asked pathetically. "I must find out the truth about my friends! Those wretches may kill Moy and Lei so they cannot talk. Please, Miss Drew."

Nancy was touched by the man's sincerity. "You're a real friend," she said. "I'll help you."

"You'll show me the way to the enclosure?"

"Yes," Nancy promised.

"When?"

"Soon! Here comes Mrs. Milton."

When Nancy told Connie Milton where they were going, the young woman strongly objected. But upon being told the trip was only an investigation prior to calling the police, she felt better.

"Dick has something in the cellar you might use to get over the wall," Connie told Nancy. "It's a rope ladder with metal grappling hooks."

Nancy was delighted to have it, since she was not certain the ladder Bess and George had hidden in the woods was still there. In any case, it would have been too heavy to lift over the board fence and to use as a means of escape.

Nancy thanked Connie, put the rope ladder into her car, and set off with Mr. Soong. It was already late afternoon when they arrived at the part of the grounds where the leaning chimney was. Nancy wanted to show him the ornament. Walking to the little knoll from which it could be seen, she exclaimed:

"The Phang ornament! It's gone!"

It was possible that the person who had put up the symbol had not wanted the Lavender Sisters to know about it. And Nancy remembered she had mentioned it to one of the women!

Quickly she attached the hooks of the rope ladder to the fence, breaking the rusted barbed wire, climbed up, and looked over. With no one in sight in the weed-filled garden, it seemed safe for her and Mr. Soong to drop down inside.

The elderly gentleman was more agile than she had supposed and dropped lightly to the ground behind her. She hid the ladder beneath a bush and said, pointing:

"We're in luck!"

The wooden door in the stone wall which ran from the old brick building to the fence stood open! Cautiously Nancy and Mr. Soong went through. Then, keeping in the shelter of the many trees, she led the way to the area where she had seen lights and heard the engine.

They encountered no one but heard muffled thuds. Presently they reached the spot. The sight ahead of them made Nancy's heart beat faster.

There was a shallow pit of sand-colored earth and flintlike layers of rock. Two Chinese, wearing mud-spattered overalls, stood ankle-deep in the pit, breaking up the rock with sledge hammers. Another man scooped up the yellowish soil with a shovel, while a fourth workman carried away the soil and broken pieces of shale in a wheelbarrow.

To Nancy the rocks had the hard, gray look of granite, and she turned to Mr. Soong to confirm her observation.

"There's kaolin in it?" she whispered.

Mr. Soong bobbed his head excitedly. "A high percentage. Excellent for making porcelain."

But Nancy did not allow her elation to overshadow the main reason for her coming to the secret spot. She must still hunt for the Engs.

"Come on!" she whispered. Keeping well hidden, Nancy led Mr. Soong from one part of the grounds to another, hoping, with each step, that the huge mastiff would not appear.

They passed a small bungalow and several pitched tents but saw no one. Finally Nancy concluded that probably the Lavender Sisters and any others in the enclosure besides the diggers must be inside the mysterious building.

"We'll go back there," she told Mr. Soong.

Reaching the brick building with the leaning chimney, Mr. Soong stared at it hopefully.

The door was closed, and the small dust-covered windows were much too high for anyone to look inside. There were no sounds from within.

"We'll go closer," Nancy said.

As she stepped forward, the door suddenly swung back and a slender, pretty Chinese girl about Nancy's age appeared. She wore a clay-spattered canvas apron over a plain gray cotton dress.

The girl stood for a moment, looking at the pit, then suddenly burst into sobs.

"That may be Eng Lei!" Nancy thought.

A man came through the doorway and put his arm soothingly around the girl's shoulder. He spoke to her softly in Chinese.

Mr. Soong's fingers suddenly closed tightly over Nancy's wrist and she saw as she turned that his eyes were fixed excitedly on the man.

"It is my friend!" he whispered. "Eng Moy!"

He started forward, but Nancy held him back.

"Before we show ourselves, we must find out what his position is here and be sure that he won't betray us," she whispered.

For a moment Mr. Soong looked upset, then he smiled. "My heart is so full of the desire to greet my old friend," he said apologetically, "I am afraid my head is forgetful. I will try to be more careful."

Nancy pressed his arm reassuringly as she studied the middle-aged Eng Moy. Coarse blue-denim work clothes, splashed with white clay, hung loosely on his thin, frail body. His face, as he spoke comfortingly to the girl, showed a quiet resignation that told of long suffering.

"The girl must be Eng Lei," Nancy murmured to Mr. Soong, her heart going out to the old gentleman as his eyes reflected the tension under which he was laboring.

He nodded eagerly. "I think you are right. But so many years have passed since I last saw Lei—she was only a child when I left China many years ago—I cannot be sure."

"What are they saying?" Nancy whispered as Eng Moy again spoke softly to the girl in Chinese.

Mr. Soong shook his head. "I cannot hear," he confessed.

A moment later the Engs turned back into the building. Nancy and Mr. Soong stole swiftly and cautiously through the entrance after them.

CHAPTER XVII

Reunion

THE room in which Nancy and Mr. Soong found themselves was small and dimly lighted. It contained nothing but a few crates stacked near a doorway. The two eavesdroppers hid behind them. Beyond was a large, better-lighted room. In this a wide workbench was arranged along one wall. On it lay tubes of paint and bowls of turpentine containing brushes.

Lined along the rear of the workbench were two neat rows of porcelain bowls, jugs, jars and vases, all glazed and beautifully decorated with Oriental designs. Above them on the wall were cabinets, their doors closed.

Eng Moy and his daughter Lei took their places at the workbench, their backs to the door. They picked up the delicate designing brushes and began working on two gracefully shaped potteries.

"Look at the vase Eng Moy just took from the cabinet!" Nancy whispered.

"Why, it's mine!" Mr. Soong whispered excitedly. "The vase stolen from Milton's shop!"

"Exactly," confirmed Nancy. "And if you look closely, you'll see why Manning-Carr wanted it. Eng Moy is copying it—and probably made the copy which Manning-Carr sold in New York."

At that moment the Lavender Sister who had ordered Nancy away from the enclosure some days before entered the room through a far doorway. She gave the Engs a hostile glance, then bent to examine their work. Suddenly she pointed to a small jar and uttered a stream of Chinese.

Stepping swiftly toward Lei, before the father could intervene, she slapped the girl's face. Then she turned abruptly and departed through the same doorway from which she had appeared.

Nancy caught a fleeting glimpse of the interior beyond, containing pottery-making equipment.

As the door closed, Nancy heard the sound of weeping. Once more Eng Moy attempted to comfort his daughter, but she resisted his soothing words.

Mr. Soong, listening to the exchange of Chinese, translated it to Nancy:

"Father, I cannot stand this hateful life any longer!" Lei sobbed. "I wish I had never been born!"

"You must not talk that way, my child," Eng Moy remonstrated gently. "You are too young to give up hope."

"Hope!" the girl replied bitterly. "Day after day, year after year I have lived because of that word! Hoping for rescue! Hoping for the capture and punishment of the men who keep us here! Hoping to see China and home again! I tell you, Father, it is no use! Hope for us is an empty word. I never want to hear it again!"

His face eloquent with distress, Eng Moy turned away. "But what can we do?"

"We have only one choice left, Father," Lei told him. "We must end it all, rather than spend our lives in misery. It is our only means of escape."

"No! Never that!" Mr. Soong cried out in Chinese.

He came from behind the crates and went quickly toward the Engs, followed by Nancy. Surprise flashed across Lei's face, then she backed away in sudden fear.

Mr. Soong went directly to Eng Moy and embraced him. "My friend! My old friend!" he murmured.

Eng Moy drew back and stared at the old gentleman. Then slowly a look of recognition dawned. "Soong!" he whispered disbelievingly.

He blinked in bewilderment, as if unable to

credit what he saw. Then he stepped forward
with a happy cry and returned Mr. Soong's em-
brace.

Introductions quickly followed. Smiling
proudly at Nancy, Mr. Soong spoke rapidly to
the Engs. When he had finished, they turned to
Nancy, their faces reflecting gratitude and hope.

Eng Moy took Nancy's hands in his and addressed her haltingly in Chinese, while Lei
smiled in agreement.

Despite the barrier of languages—for the Engs
could neither speak nor understand English—
Nancy and the Chinese father and daughter became friends at once.

"What are they trying to tell me?" Nancy
asked.

"They wish to thank you for bringing me
here," Mr. Soong replied.

"There'll be enough time for that when we're
all safely out of the enclosure," Nancy said. "We
must hurry away before we're caught!"

Nancy had Mr. Soong explain her plan, where-
by all four of them would climb over the fence
where she and her companion had hidden the
ladder. The Engs nodded eagerly to show Nancy
they understood.

Leading the way to the door, Nancy pulled it
open a crack and cautiously peered outside. A
second later she caught her breath.

Coming toward the old brick building was a man with black hair and dark skin. But the most striking thing about him was his eyes. They seemed to stare from his head like two glittering black marbles. Nancy, though she had never met him, was sure she knew his identity.

The Engs' reply to Mr. Soong's inquiry confirmed her suspicion. The man was David Carr! Nancy closed the door quickly.

"Tell the Engs they must hide us!" Nancy said.

Eng Moy and Lei looked stunned at the turn of events.

"Let's take a chance on that room beyond," Nancy suggested quickly.

Eng Moy said he would run ahead and see if anyone were in it. He reported two women were at work there.

Nancy glanced through the window. Carr had stopped to inspect something on the ground. A moment's grace.

"Ask the Engs if they can let us have some old work clothes, Mr. Soong," she instructed. "We'll take a chance getting past those women."

The Chinese quickly translated. Hurrying to a row of hooks jutting from the wall, Lei brought back a clay-spattered apron for Nancy and a similarly messy pair of overalls for Mr. Soong.

"Hurry!" Nancy said to him. "Carr may come in here any minute!"

"Let's hope we avoid detection," Nancy whispered

They swiftly slipped the garments over their own clothing and Nancy wound a scarf around her head.

"Let's hope we avoid detection," she whispered to Mr. Soong.

She opened the door to the workshop. Then, taking a deep breath, she stepped into the shop and started along the shadowy wall toward the opposite end of the room where there was still another door.

Nancy walked as casually as she could, her face slightly averted from the women, who stood at tables pounding clay. After a moment Nancy noted gratefully that Lei had slipped up beside her to help screen her from suspicious stares. Behind her were Eng Moy and Mr. Soong.

Two or three times the women workers looked up at them curiously but showed no signs of suspecting anything amiss. At last the four arrived at the end of the shop.

Going through a doorway into a short corridor, Nancy saw a large iron door. The Engs whispered something and Mr. Soong translated for Nancy.

"Behind the door is a brick vault containing genuine old Chinese porcelains, all of them stolen," he explained. "Only Carr and his brother possess keys to the vault."

Nancy felt a twinge of excitement. The mystery was unraveling fast now! And this was the first real evidence that the swindler's brother was working with him!

The group had stopped, safe for the moment. Then terror struck their hearts. Outside the wall where the four were huddled the horrible mastiff began to bay.

Had an alarm been given?

CHAPTER XVIII

Meeting the Enemy

ESCAPE was now impossible.

"Our only chance is to hide until the dog is taken away," Nancy said to Mr. Soong. "Ask your friends if there's a place where we can wait without too much risk of being detected."

Eng Moy led them to a small room at the extreme rear corner of the building. He pointed to a battered old brick wall.

Walking to the end of it, Eng Moy pulled open a rusty iron door. As it creaked back on rusty hinges, he stepped into a dank, dark cavern and lighted a candle. Then, turning, he motioned to the others to follow.

Nancy exclaimed in surprise. They were standing in a large, dome-shaped area about eight feet high at the center. The circular brick wall was dilapidated and battered, and the rough stone flooring cracked. Nancy noticed that the roof of the oven funneled into the leaning chimney.

"This must have been the smelter of the old iron mine!" she told Mr. Soong excitedly.

The elderly gentleman spoke a few words to Eng Moy.

"You are right, my dear," he reported. "When Eng Moy came to the enclosure, this old smelter was used as a kiln to fire pottery. But it seemed as if the chimney might topple over, so a modern kiln was constructed across the garden."

Lei went off to stand watch at the far door, to give notice the instant anyone might come along the corridor. Nancy, Eng Moy, and Mr. Soong sat down on the floor to await a favorable time to escape. As they marked time, the pottery maker haltingly told his friend all that had happened to him and his daughter since they had arrived in San Francisco five years before.

Eng Moy said that the man known to him as David Carr had been a business acquaintance in China. He had tricked the Engs into coming to America by making the father promises of an important position in one of the country's modern pottery plants. As the final stop in their tour of United States factories, Carr had lured them to the enclosure in the woods, and there made them prisoners.

The Engs had lived in captivity four and a half

years. During that time they had been forced to make fake Chinese porcelains, using as their models genuine, rare old Oriental pieces that Carr had stolen.

"But didn't the Engs ever try to escape?" Nancy asked.

Mr. Soong translated her question, then turned back to the girl.

"Yes, many times," he told Nancy. "Twice they even reached the woods outside the board fence before their absence was discovered. But the dog soon found them, and their poor bodies still bear the marks of the whip Carr used to punish them."

Nancy's ire was aroused anew. Poor Lei and her father had been the victims of extreme cruelty.

"Then it was Lei I heard scream for help?" Nancy asked. "The cry that sounded like *bong?*"

"Yes," Mr. Soong answered. "The two Phang characters you saw attached to the chimney also were appeals for help. Eng Moy put them there, hoping to attract someone's attention. He shaped the characters out of old scraps of iron he found."

"That, of course, is why Eng took down the old ornament," Nancy observed. "But who removed the new one?"

"My friend was compelled to remove it the day he put it up," Mr. Soong said. "One of the Lavender Sisters saw it and punished him."

Nancy's conscience pricked her. *She* had told

the woman about it and no doubt caused this punishment! Quickly Nancy had Mr. Soong explain this and offered her regrets.

"Eng Moy says he is so glad you saw it, the offense does not matter," Mr. Soong translated. "The clue of the leaning chimney is the means of your finding him and Lei."

Nancy was told that Eng Moy's signature, cunningly worked into the designs of various pieces of pottery, had also been intended by him as an appeal for aid.

Carr had made sure his prisoners were given no opportunity to learn English. Knowing that government authorities would be trying to locate him for illegally remaining in the United States, Eng Moy hoped one of the signatures would come to the attention of Federal officers and lead them to the enclosure.

"Are the other people," Nancy said suddenly, "those men and women we saw working in the pit and in the shop, prisoners too?"

Mr. Soong put the question to Eng Moy.

"The men are foreigners," Mr. Soong translated the answer. "The women are their wives. Carr and his brother smuggled them into the United States by plane. He promised them wonderful things, then he made them prisoners. Finally he threatened if they did not dig the clay and operate the machines, he would expose them and have them put in jail for life!"

At that moment they heard the iron door squeak open. Lei slipped into the candlelit smelter. She spoke breathlessly to her father and from the sudden fear that flitted across his face Nancy knew something had gone wrong.

"The Engs' absence has been discovered!" Mr. Soong told her with alarm. "Carr and the woman are out in the corridor!"

Motioning to the others to wait, Nancy stole from the old smelter into the shadowy room outside and listened.

"You fool!" cried a man's voice. "If you'd paid more attention to the Engs, they couldn't have disappeared!"

"They can't have gone far!" the Lavender Sister replied.

"Get the dog," Carr said shortly. "She and that father of hers are probably in the smelter room. My mastiff will attend to them!"

Nancy turned and ran softly back to the smelter. "They're coming!" she whispered.

Eng Moy blew out the candle, and the four waited with mounting suspense in the dark. Then, after an interval that seemed to be years, a voice spoke sharply in Chinese outside the iron door.

"It is Carr!" Mr. Soong whispered fearfully to Nancy. "He demands that the Engs come out! What shall we do?" he asked in panic.

Before she could reply that it would be best for them to slip out without betraying her and

Mr. Soong's presence, the door was pulled open.

Carr stepped into the doorway and shone a flashlight about. When he saw Nancy and Mr. Soong, his thin lips spread in a slow, mocking smile.

"So! I have caught you at last!" he said sarcastically.

The Lavender Sister, who arrived with the mastiff, gave a dry, harsh chuckle when she saw Nancy.

"Take the Engs away and make sure they do not try to escape again," her husband ordered.

The woman beckoned sharply. With a despairing glance at Nancy and Mr. Soong, the Engs followed Carr's wife through the doorway.

Nancy watched them go with a heavy heart. How happy they had been when freedom seemed so near, she reflected. And how utterly defeated they now appeared.

Carr studied Nancy and her companion silently, then spoke again in a cold, sharp voice. "I intend to do away with you two before any of your friends can get here to help you!"

CHAPTER XIX

Escape

AT David Carr's harsh words, Mr. Soong moaned.

"Nobody," Carr shouted angrily, "is going to interfere with me and get away with it! You, Nancy Drew, have interfered with my plans since the first time you saw me on Three Bridges Road."

"And I'll keep on interfering—until you and your brother are locked behind bars!" Nancy retorted.

Carr's face tightened. "Ah! So you know about my brother?"

"I do!" Nancy declared, hoping it would induce the swindler to reveal what part his brother had played in Carr's nefarious schemes.

Instead, Carr said, "You are very clever. Since you probably know it, I'll admit he stole the vase from the Townsends and the jade elephant from your home."

Nancy nodded. "Why did he bother to steal the vase when he knew it was a fake?"

"My wife is to blame for that!" he replied harshly. "Because of her stupidity, Eng Moy was able to paint his name on several porcelains I sold. My brother and I stole back as many as we could. We were afraid the signature would be traced by Federal dicks."

"You managed to remove Eng's name and sold the Townsend vase again. But who posed as Mr. Soong to collect the money orders in Masonville?" she asked quickly, hoping to catch Carr off guard. "Your brother?"

The man was much too cagey, however, to refer to his confederate by name. He addressed his reply tauntingly to the elderly Chinese gentleman, who stood listening close by.

"That was clever, eh, Soong? It's just too bad for Miss Drew his scheme didn't completely succeed. If she'd believed you guilty of selling fake potteries, she might have stopped meddling in my affairs and wouldn't be here now to face the consequences!"

"I'm glad I was able to help Mr. Soong," Nancy declared hotly.

Carr gave a mirthless, sardonic laugh, then turned to go. "I advise you not to try to escape," he warned. "The mastiff has a nasty temper and very sharp fangs! I'll be back in a few minutes and then we'll see how brave you are!"

He swung the iron door shut. Nancy found the candle and lighted it. She turned to Mr. Soong who had sat down on the floor, too weak to stand any longer.

"It's my fault you're in this dangerous situation," he murmured to Nancy. "I shouldn't have asked you to come with me."

Nancy smiled wanly. "Please do not feel bad. It was my own wish to untangle this mystery that brought us here."

She crossed to the door to listen, hoping the dog might be gone. But the mastiff outside, sensing her presence near the iron barrier, uttered a low, menacing growl.

Nancy took the candle and started to examine the battered brick walls. There *had* to be some way of escape!

Suddenly the iron door creaked slowly open. Standing in the doorway was Mr. Soong's short, inscrutable-looking servant Ching! He regarded them impassively, then gave them a toothy smile.

"Ching!" Mr. Soong arose and advanced toward him eagerly. He spoke excitedly to the servant in Chinese. But Ching suddenly gave a boisterous laugh and roughly pushed his gentle employer away.

"Fool!" he cried in English. "Are you so stupid you cannot guess who I really am?"

"Carr's brother!" Nancy exclaimed.

Ching made her a mock bow. "Exactly!"

"Now I understand several things," Nancy said. "You were the one who posed as Mr. Soong and cashed the money orders!"

"Yes, Miss Drew," Ching replied mockingly. "But my impersonation need not concern you any longer. You made a fatal mistake in coming here. Now you must pay for your stupidity." He chuckled contemptuously. "There is an old American saying, 'Curiosity killed the cat.' You see the parallel, Miss Drew, I'm sure."

"There's no use threatening us. You know my father will come and bring the police!" Nancy burst out.

"Wouldn't you like us to believe that, Miss Drew?" Ching taunted. "But unfortunately for you, I know that your father is in Washington. You see, I called his office, intending to tell him that you would be—er—slightly late for dinner."

Nancy realized how serious her plight was, but there was a ray of hope. When she did not return to dinner, Mrs. Gruen certainly would telephone the Miltons, and when the housekeeper learned that Nancy and Mr. Soong had gone to the enclosure, she would call the police.

Sparring for time, she continued to ask questions which Ching freely answered.

He said it had been prearranged between David and himself that he would get a job at Mr. Soong's. In this way he could watch the man's mail and waylay any messages about the Engs. At all times he kept track of his employer's movements.

"But once you slipped," Nancy spoke up. "A letter about the Engs did reach Mr. Soong."

"Unfortunately, yes. Then you came into the case, Miss Drew. But you shall never bother my brother or me again. As soon as we have removed our valuable property," Ching said defiantly, "we will come back and dynamite the leaning chimney. When it collapses, it will crush the roof of the smelter." He paused significantly. "Your fate will not be pleasant. But let us hope the end will be swift!"

For several seconds after Ching had departed, Nancy and Mr. Soong were too dazed even to talk. It occurred to Nancy that Mrs. Gruen would not be concerned about her absence until the dinner hour. The housekeeper would act promptly then, but it might be too late. Desperately Nancy began to try to figure some way out of their dreadful plight.

"There isn't a chance of escaping through the door with the mastiff on guard," she pointed out.

Holding the candle above her head, Nancy stared at the domelike roof of the old smelter. The opening which funneled into the leaning chimney was about two feet in diameter. Through the opening she could just see a patch of sunlit sky. A thought clicked and she turned excitedly to Mr. Soong.

"Didn't Eng Moy get up the inside of the chimney to attach the iron symbol?" she asked.

"Yes. He said he used a ladder and went up from here," the elderly gentleman replied.

There was no ladder in the smelter. Nancy again peered up the chimney. Ladder or no ladder, she promptly decided to try the climb.

"Please help me get up," she said.

Mr. Soong's eyes widened. "You don't intend to climb the chimney?" he asked in alarm.

"I must!" Nancy told him. "It's our only chance of escape."

"But you might slip and fall!"

"Nothing would be worse than the fate that awaits us here," Nancy pointed out. "But if I can make the climb, I may be able to bring help to you and your friends before it's too late."

Recognizing that there was no choice, the Chinese, exerting his last ounce of strength, permitted Nancy to stand on his back so she could reach into the opening. As Nancy pulled herself up inside, Mr. Soong looked at her anxiously.

"Be careful," he begged. "If anything should happen to you—"

"Please don't worry," Nancy reassured him. "And don't give up hope. If everything goes well, I'll be back with the police."

"Good fortune go with you!" said Mr. Soong, sinking to the floor.

Nancy began her climb. Bracing her back

against one side of the chimney and her legs against the other, she started to inch up the stack.

Her climb was made easier by the angle at which the chimney slanted. But the cement between the bricks was chipped and broken. With every movement she made, Nancy was in danger of dislodging a loose brick and plunging down the dank shaft to the floor of the smelter!

With utmost care, she crept upward. Finally, when it seemed as if her tense, tired muscles could carry her no farther, she reached the top. Then she climbed carefully down the outside of the leaning chimney to the sloping roof of the old brick building.

She was about to make the drop from the edge of the roof to the garden when she heard a noise.

"Someone's coming!" she thought with alarm.

Swiftly Nancy flattened herself against the sloping roof, and a moment later saw Carr's wife, now in street clothes, open the door in the stone wall and walk in her direction.

As long as the woman did not look up, Nancy knew she was safe from view. But the angle at which the roof sloped made her position precarious. As Carr's wife approached, Nancy's grip suddenly weakened and she started to slide down.

"I can't fail now!" she told herself desperately. "I just can't!"

CHAPTER XX

A Fitting Reward

FRANTICALLY Nancy pressed her hands harder against the roof, and just when it seemed she must tumble to the ground, her momentum stopped.

Carr's wife paused to listen, but evidently did not detect the sound as coming from the roof. Finally she returned to the door in the stone wall and went through.

Nancy breathed with relief. Landing lightly on the spongy turf below the roof, she ran to where she had hidden the rope ladder. It was still there. Hooking the ladder to the top of the wooden fence, Nancy climbed over quickly.

She tossed the ladder behind a tree and ran headlong. Taking a circuitous route to avoid detection, she finally came to the parked car. She drove as swiftly as possible along the gravel lane; then sped toward Three Bridges Road. Crossing the intersection not twenty feet in front of her was the familiar car of a state trooper!

Nancy blew a long blast on her horn and the police car stopped. She slipped out of the convertible and ran toward the trooper.

"Thank goodness you're here!" she told him. "I need help—right away!"

"What's wrong, miss?"

Nancy apprised him of the situation.

"Looks as if we'll need plenty of help," the trooper said grimly.

He radioed his district headquarters, and after a short wait they were joined by six state troopers in a patrol car. With Nancy leading the way, they sped toward the enclosure.

The men went over the fence at various locations to make their roundup complete. Nancy and two of the officers went at once to the old brick building to free Mr. Soong.

None of the criminals was in sight, but some of the workers were arrested. Since none of them could speak English, they could tell the police nothing about Carr and his brother.

"You'll have an ugly dog to tackle in a minute," Nancy warned the troopers as they went on toward the old smelter.

"We'll take care of him."

To Nancy's surprise the mastiff was gone. Nancy was puzzled. What of Mr. Soong? She darted to the door of the smelter and yanked it open. The place was empty.

"He's been taken away!" she cried despairingly.

The troopers looked at her. Had they come too late?

Nancy had a sudden inspiration. "I believe I know where everybody is," she said.

She led the men to the large corridor vault where Eng Moy had said the valuable potteries were locked up. As Nancy expected, the door would not open, but she could detect a faint whine from within. She told the men she suspected the criminals and their mastiff were inside.

"Come out of there at once!" one of the troopers commanded.

There was utter silence. Suddenly Nancy realized that if her Chinese friends were inside with the criminals, they might be afraid to answer. So she called loudly:

"It's Nancy Drew! I've come with help!"

From inside came a cry of joy from Eng Lei, but it was stifled at once. The troopers said they would batter down the door if it were not opened immediately!

At last from the interior of the vault, their faces sullen, came Carr holding the dog by the leash, his wife, and Ching. Behind them were Mr. Soong and the Engs, who blinked happily.

The story was soon told. When Carr had discovered Nancy gone, he had rounded up his wife and brother to make a getaway. But Nancy had arrived with the police too soon. By hiding in the vault, Carr had hoped to make the group think he and Ching and the others already had left.

Before leaving, the Carrs would have disposed of the old Chinese and his friends. The workers outside did not know enough to give damaging evidence against the brothers.

"You meddlesome creature!" Carr's wife burst out, pointing a finger at Nancy. "You're to blame for our capture! In another year we would have become rich enough to leave this place forever. But you had to come snooping and spoil it all!"

At that moment another of the troopers approached to report that all the workers in the place had been captured. Nancy quickly introduced Mr. Soong, who was allowed to go. All the others would have to be held for questioning, the officer said, but he was sure the Engs would be allowed to stay at Mr. Soong's home.

"Tell Eng Moy and Eng Lei good-by for me, Mr. Soong, please," Nancy said with a smile.

"But you will see them again," the old importer promised. "They will not return to China at once."

The next day Mr. Drew, back from Washington, and thankful his daughter was safe, talked over the mystery with Nancy. The Carrs and

Ching, they learned from the police, had signed a complete confession.

"One of the things I'm most curious about," Mr. Drew remarked, "is how Carr and Ching obtained possession of the enclosure."

Nancy showed her father a copy of the confession. It said the discoverer of the kaolin had been the brothers' great-grandfather. His son had worked the pit for a while but had moved away. Then his son, the father of David and Ching, had gone to China as a merchant, and the property had been sold for taxes but never used.

Records, testifying to the existence and location of the pit, had lain untouched in Shanghai for many years. Then, five years ago, David Carr and his brother had found the records and had immediately come to the United States to look over the pit. Using the name of the geologist Miles Monroe, to avoid suspicion, Carr had purchased the tract of land, despite the fact that it did not have a clear title.

"Here's something interesting," Nancy said.

The Carrs had later learned that a man named Petersen had left papers which might upset their claim to the pit. David had been given a lead to the former owner of Mrs. Wendell's house in Masonville, and this was the telephone conversation Dick Milton had overheard six months ago.

Carr, using the name Manning, had gone to her

home, taken a room, and stolen the papers he wanted, as Nancy had guessed. He had installed the secret panel leading to the empty attic next door, to keep some of the valuable potteries there, in case the enclosure in the woods was raided.

"You spiked that one early in the game, Nancy." Mr. Drew grinned. "And you figured all along that the religious colony was just a camouflage."

"Well, in a way, the discovery of the leaning chimney in Masonville was a lucky coincidence." Nancy smiled. "If I hadn't found that, I might not have uncovered the secret of the enclosure."

A week later Mr. Soong held a party in honor of the Engs. Nancy and Mr. Drew were there, as well as Bess and George, Dick and Connie, and Ned Nickerson.

Nancy noted with satisfaction that displayed on the living-room mantel were Mr. Soong's jade elephant and the dragon Ming vase which had been recovered from the swindlers.

After dinner Mr. Soong made a short, touching speech expressing the debt of gratitude he and the Engs owed Nancy. Then Lei stepped forward, holding in her hands an exquisite vase.

Against a soft-green background was pictured a slender, golden-haired girl, pitting a lance at a scaly green dragon. Behind her stood a Chinese girl and two men in long Oriental robes.

As Lei presented the vase to a surprised Nancy with a warm smile, she spoke in Chinese.

"What is she saying?" Nancy asked Mr. Soong.

"Lei is trying to tell you that she and her father made this for you. Like all Chinese work, the design tells a story," he explained. "The girl is Nancy Drew. The three Chinese are Lei, Moy, and myself whom you are protecting from the evil dragon: Ching, Carr, and his wife."

He turned the vase bottom up. "It says, 'Made in the hearts of Eng Moy and Eng Lei.'"

"It's lovely," she whispered. "Thank you," Nancy said simply. "Thank you very much."

She started to turn away, but there was a burst of applause from the smiling circle of guests.

"Speech!" George prompted, spurring the others to even greater hand clapping.

Nancy looked helplessly at Mr. Soong. "Please do," he urged, smiling.

"Go ahead, Nancy," Ned spoke up.

"I'll do my best," she promised with a little laugh. "There aren't any words to express the way I feel about this vase. It's more to me than just a gift. It's a token of friendship; a bond between me and three of the nicest people I've ever known. I'll treasure it always."

Applause burst out again as she finished, then

the circle broke up and Nancy found herself in one corner of the room with Bess, George, and Ned.

"Well, Nancy," Ned said with a teasing grin, "now that you've located the China clay and the missing Engs, what are you going to do next?"

"Next," Nancy replied, "I'm going to tell you a secret. Mr. Soong is lending Dick the money to acquire the China clay, and the Engs are going to stay in America—for a while at least—and work with him making potteries. And now," she added, laughing, "I'm ready and willing to take on any new mystery that comes along."

Although Nancy did not know it then, the mystery was to be the baffling, exciting adventure of *The Secret of the Wooden Lady*.

"Meanwhile," Nancy whispered to Bess, "I think I'll join you in the ceramics class. Now that I've learned from Ching and Carr what *not* to do in making potteries, I'd better take a few tips from Dick on what *to* do!"